The Girl on the Stairs

Also by Louise Welsh

The Cutting Room
The Bullet Trick
Naming the Bones
Tamburlaine Must Die

The Girl on the Stairs

Louise Welsh

JOHN MURRAY

First published in Great Britain in 2012 by
John Murray (Publishers)
An Hachette UK Company

1

A CIP catalogue record for this title is available from the British Library

Hardback ISBN 978-1-84854-648-6
Trade Paperback ISBN 978-1-84854-660-8
Ebook ISBN 978-1-84854-649-3

Typeset by Hewer Text UK Ltd, Edinburgh
Printed and bound by Clays Ltd, St Ives plc

John Murray policy is to use papers that are natural, renewable and recyclable products
and made from wood grown in sustainable forests. The logging and manufacturing
processes are expected to conform to the environmental regulations of the
country of origin.

John Murray (Publishers)
338 Euston Road
London NW1 3BH

www.johnmurray.co.uk

To David and Cathy Fehilly

So simple an act as death
Needs no pomp to excuse,
Nor any expense of breath
To magnify what is.

'A Burial' by Sydney Tremayne

'They say things that, if we heard them,
would simply appal us.'

The Turn of the Screw by Henry James

One

It was the kind of day that reminded Jane of her childhood, a bleak November Sunday that huddled people into their coats and set feet walking fast. Beyond the window of the cab a large man in an ice-blue ski jacket paused while the Yorkshire terrier whose leash he was holding squatted on the grass verge. Jane supposed that somewhere a lady was keeping cosy, waiting for her fat man and her little dog to return. She bet the terrier would be in his mistress's arms before the man had even extricated himself from his jacket.

It was warm in the taxi, but Jane pulled her scarf up around her face as if in sympathy with the man and his love-chore. The lights changed and the cab moved on, the rosary hooked on the rear-view mirror swinging. Petra reached out and took her hand.

'Penny for them?'

'Nothing.'

Petra unfastened a button on Jane's coat, slipped her hand beneath its folds and stroked the firm globe of Jane's tummy, but the baby had ceased the callisthenics it had been doing on the plane.

'Is it possible to think of nothing today?' Petra slid her hand free. 'It feels so good to have you here at last. My mind is buzzing.'

'That's because you're in charge. I'm totally serene.'

'Like the Madonna.' Petra nodded to the dashboard where a mass card was propped. A bejewelled Virgin Mary held a lively-looking Christ child who was naked save for a gold crown topped by a halo.

'Luckier than the Madonna, I know there's a bed waiting for me.'

'Tired?'

'A little.'

She was shattered. The queues at Heathrow and Schönefeld had been long, and Jane had been reminded of the early weeks, when she'd felt the embryo sucking all the goodness out of her.

'We'll be there soon.'

The Berlin suburbs scrolled past, clean-edged apartment blocks and neatly tended gardens, each one empty of people, as if a giant clean-up had been followed by the Rapture. Jane wondered if it was peculiarly Scottish to be wary of respectability. Order wasn't always a mask.

Petra leant in and kissed her, high on the side of her face, just above her cheekbone. Jane saw the taxi driver glancing at them in the rear-view mirror. He looked away, then back at them again, but he didn't say anything, not even when she took Petra's face in her hands and kissed her on the lips.

The apartment had the skewed look that places examined too many times on the Internet take on when viewed in person.

Jane stood in the sitting room, recognising the white couch and angled floor lamp from the photos Petra had emailed her. The dining table was white too, set on a cream rug and flanked on each side by four Starck Ghost chairs. It was hard to imagine a child here. Hard to imagine a child.

Jane shrugged off her scarf and started to unbutton her coat.

'Leave it on for a moment, baby.' Petra took her hand and led her across the parquet floor and out on to the balcony. Jane felt the skin on her face tighten as the night air touched it. 'Look.'

A streetlamp shone brightly below, illuminating the trees in the churchyard opposite. The modest *Kirche* looked too small to support its spire which loomed, reaching and iron, against the night. Beyond it, windows gleamed from distant apartment blocks, and not so far beyond them, the Fernsehturm glowed through the dark. Petra's voice was breathless with cold and excitement. 'I can't wait for you to see the view properly. I know a cemetery doesn't sound so cheerful, but St Sebastian's is more of an English churchyard, leafy and overgrown, quite charming.'

'Maybe they have a playgroup.'

'The day I viewed the apartment a bunch of toddlers were chasing each other around the headstones, so I guess they must.'

Jane pulled the hood of her coat over her head, and Petra put an arm around her, lending her some of her warmth.

'We get the sun until lunchtime and again in the evening.'

'The flat's like something out of a fashion spread.'

'You like it?'

'It's wonderful.'

Petra kissed her, lips warm and happy.

'I checked with the estate agent, the balcony's childproof.'

A delicately wrought table and a couple of spindly chairs stood to the right of the open door. Jane gathered her coat around her and sat down. She felt the unopened pack of cigarettes in her pocket. All it took was willpower.

'There's no such thing as childproof.'

'Of course there is.' Petra sat in the other chair and took hold of Jane's hand. 'This is the twenty-first century.'

Out in the darkness aeroplane lights flashed towards the Fernsehturm, miles from collision but looking like a trajectory to disaster against the flatness of the night sky. The lights vanished for a moment behind the tower's pickled-onion viewing deck, and then reappeared. Jane let out a breath she hadn't realised she was holding in.

Somewhere in the building a door slammed. She glanced back into the new apartment, half expecting to see a stranger standing in the lounge.

'Did you lock the front door?'

'Of course.' Petra squeezed Jane's hand. 'Don't worry, everything's secure. Safe as a baby.'

It was on the tip of Jane's tongue to say, nothing could be more precarious than a child, but instead she returned Petra's squeeze.

'Babies just pretend to be helpless. Haven't you seen the way they stare at you? They know everything. They could walk and talk straight from the womb if they wanted.'

Petra stood up, raised Jane to her feet and pulled her close. Jane could feel her breath, peppermint-warm against

4

the frosty evening. She lifted her face to Petra's kiss and heard her whisper, 'Our genius is very lucky to have you as one of its mothers. I can't wait to hear the stories you tell it.' She laughed and they separated. 'But try not to make them too scary.'

The larger of the spare bedrooms was opposite the lounge. They stood in the doorway, taking in the double bed, the polished hardwood floor and fitted wardrobes.

Petra shrugged. 'We can put all this in storage and buy him some kiddie furniture.'

Jane noticed the gender slip, but let it go. Time would tell. She pulled back the drapes. The courtyard outside the window was dimly lit, but Jane could make out the building beyond, a derelict mirror of their apartment block, its vacant windows sunk in darkness like sockets in a skull.

'Not such an inspiring view.'

'It's normal, backhouses at the back. The one behind us is empty, so we'll have privacy.' Petra turned away. 'You're going to love the kitchen.'

Jane registered her lover leaving the room, but she lingered on by the window. Down below, an old man crossed the dim courtyard, no more than a shadow in the gloom, and disappeared into the murk of the opposite block. Jane wondered what business anyone could have in the ruined building. She would hate to have to pass into that darkness.

The child moved. Jane pressed a hand against her stomach, feeling its kick, and wondered if it was aware of the pressure of her palm on the other side of the dark barrier. She was its universe, and its jailer. For the first time she almost under-stood how the religious could view birth as a falling from grace.

'Enjoy it while it lasts, kiddo,' she whispered. 'It's all down-hill from here.'

She let the curtains fall back into place and followed Petra through to the kitchen, preparing to exclaim at the freshness of it all.

She woke as usual in the night and slipped from bed. Petra stirred and Jane whispered, 'It's okay.' She ignored the ensuite and padded barefoot from the room, closing the door gently behind her. Outside she clicked on the hall light and paused until the energy-saver bulb glowed bright. The bathroom waited like a final destination at the end of the long hallway.

The excess of mirrors in the bathroom was intended to convey luxury, but the uninvited reflections unnerved Jane. She used the toilet, then washed her hands in the basin. This was the child's time, the hour when he or she was most active. Dance time, Jane privately called it, more rockabilly-slam than waltz. She wondered if, weeks from now, this would be the hour when it would decide to break free with no thought for fine linen or expensive rugs. She held her tummy against the kicks, feeling the tight-as-a-drum skin move beneath her palms.

'Wheesht now,' she whispered. 'Give us peace.'

The hot tap was still running, steam beginning to fog the mirrors. She washed her face, then stopped the flow and peered at herself in the hazed glass. Were her cheeks filling out? She pinched her flesh and gasped as a reflection moved in the corner of her eye; stupid to be scared by yourself. Now that the water had stopped running, Jane could feel the silence. It was deep in the night and everyone except her was in bed.

No, not everyone. There were voices through the wall. Even if her German had been better they would have been too faint for Jane to make out the words, but she could hear anger in the gunfire delivery. Late-night arguments, fuelled by drink, were always the worst. She turned away, ready to reclaim the warmth of bed, but the sound of something shattering in the next-door apartment stalled her. Her hand sought the edge of the basin, the ungiving porcelain a comfort against her skin. The louder of the voices rose, harsh and male, as if the crash had been a prelude to its crescendo. Jane thought she could detect the sound of sobbing beneath the shouting. Was it a child crying?

She stood there for a second, bracing herself to walk away, and then clambered awkwardly into the bath and put her ear to the dividing wall. The tiles seemed to confound the sound into an underwater boom. She shifted a little, pressing herself closer, the ceramic cold against her hip. Then it was as if whoever was on the other side sensed her listening, and pressed their mouth against the wall, because suddenly, loud in her ear, a voice screamed '*Hure!*' – whore. And a second, higher voice started to laugh.

Jane scrambled from the bath and hurried back along the hall and into their bedroom, not bothering to turn off the light. She slid into bed and pressed herself into Petra's warmth, face against Petra's neck, tummy cradled in the curve of Petra's back. Petra stirred and mumbled, '*Du bist Kalt*,' but she didn't pull away and Jane lay against her, feeling the weight of the child between them, until sleep crept in.

Two

Jane woke with a start to the hard click of china on glass as Petra placed a cup of tea on the bedside table. The curtains were not quite drawn and the bleak November dawn was edging its way into the room. 'What time is it?' Jane glanced at the radio alarm and saw the numbers glowing 7.03. 'It's early.'

'Sorry, sweetheart.' Petra was already dressed, in her hyacinth-blue tweed suit. They'd bought the fabric on holiday in Harris and she'd had it made up to her own design back in London, two skirts and one jacket; Petra was clever that way. 'I didn't want to sneak off without saying goodbye.'

'Sneak off where?'

'To work.'

It was beyond belief.

'I thought you'd take a couple of days off.'

'You know I'd love to.' Petra was taking her coat from the wardrobe. She slipped it on and regarded herself in the mirror. 'But I need to save my leave for the big event. We talked about it, remember?' She pulled a pink scarf from a drawer and twisted it into a complicated knot. 'I'll try to get away early. We can go somewhere for dinner. Think about where you'd like to eat. My treat.'

From now on everything was going to be Petra's treat, Jane realised.

'I haven't seen you for a month.' She hated the coaxing note in her voice. 'It's my first morning here. Stay for breakfast at least.'

'I can't.' Petra ruffled Jane's hair. Jane reached up and locked fingers with her. Petra squeezed her hand, then pulled away. 'The sooner I go, the sooner I'll return.' She kissed her fingers and placed them on Jane's cheek. 'You look very sweet lying there. You know I'd rather be with you than at work, don't you?'

Jane slid from the bed and pulled on her robe.

'But someone's got to bring home the *Schinken*, right?'

'On the button.' Petra gathered up her handbag and briefcase. 'I'm sorry I woke you. Go back to sleep. There's no need for you to get up until later.'

Jane tied her belt and pushed her bare feet into her slippers.

'Who lives next door?'

'Next door?' Petra shrugged. Jane had forgotten how infuriating she found Petra's shrug. 'Some man and his daughter. Why?'

'I wondered if there were any children in the building.'

'She's a teenager, not really a child at all.' Petra smiled, tall and slender in the doorway. She looked like a TV director's idea of a sexy female banker, a woman who knew her price and was happy with it. 'Go back to bed, baby.'

Petra shut the bedroom door gently behind her and a moment later Jane heard the front door close.

* * *

It was after nine when Jane woke again, her bladder straining. This time she used the ensuite, showering and washing her hair in the frosted-glass cubicle. The door concertinaed inwards and Jane realised that soon she'd be unable to close it for fear of getting stuck. She towelled herself dry in the bedroom and dressed in the leggings and loose jumper that had become her uniform.

She thought she heard a key in the front door and called out, 'Petra?' But there was no one in the hallway. Jane lifted a vase from the hall table and walked through the too-big-for-two apartment, already constructing an anecdote about the ridiculousness of her patrol, but knowing she wouldn't be able to relax until she'd checked every room. The place reminded her of a modern art gallery, airy and impersonal, and she suddenly wondered if Petra had ever really liked their London attic flat with its angled eaves and creaking floorboards. There was no one hiding in any of the rooms or walk-in wardrobes. Jane set the vase back on the hall table, certain that she was completely alone.

The kitchen was operating-theatre clean. Petra had filled the American-style fridge with food appropriate to an expectant mum. Jane ignored it and fried herself an egg, sunny-side-up, and toasted two slices of bread. The yolk wobbled a little as she put it on the plate and Jane felt her gorge rise. She sat at the table anyway and prodded it gently with a fork, testing the elasticity of the membrane until finally she pierced its defences and let the yellow fluid spread and pool on the plate.

'What, you egg? Young fry of treachery,' she said out loud as she lifted the plate and slid the mess into the bin.

The day stretched ahead.

She stood on the balcony and lit a forbidden cigarette. She had bought a cheaper brand than usual in some attempt at contrition; the taste was harsh and familiar, the scent of end-of-the-month economy. It was like breathing in her old self.

The trees in the graveyard opposite were bare, exposing an aerial city of rooks' nests. The birds hopped amongst the branches like an assemblage of black-coated, Free Church elders, their cries rattling the mid-morning stillness. It was winter-bleak, but Jane could see what Petra had meant when she'd described the view as charming. The churchyard was bounded by iron railings that had either escaped wartime requisition, or been restored to their original state. Beneath them, ivy colonised the edge of the cemetery, like seaweed on a shore at low tide. Tendrils crept over headstones old enough to have lost their sting, some leaning at angles, like sailors steadying themselves against the shift of a boat. There was a wooden bench set beneath the shade of a rowan tree. Jane wondered if the Germans had also believed that rowans deterred witches. She tried to imagine herself sitting there in summer, reading a book, a pram beside her, and in the pram . . .

The rooks' caws were drowned by a high babble of excited voices. A door she hadn't noticed before, set in the side of the church, had opened and a stream of toddlers poured into the yard. Jane watched them for a moment, then stubbed her cigarette out on the balcony railing, and went back into the apartment, locking the door behind her.

She wandered through to the room she was already thinking of as the child's, and stared out at the abandoned backhouse. A shutter moved in one of the windows on the second floor, shifting back and forth in the wind, knowing as an old roué's wink. As she watched, a flock of pigeons swooped through an unglazed window, into a paradise of rats and guano, she supposed. How quickly things reverted to their natural state when left alone. People too, if you weren't careful.

She would go out and buy a book; a detective novel or Tudor saga, anything that took her fancy. Mitte was a chi-chi district and there was bound to be an English language bookshop somewhere near by; indeed, now that she was thinking on it, she remembered one near Hackescher Markt. She could find a café, have someone else make her a coffee and lose herself for an hour or two. Later she could freshen up and put on one of the empire-line dresses Petra hadn't seen yet. Pregnancy might have made her breasts too tender to touch, but they had ripened to glamour-model proportions. She might as well show them off.

She was about to turn away when a young girl in a red coat walked briskly across the courtyard, carrying a black refuse sack. The girl's hood was up, but something about her high heels and erect posture suggested old Hollywood. Jane stepped to one side and watched from the shadow of the bedroom curtains as the girl entered the brick corral that housed the dustbins, and deposited her bag. The noise of the bin lid slamming disturbed another flurry of pigeons which swooped low across the yard, circling twice before making for the shelter of the abandoned building. The girl swore and turned, raising her hand as if warding off a blow. She looked towards Jane's window, but the hood of her coat conspired with the building's shadows to veil her. It wasn't until she was in the centre of the courtyard that she looked up, offering the view of her face to the sky, and Jane saw spiked eyelashes, rouged cheeks and red lips, and beneath the make-up, the soft, unformed features of a child.

Three

The only coat that still fitted her was too thin for a Berlin winter and Jane felt her jaw tense with the effort of keeping her teeth from chittering. Even the tram bells clanging their approach to Hackescher terminus sounded stiff, their chimes cut short by the cold. She waited for the *Ampelmann* to turn to green and the trail of cyclists and cars to pause, then crossed the road. Despite the bitter weather, the bars and restaurants that lined the square were still fronted by ranks of chairs and tables, sheltered beneath wide umbrellas advertising Marlboro, Silk Cut, Benson & Hedges . . . Petra had once joked that she had only suggested the pregnancy to make her stop smoking.

Jane chose a café beneath the railway arches. She settled herself at an outside table, below one of the halogen heaters she knew she should disapprove of, and tucked the blanket provided by the café up to her chest. Her fingers were numb and she had difficulty opening the pack of cigarettes and operating the lighter. A combination of guilt and taboo added to the rush of pleasure as the smoke hit the back of her throat and sank down into her lungs. This must be how adulterers felt; being bad was sometimes its own reward.

A train rumbled above, drowning out the faint beat of drum and fiddle from the Irish bar further down the archways. She took another draw of her cigarette, but the thrill of the first inhalation was gone.

A little boy, dressed as Superman beneath his anorak, dashed between the tables, chasing pigeons. These days she found herself observing children with the attention she had once paid stylish women. It was like studying another species. Their energy, the noise they made, their logic-defying tantrums. Jane imagined herself calling him over and whispering in his ear how to snare the bird by throwing his jacket over it.

What kind of a mother was she going to make?

The little boy careered into the path of a waiter laden with a tray of steaming coffees. Jane half rose to her feet, a warning on her lips. But the waiter checked his progress and the child hurtled on unharmed, arms outstretched, still intent on his quarry.

She sank back in her seat, scanning the square, expecting to see other shocked faces, or to hear the slap of flesh on flesh as the boy's mother chastised him, but no one else seemed to have noticed.

Would she and Petra allow their son or daughter to run freely like that? You risked death every time you crossed the road, and children had to learn. But how would you know how much freedom was okay? Could she cope with her own child's blood? Her own blood.

Jane stubbed out her half-smoked cigarette in the ashtray and got to her feet, leaving the almost-full pack and lighter behind. She'd promised Petra she would stop.

* * *

There were no children playing between the headstones and the graveyard had reverted to a realm of rooks. Their cries followed her progress as she neared the apartment, eager as a crew of heckling builders.

She glanced up at her apartment block. If it hadn't been for the date, *1910*, etched above the doorway, a stranger might have thought it recently built. Winter sunlight bounced off the building's façade, making the white stucco sparkle. It looked like an architect's drawing of upper-income living, except that an architect would have included some people in the picture. Jane stared at the windows of her and Petra's flat, wondering what she would do if she saw someone moving behind the blinds, but there was no movement, no sign of life. The windows of the neighbouring apartment were also still, turned black by the glare of the sun.

It was strange that the building's blank windows and empty balconies should make her feel uneasy. When she was a girl, she'd hated *windaehingers:* women who leant from tenement windows watching the street below. Some days it was as if you couldn't walk straight from the weight of their stares on you.

The sensation of being watched was with her now. Maybe it was the child making itself known; sometimes she felt as if it were monitoring her before deciding whether to be born. She resolved to save the detective novel she had bought till later and spend the rest of the afternoon with the childcare manual Petra had given her.

Jane paused, caught by the flash of brightness amongst the blue-green ivy in the churchyard: a bunch of spring flowers, irises and daffodils, propped beneath a headstone. For a

moment she was confused by their freshness, then she realised they were plastic. She wondered if the body below had
decayed while the tribute endured.

The rooks had grown quieter, their cries ebbing to a grum-
ble, as if they liked her no better, but had grown bored with
declaring it. Now they were starting up again, their caws
building to an alarmed chorus. Jane glanced upwards,
wondering what it was that had disturbed them. The wind
was rising, the treetops gusting into a dance. Jane raised a
hand to brush a strand of hair from her face and felt a sudden
rush against her cheek as a small missile flew from the graveyard and landed on the road beyond. She knew it was a stone,
even before the second piece of gravel hit her in the face.

In another life she would have raced through the gate with
no thought of what she was going to do if she caught the
stone-thrower, but now she pulled up the hood of her coat
and swiftly crossed the road to the apartment block, her hand
fumbling in her pocket for the key.

Safe in the darkness of the lobby, she leant against the wall,
waiting for her heart to slow to its normal rate.

'Bastard, bastard, bastard.'

It was only some kid with a catapult and a comic-book
sense of humour. She touched her face. The skin along her
cheekbone was tender. It would leave a bruise. She shook her
head. It was a look she would have preferred to avoid: bruised
and pregnant.

'Bastard.'

Jane opened the door of the building and looked at the
graveyard across the street. It was quiet again, but she couldn't
shake the feeling that someone was watching her and

laughing. Tomorrow she would walk there. If needs be, she would buy her own catapult.

The lobby was dim. Jane reached out to hit the light switch and stalled with her hand on the button as she spotted a second, almost identical switch at its side, realising she had been about to ring the downstairs apartment's doorbell. She corrected herself, making a mental note not to repeat the mistake, and then slowly climbed the staircase, the wooden steps sounding hollow beneath her boots. The building might look newly made from the outside, but inside cracks were spidering across the carefully applied plaster. It wouldn't be long before the gleam rubbed off the renovation's cosmetic sheen. Jane was surprised that Petra hadn't been put off by the decay lingering just beyond the stylish veneer.

The light timed out, leaving her in gloom. Jane rested her book bag on the ground and leant against the banister, starting as it shifted against her weight. She saw herself for a moment, a pregnant woman leaning against a banister on a shabby swirl of stairs. It was dizzying.

The door to the neighbouring apartment opened as she reached their landing. The man who emerged was tall, with the kind of casually ruffled haircut that required styling products and time in front of a mirror. The walking stick he leant on contrasted with his athletic frame to give him the air of an adventurer; a racing driver or pilot brought low through recklessness. He looked her frankly up and down, his eyes hesitating on her stinging cheek.

'Frau Logan?'

'Ja.'

She wanted nothing more but to lie down and close her eyes.

'You have a delivery.'

The man had glanced at her stomach as he spoke and for a second she thought it was a clumsy joke, but he ducked back into his flat, his limp awkward and swinging. How could he know she was British from just one word?

The bouquet was ridiculous in its extravagance. A dozen budding red roses fastened by a ruff of cellophane and decorated with angel's breath; baby's breath.

'Thank you.'

The arrangement was so big she had to cradle it in both arms.

'Someone's way of saying sorry?'

'What?'

'Your face.' He touched his own cheek.

'No.' She raised her hand to where the stone had hit. 'This only happened a moment ago.' She forced a smile in lieu of the explanation she was too tired to produce. 'A stupid accident. I think the flowers are a welcome-to-Berlin present from my *Lebenspartner*.'

The man nodded, but his expression remained grave.

'Welcome then from me too. How long do you have?'

'Nine weeks.'

He was standing too close and it took all of Jane's effort not to step backwards on to the edge of the stairs. She lowered the bouquet and the man stepped beyond its reach. His smile crinkled the corner of his eyes and Jane imagined him practising the expression in front of the mirror.

'Dr Alban Mann.' He held out his hand. 'I can recommend a good obstetrician, if you don't have one already.'

'You?'

'No.' His smile widened. 'But you can call on me if you need to.'

Jane took her key from her pocket.

'Let's hope it doesn't come to that.'

'You're very white. Are you sure you're okay? '

'I'm Scottish. We're well known for being peely-wally. It's our thick skin.'

'Peely-wally?'

'Pale.'

Below them the door to the building slammed and footsteps sounded a quick ascent against the hollow stairs. Dr Mann glanced towards the stairwell, a frown creasing his forehead, giving the lie to his trendy haircut and young man's clothes. Jane remembered a fairy tale about a mother who had gone to lift her baby from its cradle and found it transformed into a wrinkled old man. In the story the mother had let the old man drink from her breasts, until he drained her dry.

The girl's face had been cleansed of make-up, exposing perfect skin of the kind favoured by advertisers of natural beauty products. She was still wearing her red coat but her high heels had been replaced by a neat pair of black pumps. She came to a sudden stop at the top of the stairs, hesitating there, as if surprised to see Mann and Jane, and unsure of what her response should be. A rucksack swung from one shoulder. Jane wondered if it contained the unsuitable shoes.

Alban Mann was smiling again. He said, 'This is my daughter, Anna.'

Jane was surprised by a sudden stab of sympathy. She had

21

hated puberty, the intrusion of blood and breasts, the whispering sisterhoods and invitations from men in slow-crawling cars.

She smiled. 'Hello, Anna, I'm Jane, one of your new neighbours.'

'Hello.' Anna Mann went to her father and put an arm around his waist. She leant against him and he kissed her lightly on the top of her head. The girl looked up at him, lips slightly parted, then quick-glanced at Jane's bump. Some emotion twitched at her mouth. Amusement or embarrassment?

Jane felt a blush spreading from her neck to her cheeks. Stupid, stupid, stupid, to be self-conscious in front of this girl, after all she and Petra had gone through.

Beyond the door to her apartment the telephone started ringing.

'Excuse me, I must answer that.'

Jane turned the key in the lock. She hurried down the long hallway, almost losing her footing on the polished hardwood floor, and skidded into the sitting room, flinging the bouquet on to the couch and grabbing the phone before Petra could hang up.

Four

'Less than a week in Berlin and you've already beaten the poor girl up.' Tielo squeezed Jane's hand to show he was joking. 'Come and live with me in my beautiful new home. I love children and my wife refuses to give me any more.'

Jane saw him throwing Ute a naughty-boy smile and her answering shake of the head, the kind of look one might give a mischievous three-year-old. Tielo stroked his palm across Jane's stomach. 'I like round women.' He gestured at the curved edge of the room's outer wall. 'Round women and round houses.'

The converted *Wasserturm* where Petra's twin brother and his family had moved was airier than Jane expected, but in the hours they had spent there the dark had crept in and now the only light came from the candles guttering on the coffee table. The room's lack of corners was disorientating. Jane looked out at the blackness beyond the window and thought they could be floating on the outer edges of the universe. She slid her hand free of Tielo's and got up from the couch.

'I have to use your beautiful new bathroom.'

Now that she was standing she could see the trees outside

the window, turned to copper by the streetlamps. A string of multicoloured lights shone faintly from the Jewish restaurant on the other side of the square.

'You will notice that the lavatory is also round,' Tielo said, his voice loud and boozy.

Petra touched Jane's leg as she passed. 'Poor clumsy girl.'

Tielo put an arm around his sister.

'Poor battered wife. She doesn't have the speed to dodge your punches any more.'

Petra slapped her twin's cheek lightly. 'Neither do you.'

'Sure about that?'

Jane shut the door on her lover's laugh, not waiting to see what form Tielo's reprisal would take. They had been speaking English for her sake, now they would switch to German, their own language.

She took her time in the bathroom, washing her face and refreshing her lips with a lipstick she found in the cabinet. It was paler than her usual colour. Little changes could transform you. She pressed her grazed cheek against the glass.

Back in London, a different Jane was wearing red lipstick and dancing in a basement nightclub, vodka-bright and ready for anything.

It was pathetic to get annoyed with people because they were drunk and you weren't. Jane dabbed a little of Ute's foundation on her bruise and practised her smile in the mirror. It looked tight, but it would do. She flushed the toilet again and went out.

Ute was leaning against the wall in the hallway staring at the map of the world Tielo had hung deliberately low, so Peter and Carsten could see it properly. She'd had her hair cut since they'd last met. One of those boyish crops German women seemed to favour after they became mothers. It suited her. Ute straightened up and slid her hands into the back pockets of her jeans. Her flowered blouse was fastened to her navel, offering a glimpse of toned stomach. They'd exchanged a drunken kiss once at a Hogmanay party, their tongues touching until one of them, Jane couldn't remember which, had pulled away.

'Sorry.' Jane smiled, hoping Ute wouldn't recognise her lipstick. 'I didn't know you were waiting.'

'I'm not. I just wanted to make sure you're okay.'

'Fine. A little tired. You know how it is.'

Ute nodded. 'With Carsten I was so tired I thought I might kill Tielo and Peter, just to rest.'

'Really?' Jane laughed. 'I suppose you must often feel like killing Tielo.'

'No.' Ute looked bemused. 'Only then, and only because I was tired. I knew exactly how I would do it. I would wait until they were both asleep, then I would go into the kitchen and get a knife – the Sabatier knives you and Petra gave us would be sharp enough. Then I would cut their throats, Tielo's first, and then Peter's. Afterwards I would lie down on the bed and sleep. I used to imagine it sometimes late at night when I could hear Tielo snoring while I walked the floor with Carsten.'

Beyond the living-room door Tielo and Petra were laughing. Jane wanted to go through to them, but she asked, 'And the baby?'

'Carsten? I would have smothered him. Babies are easy to smother.' Ute laughed, her teeth white and even. 'Everyone feels that way, it's normal.' Her voice dropped to a whisper.

'The important thing is not to do it.' She squeezed Jane's arm, as if they were conspirators. 'I have to check on the boys. Petra and Tielo are making enough noise to wake the dead.'

In her mind's eye Jane saw sweet Ute lying down on blood-stained sheets and closing her eyes.

'Shall I come with you?'

'No.' Ute's voice was warm. 'You rest while you can.'

It was as if she was being initiated into a club she didn't want to join.

'Petra and I are going to co-parent.'

Ute's smile was patient. 'I know, but she will be working all day and you will be home. When the child cries in the night you'll be the one with the milk and Petra will be the one with the early-morning meeting.'

Jane looked at Britain on the world map. Scotland was a tiny country, smaller than her thumbnail.

'Do you ever regret having Peter and Carsten?'

'No, never.' Ute looked as if she was going to say something more, but instead she smiled and pulled Jane into a hug. 'I'm sorry. Just because Tielo's a selfish bawbag doesn't mean Petra will be one too.' They laughed together at the Scottish insult, a favourite in the repertoire Jane had taught Ute and Tielo years ago in a Bavarian *Biergarten*, before any of them had thought of children. Ute stroked Jane's hair away from her face. 'And you'll have a beautiful baby.'

'I won't care if it's ugly.'

'Any child you two produce together will be beautiful.'

The sound of singing wafted through from the front room, Petra and Tielo joining in some childhood song Jane didn't recognise. She returned Ute's squeeze and pulled away, not bothering to remind her of the basics of biology. After all, that was exactly what she and Petra were doing, producing a child together.

'Thanks, Ute, let's hope it looks like Petra.'

'You're both beautiful.' She put an arm around Jane's shoulder. 'The boys can wait. Let's see if we can persuade these big children it's time for bed.'

Petra leant against her in the taxi. Jane smelt the brandy on her breath and felt the old queasiness rising in her gut, but she let herself be pulled into a clumsy kiss, teeth on lips.

'I'm sorry we kept you up so late.' Petra placed a finger on Jane's lower lip and rubbed where she'd bitten. 'Sorry.'

'It's okay, it's good to see you both so happy together. It makes me imagine how you must have been as children.'

'Tielo is such a silly idiot.' Petra gave the word a comic inflection – *iddy-yot*. 'I don't know how Ute stands it.'

'She loves him. So do you. Tielo is very lovable.'

'He's an idiot.'

Iddy-yot.

'A lovable idiot.'

'Very lovable. I love him even though he's a fool. What do you think of their new apartment?'

'Nice. When you said water tower, I thought,' Jane shrugged, 'I thought water tank, but it's lovely. Tielo must be a rich idiot.'

'No, just lucky. Particular places can be slow to move. There are bigger idiots than Tielo around.'

'What do you mean?'

'He didn't tell you?' Petra laughed. 'He was probably trying to be sensitive. Everyone knows how embarrassed British people get when Germans mention the war.'

Jane ignored the old jibe.

'Why would Tielo's apartment go cheap?'

'Some people don't like buildings with a past. They worry ghosts will come creeping to their bedside while they sleep.'

The taxi stopped at a red traffic light on the intersection of Schönhauser Allee and Torstraße. It was after midnight and cold, but the outside tables were still busy with late-night drinkers. Jane watched a young girl raise a cigarette to her lips. She saw the flare of its tip as the girl inhaled, then the rush of smoke and breath as she let go, laughing at something one of her companions had said. Tielo's ghosts rose vaporous in Jane's mind's-eye, delicate tendrils like mist on a marsh. She rolled down the cab window and breathed in the early-morning scent of the city.

The lights changed and the cab drove on. They passed Rosa-Luxemburg-Platz and Jane thought of Rosa falling through the water. Had she been dead when they dropped her into the canal? She asked, 'Why would Tielo's building have ghosts?'

'Everywhere in this city would have ghosts if they existed, everywhere in every city. What about your Glasgow?' Petra's voice held a sudden, unfamiliar, bitter edge. 'A murder on every corner.'

'I bet our Ned-ghosts could take your Nazi-ghosts at square goes.'

'They are not my Nazis.'

'Oh for Christ's sake, Petra, lighten up. I said Nazi-ghosts, I was hardly being serious.'

The taxi was in Mitte now, shop windows scrolling by: *American Apparel, MAC, Adidas, Muji, Hugo Boss*... Mannequins in designer clothes giving out frozen attitude beneath the harsh display lights.

Petra sighed. 'It's not a nice story. The Nazis used the *Wasserturm* as a prison during the war. They tortured people in the basement; there's a plaque dedicated to the victims on the entrance wall. I thought you'd notice it.'

'No, I didn't notice.' Jane heard Petra's cool tones in her own voice. 'And Tielo and Ute knew this when they moved in?'

'Yes, of course.'

'Rather them than me.'

The impatience was back in Petra's voice. 'We're living in an old apartment in an ex-Jewish district. Tielo and Ute know what happened in their building, but we have no idea of what went on in ours. That's something you have to accept if you want to live in this city. The past is past; Berliners have learnt to come to terms with it.'

'They put up commemorative plaques.'

'What would you prefer? We torture ourselves for the sins of our ancestors? My granddad was a Nazi. You want me to kill myself?'

'Of course not.'

'Your country fire-bombed Dresden. A whole city reduced to flame, for what?'

Jane closed her eyes. It always came back to Dresden.

'I know, for revenge. I'm not proud of it.'

'But you're proud of Glasgow, a city built on slave trading and arms dealing. Where are the plaques to that?'

'All I meant was I'd find it hard to live in a building where I knew people had been tortured.'

Petra turned to look at Jane, her face hard and angry.

'In Berlin you can never be sure. Perhaps you are.'

They were driving into their road now. Jane glimpsed a pair of streetwalkers on the corner dressed in high-heeled boots, tight shorts and tighter corsets. She wondered where they took their clients. Did they slip into the graveyard or was there an apartment nearby which they shared, temporary couples queuing in the hallway until a room was free? Would it be a relief to them to be hired by a woman? She would never dare, would never want to dare.

The *Kirche* was on their left now, headstones dark against the night. She imagined snipers hiding amongst the monuments, a bomb hitting the graves, the already-dead flying into the air; resurrection and judgement day.

The taxi drew to a halt outside their building. Petra paid the driver and they left the warm interior of the cab, avoiding each other's eyes as they stepped out into the chill night.

They made up in bed, Petra's hand snaking across the gap between them, stroking an apology on to Jane's face before sliding gently, gently down and caressing her breasts. Jane let herself be kissed, then kissed back, running her fingers along the familiar swoop and rise of Petra's waist and hips. Petra rolled on to her stomach, her fingers feather-touching Jane's belly, her tongue following the trail her fingers had set. Jane gave herself over to her lover's touch, closing her eyes, though it was dark already, feeling her head press against the pillow and her body arc as a sound escaped her lips and the child fluttered inside her.

She woke in the night to the sound of heavy feet jack-booting up the stairwell and lay in the dark, wondering if the pounding and desperate shouts had been part of a dream, or whether they came from somewhere beyond their room. Petra was right; only fools believed in ghosts. Jane's heart beat hard in her chest, pulsing to the same rhythm that had woken her.

Dogs could hear noises pitched too high for human ears. Could some people hear sounds from the past? Screams and shouting so desperate they lingered on, only audible to those tuned in to the right frequency?

It was silent now, save for the regular in-and-out of Petra's breathing. They sometimes joked that she would sleep through an earthquake. Jane slipped from bed and went naked to the child's room.

The room was north-facing and chill, but it was a good size, and nicely proportioned. The cot could go against the wall that divided it from their bedroom. They would find a low chair to set beside it, where she could nurse, and a CD player so that she and the child could listen to music together. It already had its favourites, more active to Nirvana and The Foo Fighters than to Mozart.

The bedroom's best feature was an oak mantelpiece carved with fruit and flowers. The fireplace itself had been boarded up. Jane knelt by the hearth and tapped her knuckles against the board, wondering what lay behind, and if it might be opened and a stove installed. It sounded vaguely hollow, but it would take an expert to tell. She noticed a face gleaming amongst the carved flora and gasped. Her eyes adjusted and she saw other faces, gleeful and androgynous below ivy-tumbled hair. The smiles looked benevolent but Jane could imagine them altering with the shadows, and she hoped they wouldn't disturb the child's dreams. She straightened up, steadying herself against the mantelpiece, and saw her own name scrawled in the dust. Petra must have done it, alone and thinking of her, but the sight of her name in the unused room unnerved Jane and she rubbed it away with her fingertips.

She turned off the light, ready to go back to bed, but instead drew the curtains and stood by the window, staring out at the backhouse. The building was nothing in the dark, just black on blackness, but she knew it was there, staring across the yard, the open shutter winking at her in the breeze. She shivered. Would she really leave the child alone in here at night? She wasn't sure she would dare to, not after all these months of letting it lodge in her womb.

Light was creeping in, the building opposite growing visible. She wondered why it had been left to decay while surrounding tenements were developed into lucrative apartments. Petra was right. This had been a Jewish district before the war; later it had been in the Soviet zone, consigned to the Eastern side of the wall. Some properties here had been confiscated and reassigned so many times there were questions as to who actually owned them. Perhaps the backhouse was at the centre of some legal dispute. In this city you could never be sure of what had happened. Did pain force itself into the walls of buildings, screams captured like an image on a photographic plate?

There was a sudden movement behind one of the broken windows. Jane narrowed her eyes, trying to detect what it was that had caught her attention, but the room behind the fractured pane remained black and impenetrable. It was a bird, she decided, roused from its roost by the incoming dawn. As if to confirm her thought, a flock of pigeons whirled into the courtyard, circling once, before swooping into an upper storey. She glanced back at the broken window and caught another flash of movement. And though she knew the child's room was too dark and too far away for anyone to make her out, Jane was filled with the sudden conviction that someone was staring at her. She snapped the curtains shut and hastened back to bed and the shelter of Petra's body.

Five

The bath salts Jane had found in the bathroom cabinet smelt sweetly of lavender. She had assumed that Petra had bought them, but their scent was slightly cloying, reminiscent of something just beyond memory's reach, not Petra's style at all. Jane would smell of someone else now, the unknown tenant who had lived here before them. Jane sank beneath the suds, resolving to throw the half-empty packet away.

She surfaced, brushing her wet hair from her face with her hand, and lay looking at her bump rising from the water like a volcanic island in a soapy sea. She had an idea that the child liked the warm water, or maybe she simply felt closer to it, submerged in liquid, just as it was submerged inside her. She stroked the bar of soap across her belly; its smoothness suddenly distorted by a kick, or was it a punch?

When did consciousness arrive? No one remembered being in the womb, but then few people remembered their first year of life. Did the child have thoughts, curled there in the dark? Did it dread its birth the way some people dreaded death?

The mound of her stomach obscured her view of her lower body. Jane leant forward, soaping her thighs, raising one foot, then the other, washing the staleness of the night from her skin. The bathroom mirrors had fogged, but she could see the alien she had become, misshapen and vaguely pink behind the misted glass.

The paperback she had intended to read lay precariously on the edge of the bathtub, next to the lit scented candle. She considered reaching for the book but closed her eyes for a second, thinking again of the baby. She could understand those teenage mothers who hid their pregnancies, hoping they would disappear and take the disgrace with them. It seemed impossible that it would ever claw its way free and she would see the face of the creature that had crouched within her all these months. Twisted goblin features imposed themselves on her imagination and she opened her eyes.

The sleepless nights were taking their toll. She had read somewhere that it was nature's way of preparing you for what was to follow. If so, nature was a bitch. Jane shut her eyes again, not intending to sleep, just wanting to ease the sting of tiredness. The lavender scent was stronger, but she minded it less now. It belonged somewhere in her childhood; a smell of respite and safety. A vague memory surfaced of someone tucking her into bed. The sheets had been cold and unfamiliar, so sweetly perfumed she had worried she might taint them.

Jane woke with a start, her right arm splashing as it sought for purchase on the side of the tub. There was water in her nose and she spluttered, coughing, as she forced herself upright. For a moment she thought it was a repeat of last night's dream that had woken her, and then she heard the shouts, hard and guttural, on the stairwell.

The water was cold, her limbs had stiffened and it was difficult climbing from the bath. She felt a leap of dismay at the inch that had burned from the candle. Would she have woken if it weren't for the commotion outside? She wrapped herself in an oversized bath sheet, resolving to keep her carelessness from Petra.

The shouting was louder now, a male voice incoherent with anger. Jane roughly towelled her body, feeling some of the life returning to her skin. She slid her feet into her slippers, pulled on her bathrobe and crept down the hallway. The spyhole in the door offered an unhelpful view of the corridor. She could recognise the voice now. Jane leant against the door, water dripping down her neck from her wet hair. From what she could hear, it was only shouting; perhaps she should steal away and leave Dr Mann to his rage. She put her eye to the spyhole again and saw an edge of banister, a glimpse of wall and ceiling. She heard Anna's voice, soft and slightly pleading.

Jane cursed quietly. 'Fuck.' It was none of her business what people got up to in their own home. Teenagers were a trial and the best of parents lost their temper, as she would no doubt discover in time. The wisest thing for her to do was to walk away, turn on the radio and make a warming cup of tea. It was the thought of the radio that did it, music blaring as the punishment was meted out. Jane put her hand on the latch and opened the door.

Alban's face was blood-flushed and distorted with anger. He turned his stare on Jane and she took an involuntary step backwards into her hallway.

'Is everything okay?'

She heard a tremble in her voice. When did she become such a coward? It was like being a child again.

'This is nothing for you to worry about, Frau Logan.'

Alban's voice had a shake to it too. His hands were bunched into fists.

Anna stood at the top of the stairs. She was dressed demurely, her red coat fastened to the neck, but there was something provocative in the jut of her hip. Her mouth was slightly open, her expression blank. Jane suddenly wondered if the girl was stoned. She asked, 'Is everything okay, Anna?'

The girl shrugged without meeting her eyes and Alban Mann said, 'Everything is fine, Frau Logan. I'm sorry our family row disturbed you. You should go inside. It's not good for you to be out in the cold with wet hair.'

He was right, she had started to shiver, but Jane held her ground.

'I'd like to hear it from Anna, if that's all right with you, Herr Mann.' She looked at the girl and lowered her voice, striving for intimacy. 'Are you okay, Anna, or is there some-one you would like me to call?'

The girl turned to face her and Jane saw a small blue-black bruise high on the side of her face. She stared at Jane's tummy, bulging beneath the hastily tied bathrobe, and her mouth twitched as it had on their first meeting. She looked as if she was about to giggle, but when she spoke her voice was valium-flat and free of emotion.

'My father thinks I should stay at home.'

The girl's English was slow and heavily accented. Jane kept her own words simple, wishing she had stuck to her resolution to learn German.

'What happened to your face?'

Anna touched her bruise. 'A boy threw a stone at me. What happened to yours?'

'Nothing.' Jane felt out of her depth. It was possible that she and the girl had been hit by the same stone thrower, but her father had sounded angry enough for violence. She looked back at Alban. 'Shouldn't she be at school?'

'Anna is home-schooled, and you're right, she should be at lessons.' He turned his gaze on his daughter. '*Komm nach Hause,* Anna.'

The girl stared at her father and Jane was reminded of a fox she had found on her London doorstep late one winter afternoon. She had been on her way home from the book-shop, a bag of groceries in her hand. The creature had frozen and she had been struck by its beauty. Jane had hunkered down, holding eye contact with the pointed face, and slipped a rasher of bacon from its wrapping. She had flung it at the fox and watched as it warily sniffed the offering, then gulped it down. Jane had flung the strips of bacon towards it one by one, until she was left with the last rasher which she dangled at arm's length. The fox had stared her in the eye, and for an instant she had thought he was going to take it from her hand, but then he had flinched and galloped into the night.

'Anna . . .'

Alban's voice had lost its edge and taken on a soft, coaxing tone.

The girl smiled and for a moment it seemed that she might go to her father, but then she shook her head, turned and ran down the stairs, the clatter of her footsteps cut off by the bang of the entrance door.

Jane thought Alban would give chase, but he reached for his cane and she remembered. The slam of his door echoed his daughter's escape.

She put a coat over her dressing gown and stood on the balcony fingering the cigarette pack in her pocket. Her own mother had smoked, but then she hadn't known any better. Jane did. She balanced the packet on the edge of the balustrade and whispered, 'Goodbye cruel world,' as she flicked it over the edge.

It only took a few minutes to pull on underwear, leggings and a loose black jumper. Jane tied her still-damp hair back in a ponytail, shoved her feet into her boots and grabbed her coat. She was picking up the dented pack from the pavement when the rooks' calls made her look towards the church. A quick flash of red flitted amongst the gravestones and was gone. She toyed with the cellophane wrap. It was a family quarrel and none of her business.

The metal gate gave a Hammer Horror groan as she pushed it wide and entered the graveyard. The *Kirche* lay up ahead, dark and silent. Jane walked towards it, boots crunching against the gravel. The day was cloudy, but the building still cast a shadow and the path was sunk in gloom. Above, the rooks took flight, splitting the silence. Her cheek throbbed. She stooped, picked up a handful of stones, slipped them in her pocket and followed the pathway round to the side of the church. The timber front door was locked and unyielding; the painted side entrance also refused to budge. There was no sign of Anna. The girl was probably gone by now, off to the house of a friend whose parents worked away from home during the day.

Was that when she had first started smoking – stolen schoolday afternoons at other kids' houses; drawn curtains and horror videos; pooled fags smoked from upstairs windows? Jane smiled at the memory. They'd always got caught in the end. Nosy neighbours shopped you or the grown-ups noticed tell-tale signs of occupation that kids were too stupid to see.

A weeping angel crouched at the base of a large cross, her arms raised to the sky in supplication. The angel's wings were as long as her body, her face beautiful and tortured, like a female Jesus. The sculptor had done a good job; there was a sense of lightness to the stone folds of her gown, clinging around her athletic, but most definitely female, form. Jane realised that her gaze was lingering on the angel's backside. She laughed and whispered, 'Churchyard porn.'

Rain was beginning to spot the ground. Jane stood in the shelter of the church's side door, realising that it was a relief not to find Anna. She breathed in, enjoying the damp air on her face, the fertile loamy smell rising from the graveyard; took out a cigarette and lit it. Recently everything seemed to remind her of her childhood. She wondered if it was a consequence of the impending birth, her mind trying to turn her towards the child. The wind was rising, the trees setting into a roar, the circling rooks adding to the din. She was beginning to like the birds' aggression. They were reassuringly constant, like a favourite aunt who always welcomed you with a threat, but never followed through.

'Hallo, kann ich Ihnen helfen?'

Jane turned, startled, and saw a man standing in the shadows. She was suddenly aware of how she must look, huddled in the church doorway, her bruised face free of make-up, hair pulled back in no style at all. She dropped the cigarette on the ground and crushed it surreptitiously beneath her foot, hoping the man hadn't noticed.

'*Nein, danke.*'

'Are you okay?'

How would she ever learn German when everyone answered her in English?

'Yes, fine, just sheltering from the rain.'

Jane pulled her hood up and made to move, but the man blocked her way. The rain had grown suddenly heavier and his hair was plastered against his head, his black waterproof coursing with raindrops. She glanced towards the road, grey and deserted beyond the trees. It wasn't so far, but if he wished to, the stranger could make it all the distance in the world.

'Excuse me, please.'

The man's voice sounded weary. 'You can come in, if you want.'

'No, thank you.' Inside her pocket Jane fitted her keys between her fingers, arming herself with a makeshift knuckle-duster. 'I have to go home.'

'Okay,' he nodded, stepping aside. 'But there is help for you here, if you need it.'

He pushed a strand of wet hair from his face and Jane saw that he was Alban Mann's opposite: a young man adopting the sober style of a generation before him. She asked, 'Excuse me, but are you the minister?'

The man nodded. He frowned, as if bracing himself to hear what had brought her there.

'I'm Jane Logan.' She shifted to make room for him in the lee of the doorway, but he remained out in the rain. 'I live over there.' Jane nodded in the direction of the apartment building, unsure of why she was explaining herself. 'I thought I saw my neighbour's young daughter here and wanted to say hello.'

'You haven't been sleeping here?'

'No.' She laughed, too amused to be offended. 'It's a while since I slept in church.' He frowned and she added, 'Sorry, that was a silly joke. I told you, I live over the road.'

The priest nodded, as if not quite convinced.

'I am Father Walter. I would prefer to leave the door open, most pastors would, but then people sleep here. If it was just that, it wouldn't be so bad . . .' He let the sentence trail away.

Jane wondered if it was the street girls he was worried about, and if he had thought her a loose woman brought low. It was a story to tell Tielo the next time they all got together.

The priest took a key from his pocket, and then hesitated.

'Let me walk you to the gate.'

'Are you seeing me off the premises?'

She hoped Father Walter didn't detect the laugh in her voice. Was she flirting? What was it about stern men that brought out the silliness in her?

'You are welcome here, Frau Logan, but the graveyard isn't the best place for you to be on your own. Wait,' he turned the key in the lock, 'I will fetch an umbrella.'

'It's fine, I've got my hood . . .'

42

But he was gone. The feeling of wellbeing of just a moment ago deserted her, and Jane resisted a sudden urge to follow him into the dim interior of the church. She blew on her hands, trying to thaw them with her breath. It was the second time that day she had let herself get cold to her bones. Was the child still warm in her womb?

Father Walter's brolly was not quite wide enough to shelter them both and they walked down the path, huddled together like reluctant newlyweds. He crossed the road with her, the contrast between his young face and old-man garb growing stranger beyond the bounds of the *Kirche*.

'Why did you say it wasn't safe for me in the churchyard?'

He shrugged. 'Solitary places are not so safe for women on their own.'

'We're in the centre of the city.'

He nodded. 'Strange things can happen in the centre of cities. Your husband, is he American too?'

It still amazed her that foreigners couldn't distinguish her accent of hard consonants and brisk rhythms from an American drawl.

'I'm Scottish.' She smiled brightly, keeping the irritation from her voice. 'My *Lebenspartner* is German, originally from Wannsee.'

Put that up your flue and smoke it, she thought. But Father Walter's expression didn't alter.

'You are both welcome at our services.' They halted outside the door to the apartment block and he sheltered Jane as she selected the right key. 'The girl you were looking for, what is her name?'

The rain was heavier now, battering loud against the

priest's umbrella, and they were standing so close they might have been mistaken for lovers. Jane looked up and saw an angry scratch on Father Walter's chin where he had cut himself shaving.

'Anna.'

The priest nodded again, as if it were the answer he had expected. Jane turned the key in the lock and then stood in the doorway and watched as he crossed the road and made his way between the tombstones, black and cheerless as the rooks. Her eyes scanned the churchyard for a flash of red, but the graves stood grey and unmoving against the shivering grass.

Six

They had just finished dinner when the doorbell rang. Petra raised her eyebrows and went from the room, paying no attention to Jane's 'Let it ring'.

Jane had spent the afternoon trying to ignore the growing conviction that she was getting a cold. She had lain under a blanket on the double bed in the child's room, half reading her novel, half listening for the sound of high heels crossing the courtyard. She had woken with a start, woozy and ill-tempered, to the electronic trill of the telephone in the next room, stumbled into their bedroom and had actually lifted the receiver to her ear when the sound was replaced by the faint peal of her mobile. It died as she slid it free from the pocket of her jacket, hanging where she had thrown it, on the back of a kitchen chair.

Petra's message was quick and businesslike, set against a background of street noise. It had been a hell of a day. She was dropping by the gym on her way home; Jane should have supper without her.

'Sorry, baby, but it's the price you pay for a hot girlfriend.'

Jane listened three times, almost sure that Petra's laugh had been echoed by a second bark of amusement, but the hum and growl of traffic was too strong to be certain. It had taken all her willpower not to throw the phone at the wall. Instead she raked the fridge for vegetables and made a pot of soup, hoping the activity would calm her.

Petra's cheeks glowed, rosy as a polished apple, when she eventually came through the door. Jane hugged her, breathing in the outdoor chill still clinging to her coat, and the sharp mineral scent of an unfamiliar shower gel. Petra placed her hands either side of Jane's tummy and gave her a fresh-mint kiss. She glanced at the table, set with cutlery in the sitting room, and for a moment Jane thought she was about to say she'd already eaten, but they dined together in not quite silence. And when Jane asked how the gym had gone, Petra revealed that she'd not been at her usual spin or Pilates class, but for an impromptu game of badminton with Claudia, a previously unheard-of colleague.

The child moved swiftly in Jane's stomach, as if it too had been stung by a stab of jealousy. She winced and Petra swallowed her last mouthful and asked, 'Are you okay?' The doorbell cut through Jane's shake of the head and Petra laid down her spoon, saying, 'Saved by the bell,' in a bland voice that made Jane want to fling her own half-full bowl at her.

Now she could hear the low rumble of Alban Mann's voice in the hallway, followed by Petra's higher tones. She recognised the answering rhythms in their accents and stroked her tummy, willing the child to hit her again.

'A visitor for you.'

Petra ushered Alban into the room, making a questioning face behind his back. She was lithe and glowing, the effects of the badminton game still working on her, and Jane was suddenly aware of her own ungainly shape. The dishes were still on the dinner table. Jane began to stack them, but Petra took the plates from her.

'I'll do that. Coffee?' She turned the full force of her charm on Herr Mann. Petra's charm was hard to resist, but Mann shook his head.

'No thank you. I apologise for interrupting your meal.'

'We'd finished.' Jane passed her cold bowl to Petra.

Mann stood awkwardly in the centre of the room. Jane knew that if she were to settle herself in one of the armchairs then he would also sit, and some of the embarrassment would evaporate. She remained standing.

Petra glanced between them and put the small pile of plates back on the table. 'Is everything okay?'

'I came to apologise for this afternoon.'

Petra said, 'What happened this afternoon?'

Jane ignored her. 'There's no need to apologise to me.' She heard her own emphasis on the final word, 'to *me*', and thought she sounded like a prig.

'Did something happen I should know about?' It was the voice Petra used on the phone to recalcitrant work colleagues; cold and glittering, hard as glass.

'Dr Mann and his daughter had an argument in the hall-way, it was nothing.'

Petra's teeth gleamed in her smile; an invitation for Alban Mann to leave. 'Everyone argues. It was gracious of you to apologise.'

Mann's eyes met Jane's. 'Anna is a difficult child. I do my best but sometimes . . .'

'Sometimes you want to slap her.'

'Jane.' Petra's voice was almost all breath, but Alban Mann's expression remained calm.

'Sometimes I want to hold her so tight no harm can come to her. When you have your own child you'll understand.'

Jane trembled with the urge to punch him. How dare he bring her child into it?

Mann's eyes glanced around the room, then back to Jane. 'I also wanted to ask if you'd seen Anna.' He smiled, but the slick charm he'd exerted on their first meeting was gone.

'She isn't home yet?'

'No, not yet.'

'Shouldn't you call the police?'

Mann gave a weary shrug of the shoulders.

'When she was younger the police would bring her back. Now they tell me she'll come home by herself. Sometimes I go looking for her. Sometimes I sit and wait.'

'How old is Anna, Herr Mann?'

'Thirteen.'

The make-up had made her look younger. Thirteen was old enough to feel grown up. You could get into a lot of trouble at thirteen.

'It's not for me to presume, but maybe if you cut her a bit of slack she'd be less inclined to be rebellious?'

There it was again, the priggish tone stiffening her language and reminding her of a particular teacher who had delighted in giving her detentions.

Mann looked away from her, his gaze scanning the pile of plates, the squashed cushions on the couch where she had awaited Petra's return, and Jane wondered if he suspected

Anna of hiding in their apartment. She said, 'I'm sorry we can't be of any help.'

'Thank you.' Mann nodded as if he had accepted something that had been inevitable all along. 'I'm sorry to have disturbed your evening, and your afternoon. Please, don't worry.' His eyes met hers. 'My daughter will come home when she's ready.'

Petra walked him to the door. Jane let herself sink into the couch. Across the city people were clinking wineglasses in restaurants, meeting friends in pubs and *Biergartens*; nightclubs were gearing towards opening their doors, but for her the day was almost over and she was glad of it. She thought of the empty street outside their window, the grass shivering beneath the gravestones, and the rooks, heads tucked beneath their wings, rocked to sleep in the swaying treetops. Where would Anna sleep that night?

Cities had always had their watchers, waiting in the shadows, ready to make the most of whatever flotsam drifted their way. They had always had their lost girls, too, falling into arms that were all too eager to catch them, though they never held on for long.

Had the minister really thought her a pregnant streetwalker in need of shelter? They were pretty, these girls, much younger than her, most of them; perhaps she should take it as a compliment. Jane let her fingers run lightly across her tummy and thought again of Anna, the bruise just below her eye that almost mirrored her own. The girl was out there alone in the dark, and yet her father was reluctant to call the police.

Petra walked in, shaking her head, and dropped on to the couch beside her.

'In America you get a welcome basket from your neighbours; in Berlin you meet them fighting on the stairs. Let's keep our distance.' She turned and looked at Jane, as if suddenly seeing her properly for the first time. 'Are you okay?' She touched Jane's face gently, put her arms around her and drew her close. 'You're not upset because a teenage tantrum got out of control?'

'I don't like Alban Mann.'

Petra pulled away, the better to look at her.

'It's normal to rebel at his daughter's age, normal too for him not to like it. Fathers always want their daughters to remain little girls. Imagine,' she stroked Jane's cheek, 'for years you're the only man in this perfect creature's life, then suddenly she grows breasts and starts looking at boys, or worse, at girls. You've no idea of the arguments I had with my father. The only thing that could stop us was my mother's tears.' She looked away. 'Sometimes not even that.'

'I heard him through the wall, calling her a whore.'

Petra shrugged. 'Maybe she is.'

They were apart now, facing each other on the couch as if they were about to box or play cat's cradle.

'She's a child.'

'Are we talking about the same girl?' Petra snorted. 'I've passed her on the stairs with her skirt up to here,' she touched her leg high on the thigh, 'wearing more make-up than all the girls on the MAC counter combined. If I was her father I'd do more than shout, I'd invest in a strong lock and an electronic tag. No wonder the poor man looks shattered.'

50

'She has a bruise on her face.'

'So do you.' Petra stroked Jane's cheek gently. 'You also have a vivid imagination.'

Jane could feel the conviction leaking from her voice.

'Abused girls are often highly sexualised.'

'Every cloud has a silver lining.'

'That's not funny.'

'I know.' Petra caressed Jane's bump, her fingers soft and soothing. 'I'm sorry. I don't like you getting upset.'

'It's not good for the baby.'

'Not good for anyone.' Petra pushed Jane's top up and kissed her exposed skin. 'Anna is just a stroppy teenager and Herr Doktor Mann is just a father out of his depth. Forget them.' Petra slid the waistband of Jane's trousers down, exposing her hip bones, and ran her tongue along the sensitive part of Jane's tummy, just above her knickers. 'You'll feel better after a good night's sleep.'

'I'm not sure I'll be able to sleep.'

'Of course you will.' Petra pressed her face gently against Jane's stomach and smiled as the child hit out.

'He's getting stronger all the time.'

'He or she.'

'He or she is getting stronger all the time.'

'What does it sound like?'

Petra adopted a pseudo-scientific expression. 'Hmm, let me see.' She rested her ear on Jane's belly and then looked up, her face creased with delight. 'I think he's singing.'

Jane laughed. But Anna was still in her mind and she didn't ask about her child's song.

* * *

She woke at 3.00 a.m, unsure if the banging that had roused her had been in her head or on the stairwell. The room was in darkness, Petra's even breaths the only other sound. Jane lay still, letting the pounding in her heart subside. Was Anna home yet or still wandering the streets? There were worse things than wandering the streets. People were quick to offer shelter when you were young and pretty. Was she lying in some stranger's bed, their door bolted, the key hidden? Jane slipped from between the sheets, noticing that Petra no longer stirred when she left their bed.

The child's room was cold. Jane took the woollen coverlet from the bottom of the bed, wrapped it round her nakedness and stood at the window, looking out on the night. The child moved, testing the boundaries of its world. That was probably all Anna was doing, testing the boundaries. Jane put her hand to her cheekbone. Checking the tenderness of her bruise had become as much a habit with her as touching her stomach. Were these her boundaries, her body, this apartment? If she were Anna's age and free to live her life again, what would she change?

It was morbid to think like that. She would fetch a book and get into the spare bed; that way she could read herself back to sleep without disturbing Petra. She turned and saw her own face, pale in the mirror, and behind it a flicker of light so brief she was unsure if it was a spark of her imagination. Jane pulled the coverlet closer and stood sentinel at the window, like a fisherman's wife waiting on the quayside after a storm.

There it was again, the faintest glimmer on the other side of the courtyard. Was it a light from somewhere in her building reflecting on a broken window in the derelict backhouse?

It flickered again and disappeared. The windows in the back-house were almost all free of glass. It shone again, faint and wavering; could it be the wind breezing through an unglazed window, causing a flame to tremble?

She pressed her fingers against her bruise. It might not be Anna. The night was cold and there were plenty of down-and-outs in Berlin. But the possibility that it was the girl fixed Jane's eyes on the faint glimmer. What would persuade a child to hide in an abandoned building amongst the pigeon droppings and scuttle of rats? What could be so bad that you would prefer the company of ghosts to home?

Jane stroked her stomach through the soft weave of the blanket. A mother's first consideration was to her own child. The light shimmered, faint and persistent as a wrecker's lantern. Only a fool would put their unborn in danger for the lure of a trembling flame. It was impossible.

She tiptoed softly back to their bedroom, retrieved her boots, leggings and jumper and pulled them on in the hall. There was a torch in the cloakroom. She shoved it into her jacket pocket and stole out of the apartment.

Seven

The landing light lasted until she was on the second floor, then plunged her into darkness. Jane clicked on the torch, trying not to recoil at the crazy shapes thrown against the walls by the banister and twisting stairs. She reached the ground floor, followed all the way by her own black shadow, and cursed, remembering that she should have brought the key to the back court. But the door opened easily and she saw that a piece of gaffer tape had been stuck across the latch, stopping the door from locking automatically when it closed. Out of curiosity she tried the building's front entrance and found it locked. The person who had disabled the door to the courtyard had needed a key, or an accomplice with a key. Had they come from within her building?

Jane turned off the torch and slipped out into the cold of the back court, closing the door gently behind her. The courtyard was shadowed on all four sides by tall tenements. She breathed in night and darkness and was touched by a feeling of déjà vu. There were so many places Jane couldn't remember. Perhaps she was recalling somewhere she had lived as a child, or maybe it was simply a sense of all the other people who had crossed the yard in the dark, not knowing whose eyes were upon them.

Jane looked up towards the looming bulk of the back-house, hearing the sound of her own breath, shallow and uneven. The light was gone from the window. This was her cue to turn back, but she stepped on, into the dimness of the courtyard, tensing against the cold and the sensation of unseen eyes. The backhouse door gaped; beyond it, nothing but blackness.

She kept the torch off and stepped into the building, putting one foot gingerly in front of the other, feeling broken tiles underneath her boots. The place smelt as she knew it would, of the sharpness of urine overlaid with damp mortar, rotting newspapers and decay. There was a scent below that too, sweet and nasty, an odour for dogs to roll in. Would the girl really hide herself here?

Something rustled beneath the stairs and Jane forced herself not to cry out. Was it true that rats would leap for your throat? She clicked the torch on and pointed it at the floor, guarding the beam with her hand. The stairwell was a mean reflection of the one in their apartment block, scaffold steep, with less space for the sweeping curves that graced their lobby.

There was the sudden sound of boots on the bare floor-boards above. Jane turned the torch off, plummeting back into darkness. A faint voice, light and female, came from somewhere upstairs. Anna's name was half formed on Jane's lips, when a second voice sounded above her, deep and hoarse, and unmistakably male.

'Christ.' She shrank against the wall.

Upstairs the woman laughed, as if in response to Jane's alarm. The man said something quick and urgent and the woman answered him, all business now. There was a pause and then the thudding started, slow at first, but developing into an unmistakable rhythm.

'Fuck.' Jane's curse was lower than a whisper. She was filled with a childish urge to laugh. Jesus, this wasn't a dinner-party story.

Her eyes had almost adjusted to the darkness; she crept back the way she had come, towards the door, tensing at the sound of fragments of glass crunching beneath her boots. Upstairs the tempo increased and then came to a halt. That was her cue to up-pace. Jane stepped quick and sure towards the lighter shade of black. She was almost there when her foot kicked against something. It rattled as it bounced, loud as an orchestra in the empty hallway.

There was a shout from above followed by the hollow thud of heavy boots, an echo of the dream that had woken her. Jane pulled up her hood and dashed across the courtyard, one hand on her stomach. She barrelled into the lobby, ripping the tape from the back-door latch and letting the lock slam to. She clicked the light switch on but the hallway remained in darkness. She cursed as she realised that, in her rush, she had pressed the doorbell of the ground-floor flat.

'Fuck.'

Jane hastened towards the stairs, but it was as if the occupant had been waiting for her to call because the door opened and a wizened face peered from within. The old person smiled and beckoned to her. Jane looked at the stairs looming steeply above and ducked into the apartment.

Eight

'*Sind es die Russen?*'

The old lady was tiny and layered with clothes. Jane glimpsed the frill of a long nightie beneath a pink sateen underskirt, which was in turn topped by a dress patterned with sunflowers. A raincoat completed the ensemble.

'Sorry?'

'The Russians.' The woman's English was clear and barely accented, but her voice was a whisper. 'Are they after you?'

'No,' Jane faltered. 'I don't think so.'

'This wouldn't stop them.' She touched Jane's belly, her smile as cheerful as her summer frock. 'They're pigs.'

'I've heard that.' Jane kept her own voice low, listening out for the sound of a commotion outside. 'I'll just hide from them here for a wee moment, if you don't mind.'

'No, not here.' The woman's eyes were wide. 'Where could you hide here?' She waved an arm and Jane took in a small hallway, made smaller by the overstuffed bookcases that lined both walls. 'No,' the old woman took her hand in a surprisingly strong grip and propelled her along the lobby, 'you must come through.'

The sitting room felt stuffy after the chill of the

backhouse. The bookcases continued through here, but the space was dominated by a large double bed tumbled with blankets. All three bars of the electric fire glowed red, too close to the mattress for safety. A smell of burnt dust, cooking and stale cat litter percolated the room. The old lady roused an elderly tabby from one of a pair of armchairs.

'This young lady is going to have a baby, Albert, so you will need to make space for her.' She looked anxiously at Jane as if something had just occurred to her. 'You're not going to have it now, are you?'

'I've a while yet.'

'Good.' The old woman moved a bundle of newspapers and settled herself on the other chair, beaming with delight. 'I'm not sure I would remember what to do.'

'Were you a nurse?'

'No, I'm a teacher.' The old woman stood up. 'I mustn't be late. It sets a bad example.'

Jane glanced at the clock on the mantel.

'You're all right; it's only three forty-five.'

'Then I've missed the whole day.'

They had been keeping their voices to a whisper but now the old lady's voice was rising with distress. Jane pulled herself to her feet and put a comforting hand on her arm.

'Three forty-five in the morning, all your pupils will be safe in bed.'

'*Beruhige dich, Heike.*'

Jane gasped as the mound of bedclothes moved, like an ancient hillside preparing to reveal the sacred army hidden in its depths. An old man emerged from beneath the blankets, his face creased with sleep. He eased himself up painfully, bolstering his back with the pillows, his eyes half closing against the light.

'It is the middle of the night, and anyway, it's the school holidays.'

The old lady sat back down, easily mollified.

'Look, Karl, we have a visitor, a nice pregnant English lady.'

The man rubbed his eyes and groaned. His head was bald and patched with age-spots; his mouth, wide and thin-lipped, would have been a gift to a clown. He placed a pair of glasses on his nose and looked at Jane, apparently unsurprised to find a foreigner at the bottom of his bed in the middle of the night.

'My wife likes to talk English. She is a very educated woman. I thank you for bringing her home. Normally I notice if she goes out in the night, but tonight I slept.' He rubbed his face again and his wide mouth drooped sadly. 'That is a problem.'

'No . . .'

Jane wanted to explain but the old lady was on her feet again.

'She's running from the Russians.'

'The Russians?' The old man glanced at Jane and for a second she thought he was about to humour his wife, but then he said, 'They are not as active as they once were, Heike.'

Jane could feel the strain of the night working on her. She wondered if Anna was after all asleep upstairs in her own bed, but she said, 'Anna Mann has gone missing and I thought I saw her in the backhouse. I was mistaken, but I'm afraid I pressed your doorbell instead of the light switch when I came back in.'

'You went into the backhouse in the dark on your own?' Surprise mingled with concern in his voice, or was it anger?

'I didn't like to think of her out there in the cold.'

'Frau . . . ?' The old man hesitated, unsure of what to call her.

'Frau Logan . . . Jane, I live upstairs.'

'I know.' He nodded. 'We have seen you and your sister. She keeps long hours, and you keep house. We are Frau and Herr Becker.' His gaze moved to her belly and lingered there. Jane wondered if Herr Becker was going to ask her where the child's father was, but he continued, 'I will give you some advice. It is not a good idea to wander around here in the middle of the night.'

'I thought that Anna . . .'

He cut through her words, quick and sabre-sharp.

'Better you leave Anna Mann alone.'

'She's only a child . . .'

Frau Becker's voice was petulant. 'Who is Anna Mann?'

The harsh edge in her husband's voice blunted into softness.

'You know Anna, Greta and Alban Mann's daughter.'

The old lady smiled and Jane realised they were entering Frau Becker's realm: the past.

'I liked Greta. People shook their heads when they talked about her, but she was so pretty, I would have liked to marry her.'

'Lucky for both of us, I married you first.'

Herr Becker propped himself up on one arm. His pyjama top hung open, exposing a thicket of white chest hair.

Jane asked, 'What happened to Herr Mann's wife?'

Herr Becker stared at Jane and she noticed how small and dark his eyes were. She thought he was about to ask if it was any of her business, but then he shrugged.

'When Anna was two years old, Greta walked out in the middle of the night.'

Frau Becker giggled. 'Alban Mann killed his wife and buried her beneath the floorboards in the *Hinterhaus*.'

'That's an old joke, Heike.' Herr Becker's voice was firm, as if he were addressing a recalcitrant child whose treat he didn't want to spoil, but whose excitement must be checked. 'You remember Greta, she liked to drink and dance and have a good time. Babies get in the way of all that.' He looked at Jane. 'It is my opinion she went to Hamburg, or maybe America.'

'It's not a joke.' The old lady stared at Jane fiercely, offering a glimpse of the kind of teacher she might have been. 'He strangled her, up there in his apartment, next door to where you sleep.'

Jane whispered, 'What makes you think he murdered her?'

'I would if she were my wife.'

'You're being silly, Heike,' Herr Becker chided. 'A moment ago you were saying you would have liked to marry her.'

'I've changed my mind. I want a wife who will cook and clean and make my dinner.' She looked up as if she had suddenly remembered something. 'When is dinner-time? I'm hungry.'

61

'We will eat after we've slept.'

It was Jane's cue to leave but she asked, 'Did the police have any idea of what might have happened to Greta?'

'Police?' The old woman was incredulous. 'No one called the police.'

Her husband's voice was firm. 'Because there was no crime.'

'She went no further than the courtyard and there she stays.' The old woman laughed. 'You check beneath the floorboards in the *Hinterhaus* if you want to know about Greta Mann. I wonder if she still has her lovely hair.'

'Heike,' Karl Becker's voice was sharp. 'You'll frighten the young lady.'

'No,' Jane tried for a smile. 'It's okay. It's late and you've been very kind to me. I should let you go back to sleep.'

The old woman got to her feet. 'I have to get ready for school.'

'It is vacation-time, remember?' Herr Becker reached beneath the bed and passed his wife a battered textbook. Jane caught a glimpse of a boy in lederhosen and a girl in a checked pinafore on its cover. The boy was chalking something on a blackboard, while the girl played pupil. The old man said, 'Why don't you plan what lesson you will give the children when they come back?'

Frau Becker looked at her husband suspiciously, but she began to leaf through the book's pages, too quickly to take in their detail. Herr Becker slipped from the bed, pulling on a heavy grey-and-black dressing gown, not quite big enough to fasten around his paunch.

Jane got to her feet.

'Goodbye, Frau Becker, thank you for letting me hide here.'

But the old lady was absorbed in her book, and didn't reply. The tabby jumped on to the chair, settling itself in Jane's warmth. She rubbed the cat between its ears. It turned and hissed, baring its teeth at her. Jane felt its breath, warm and alive against her skin, as she snatched her hand away.

Herr Becker said, 'I'm sorry. Old age has made Albert bad-tempered.'

Frau Becker looked up from her book.

'Albert was always bad-tempered. He's the same as ever he was.' Her voice took on a sing-song tone. 'I'm the same as ever I was, and you are the same as ever you were. Time makes us older and our bodies rot, but we stay the same inside.'

Herr Becker glanced at his wife, but made no reply. He put a hand on Jane's shoulder.

'I will escort you home.'

She glanced up, saw the sheen of night-time sweat that greased his skin, smelled the sour scent of him. His breath touched her face and it was as warm and unwelcome as the cat's bite.

Frau Becker sing-songed, 'People who die young stay beautiful for ever. Who gets the best of the bargain, those who die or those who stay?'

Neither of them answered her. Jane said, 'I've put you to enough bother, Herr Becker. I can find my own way out.'

But the old man followed her, keeping close in the corridor shrunk with the weight of books. He unlocked the door and then turned to face Jane, blocking her exit.

'You mustn't listen to my wife, she is a very clever woman, but in recent years . . .'

'Yes.' She interrupted to save him the pain of an explanation. There was the sound of a cupboard door slamming in the sitting room, and Frau Becker started to sing in a high, wavering voice. Her husband looked towards the noise but remained standing by the door, steeling himself for the task ahead. Jane knew she should let him go but she asked, 'This belief about Herr Mann and his wife, is it a recent fancy?'

The old man shook his head.

'Anyone who cared to look would see that Greta was unsuited to motherhood, anyone except for her husband. Things have changed a lot here. The city has become a carousel, but Alban Mann stays. I think in his heart he still hopes the carousel will turn full circle and bring Greta home to him.' His wide mouth stretched into a smile and he looked again like a sad clown. 'Who knows? Perhaps it will.'

Herr Becker moved to let Jane pass. His hand stroked against her thigh, but the corridor was so narrow she could not be sure whether it was by accident or design . . .

'Frau Logan . . .'

'Yes?'

His eyes met hers, hard and dark, like the eyes of a younger man, still moved by ambition.

'Please remember what I said. Stay away from the backhouse, especially by night.'

'Why?'

Herr Becker lowered his voice. 'Abandoned buildings are like abandoned people. They grow bitter and start to keep bad company. Haven't you seen shadows crossing the court-yard at night?'

'Perhaps. Whose shadows are they?'

The old man shook his head.

'I know enough to keep my windows locked and my door bolted. Whatever goes on there is none of our business.' He smiled, closing the subject. 'It's late and whoever you were avoiding has gone now.'

He took her hand, his palm warm and damp against hers. Jane returned his smile, pretending not to feel the pressure of his grip tightening as she pulled her own hand free.

'Please don't worry, I can make my own way home.'

She listened for the sound of the Beckers' front door shutting as she climbed the stairs, but the old man must have closed it softly because, although she stopped on the landing to listen, she didn't hear the latch clicking home.

Jane let herself quietly into the apartment, surprised to see the lightening grey of a winter dawn stretching though the windows. There was a figure, standing by the window, a silhouette in the shadows. She gasped and then laughed with relief as the figure turned and she recognised Petra.

'Where in hell have you been?'

'Out.' Jane's smile withered and all of her resentments at Petra's early starts and late nights at the office were in the word. 'I went for a walk.'

'At this time in the morning?'

'Why not?'

'Why do you think? Because it's dark, you're pregnant and you gave me a fright.'

'I didn't realise pregnant women were under curfew in Berlin.'

She wanted nothing more than to get back into bed and forget her strange adventure. The dust of the backhouse was still on her skin. She went through to their bedroom and started to strip off her clothes. Petra followed her.

'I thought you were getting better but you're still fucking irresponsible.' She paused, stepping neatly into the well-worn rhythm of their arguments, but Jane remained silent. After a moment Petra snapped, 'You're all right, you can sleep through the morning, but I have to be at work in a few hours.'

'Think of it as practice for when the baby comes.'

Jane pulled her jumper over her head, and then wriggled out of her leggings.

'I can't believe you're already using our child as a weapon.'

Jane wanted to scream that it wasn't their child yet, it was hers, but that would be untrue. She pulled off her underwear and stood there naked, feeling fat and ungainly but determined not to hide herself.

'I'm awake every night. I just felt like getting some fresh air. I'm sorry I woke you. Perhaps I should sleep in the other room.'

'Yes.' Petra plucked Jane's dressing gown from the back of the bedroom door and flung it at her. 'Perhaps you should.'

Nine

Jane woke with a start, and the feeling that somewhere in the apartment a door had slammed. She pulled on her dressing gown, wondering if Petra had left for work, and saw the note on the table next to the bed.

Sorry I overreacted, I'm useless without sleep.

Love you, P x

P.S. I love that you're irresponsible, but sometimes you scare me.

'Sometimes I scare myself.'

Was she speaking to herself, or to the child? Jane touched her tummy, as she did these days when she woke. Sometimes it felt as if she and the baby were co-conspirators against the rest of the world. Christ, she was like a lonely child inventing an invisible friend.

She got up, shoved her feet into her slippers, and went to the window. The backhouse was calm today, the open window frozen in place. It seemed taller and darker and, though it wasn't possible, closer. Had she really crossed the courtyard in the dark and gone inside? Jane drew her robe tight. The radiator beneath the window was warm to the touch but the child's room retained its vacant chill, as if no one had entered it for a long time.

She looked again at the derelict building opposite, realising that even in summer its shadow would stretch into the room, smothering all chance of warmth. She had thought the backhouse an inferior copy of their smarter, newly renovated block, but perhaps the opposite was true and their building was a reflection of the decaying tenement. The notion made her feel small, and the child within her smaller still, a lone fish stranded in inland waters.

A pigeon swooped across the courtyard and fluttered for a moment on a windowsill before flying in through the open window. The building's stare faltered, the spell was broken and Jane turned away. It was one thing to abandon a building, quite another to desert a child.

She went into the room Petra had turned into an office, logged into her computer and found Alban Mann's number in an online directory. The phone call was short and businesslike.

Anna had arrived home late last night. She was safe in bed, still sleeping off her adventure. Mann seemed to have regained his poise. He reassured Jane, in smooth tones tinged with amusement (how dare he be amused?), that he was grateful for her concern, but everything was back to normal.

'All's well that ends well.'

Jane heard the smile in his voice, his pleasure at finding the right phrase in a foreign tongue, and felt the conversation drawing to a close. She blurted, 'Anna wasn't locked in the backyard, was she?'

'No.' Mann sounded puzzled. 'Why do you ask that?'

'I thought I heard something in the courtyard and wondered if it was Anna,' she lied. 'But when I looked out, there was no one there.'

'I heard something too. Running feet and slamming doors, but Anna was home and my thoughts were with her.'

'Of course.'

They said their goodbyes, formal as a couple after a one-night stand, and Jane wondered why, however polite Alban Mann was, she found it hard to believe anything he said.

This time the door to the *Kirche* was open. She slipped in, smelling the unfamiliar scent of worship: polish, stale incense, fading flowers and something else, perhaps simply the smell of cold without damp.

A suffering Christ was nailed to the cross above the altar, his face flung back, ghastly and horribly lifelike; deathlike. The child sent out a kick. Jane felt the urge to look away from the tortured image but she forced herself to take in the rent in his side, the blood leaking from his brow, the eyes falling back in the lolling head. It was just paint and wood and she hated the thought that the child might be forging a weakness inside her.

A small carousel of postcards stood on a table littered with leaflets at the back of the pews. Jane gave the rack a shove, but it refused to spin. It didn't matter. There was only one image for sale, repeated over and over like an Ersatz-Warhol: a foreshortened view of the church, taken in black and white on a *dreich* day. The church spire loomed tall and threatening above the gravestones, like a tool of vengeance. All it needed was a terrified girl fleeing down the pathway in her night-gown to turn it into a perfect horror-movie poster.

It was the kind of thing that would amuse her old work-mates back in the bookshop in London. Maybe she could atone for the promised emails still unsent, the Facebook page she would never establish. Jane felt in her pocket for some change and when she failed to find any, slipped a postcard into her pocket with a quick glance at Jesus.

'Forgive us our trespasses as we forgive those who trespass against us.'

It was the only prayer she knew by heart.

'Frau Logan.'

The priest was at her elbow. Jane felt her face redden. Her hand clutched the stolen card in her pocket.

'I'm sorry. I didn't mean to frighten you.'

'No,' she laughed. 'It's okay. That's the second time I've done that recently. I didn't hear you coming.'

Had he seen her? She felt the weight of the store detective's hand on her shoulder, the shame of the police interview. When would she learn?

'These shoes.' The priest lifted a foot to display rubberised soles. 'Perhaps they make me too silent.'

'I guess it means you don't interrupt the peace of the church.'

She was talking to him as long-married women often talked to their husbands, as if he were a child.

'I don't mean to interrupt your worship.'

'No.' It was hard not to smile at the suggestion. 'Actually, I was looking for you.'

The worry was back in the priest's face. He glanced towards the altar as if seeking an eyewitness.

'Would you like to take confession?'

Jane gave a polite smile.

'No, thank you. I noticed you have a nursery and wondered if you had any facilities for even younger children.'

'You want to leave your baby here?' He sounded horrified.

'No, I'd like to get to know other mothers. I thought you might have a group where women and their babies meet other women and their babies.'

It sounded ridiculous, but the priest looked relieved.

'Of course.' He hesitated as if unsure of the best course, but another glance at the altar seemed to decide him. 'There is a register.'

He turned and walked towards the back of the church. Jane returned the postcard to the rack and went after him.

A heavy wooden dresser, topped by glass-fronted book-shelves, took up one wall of the priest's inner sanctum; an oak table surrounded by mismatched chairs dominated the rest of the space. The priest had switched on a pendant light and its tobacco-tinged glow revealed the shadows of dead flies littering the inside of the glass shade. The smell of polish and incense was stronger here and Jane was gripped by a fresh pang of nausea. The priest pulled out a chair for her and started to root amongst the ledgers on the shelves.

It was a cold day, but the room felt close. Jane sat down, noticing a small desk where she supposed he must write his sermons. She wasn't sure she could bear to work there, with the church at her back. Above the desk was a narrow frosted-glass window, guarded on the outside by metal bars, as if the church's architects had thought that one day there might be a siege. Another Christ looked down from a picture by the door, his blond hair curled in a demi-perm, one hand touching his exposed heart, the other raised in a blessing. His eyes were an impossible shade of cornflower blue that only newborns had.

Jane felt her stomach lurch and looked at the window again, trying to make it her horizon. She didn't even want to join a mother-and-baby group; had only come to show Petra that she was making sensible preparations for the child's arrival.

'Are you okay?' The priest's worried look was back.

'Just a little warm.'

'Some air might help?'

He took a window pole that had been propped against the side of the dresser, pushed the sash up and pulled out his desk chair, offering it to her.

'Thank you.'

Jane moved to the seat by the window, breathing in the scent of rain and earthy dampness that filtered into the room. Some handwritten pages were splayed across the desk next to a discarded ballpoint, the handwriting small and tightly coiled, like a cipher that might read clearly in a mirror. A Bible tagged with bookmarks lay shut beside them and next to it a bright-red hair clasp shaped like a bow. Jane picked up the clasp, just as the priest lifted the volume he had been looking for from the shelf and turned towards her. When he saw what she was holding, his anxious smile died.

'I'm sorry; I couldn't help noticing this.' She was unsure whether it was worry or anger that now wrinkled the priest's brow. 'I hope you don't mind,' she gave a nervous laugh. 'As you know, my German isn't good enough to read your papers.'

'Of course.' The priest placed the ledger on the table and started leafing through it. For a moment his features were hidden, but when he looked up his composure was restored. 'I found it outside and thought perhaps it belongs to one of the mothers.'

'It's mine.' Jane slid the cheap clip into her hair where she had no doubt it looked ridiculous. 'I must have dropped it when I was here last week. My hair got soaked in the rain.'

The priest stared at her for a moment and then shut the ledger with a finality that felt like a judgement. He replaced the book amongst its fellows on the shelf.

'I'm afraid our mother-and-child group is completely full.'

'Could I be added to the waiting list?'

'The waiting list is long; it would be better to join another kindergarten. There are many in this district.'

Jane got to her feet, raising a hand to the clasp to make sure it was still there.

'I won't take up any more of your time.'

The priest opened the door to the church for her, his expression as bland and unreadable as the look on the face of the blond Jesus as he plucked his bleeding heart from his chest.

The heels of Jane's boots rang against the tiled floor of the aisle as she made her way from the church. She tugged the plastic bow from her curls and looked at it again, before slipping it into the pocket of her coat. She was almost sure that she had seen it before, tucked into Anna Mann's sleek, black hair.

Ten

It was Petra who spotted him first. 'Look,' she said, pointing an indiscreet finger at the street beyond the cab window. 'Isn't that your friend?'

They'd been to the Kino International. Petra had guaranteed that the film would be in English, but it had been dubbed into German and Jane had been unable to keep track of the plot which had taken on a dreamlike, vaguely nightmarish quality. She hadn't expected the heroine to be murdered and the way the girl's pupils widened as her assailant pushed the knife into her belly was still with her.

She leant across Petra and saw Alban Mann leaning on his stick at the corner of Sophienstrasse, deep in conversation with two women. The night was cold and Alban wore an overcoat and jaunty tweed cap, but the women were jacketless, dressed in skin-tight trousers, high boots and white corsets. Their long black hair looked as if it had been dyed from the same bottle. Jane wondered if they were wearing wigs and if they dressed alike to encourage the impression that they were sisters. Perhaps they *were* sisters. Alban said something and the girls laughed. One of them put a hand on his shoulder, stepping closer.

The lights changed to green, the line of traffic edged slowly on and their cab moved with it. Jane twisted round to catch a final glimpse of Alban through the rear window. The girls had an arm around each other now; one toyed with the other's hair.

'I told you he was a creep.'

'You implied he was an incestuous child molester.'

'I think that strengthens my case.'

'Really?' Amusement deepened Petra's voice. 'Those women looked older than eighteen to me.'

'They're prostitutes.'

'And I thought they were collecting for the Salvation Army.'

'It's not funny; the kind of man who pays women for sex? Who knows what he's capable of?'

Petra took Jane's hand in hers and kissed it.

'I love you. You're so passionate and so naïve.'

Jane pulled away. 'Don't patronise me.'

It was growing dark and the office workers who had crowded the pavements when Jane had set out to meet Petra had been replaced by the going-out crowd. There were fewer suits and briefcases in the mix, but it was the body language that revealed night-time's coming in. No one was pinned to the cross any more. Shoulders had more give in them, walks were looser, and there were more couples; holding hands, wandering into bars and restaurants, joining other couples in an unspoken celebration of the freedom at day's end.

Petra said, 'I'm not patronising you. Practically every man has paid for sex at some point, every woman too when you think about it. At least these girls are honest about the transaction.'

'I've never paid for sex.'

Petra raised her eyebrows. 'All those times you're extra nice to me?'

Jane knew she was being teased. She kept her voice neutral, but irritation clipped her words.

'Love isn't an exchange.'

'No.' Petra's hand snaked across the seat, on to Jane's lap and down the inside of her thighs. 'But I bought your cinema ticket so I hope you're going to put out when we get home.'

'Fuck off.' She lifted Petra's hand and let it drop. 'If I thought you were serious I'd get out of the taxi.'

The cab stopped at a junction. An old man sat in a wheel-chair outside a pharmacy, a paper cup in his outstretched hand. Strange to think that he had been a baby once, that everyone had: the slim blonde girls in skinny jeans and fitted jackets who tied their scarves so cleverly, the cyclists gliding round the junction, the young couple kissing at the kerbside regardless of the green *Ampelmann*, the Roma women kneel-ing on the pavement.

Petra said, 'I am serious.'

Jane thought about opening the door and stepping into the street, but she was on the road side of the cab, rain had started to spatter the windows and she knew she would only make for home anyway.

'Don't go.' Petra leant over and kissed her on the sensitive spot just above her ear. She placed a proprietorial hand on Jane's tummy and stroked it gently through her coat. 'It would be impossible if you got a chill now.'

Jane looked at her. 'Are you worried about me or the baby?'

'Both. Why?' Petra's smile was wicked. It made her look like her brother Tielo. 'Are you jealous?'

'Of course not.' Was she? Jane looked out at the rows of apartment blocks scrolling past. She remembered standing outside a high-rise in the rain, looking up at the lighted windows above, trying to imagine the lives within. How old had she been then? 'Do you think Alban was renting those girls?'

'Who cares?' Petra sighed. 'Maybe he's a time-waster who gets his kicks from talking to whores.'

'They seemed to know him.'

'I imagine whores are good at making strangers feel at home.' Petra turned to face her. 'You're fascinated, aren't you? Would you like us to invite one back some time?'

It was another tease, but Jane muttered, 'Don't be disgusting.'

Later that night in bed, when Petra started to kiss the back of her neck, the memory of the two girls drifted into Jane's mind. She remembered the Sleeping Beauty contrast between their long black hair and pale skin, so like Anna's colouring. She saw them again as they leant towards Alban, laughing, the light touch on the shoulder that drew him closer, the girl's fingers playing with her companion's curls. And it took all of her will to push the image away.

Jane woke in the early hours. She left their bedroom and stood for a while in the jewellery-box brightness of the bathroom, listening for signs of life in the next apartment. But the only sound was a faint trickling in the central-heating pipes and after a while she turned out the light and went through to the child's room.

There was no flickering glow, no movement at all in the darkness that was the backhouse. She thought she'd been dreaming of Anna's mother, Greta, lying beneath the floor-boards on the second floor, but in the dream Greta had been confused with Alban's whores and the murdered girl in the film; the way her eyes had widened when the knife went in.

The door suddenly opened and Jane gasped, even though she knew it was Petra.

'What is it?' Petra put her arms around Jane, cradling her bump.

'I couldn't sleep.'

'Uncomfortable?'

'Not really.'

There was no point in trying to explain.

'It's cold in here.' Petra rubbed her face against Jane's shoulder. Her voice was hoarse with sleep. 'We should do something to this room. We haven't even got a crib yet.'

'Ute said we could have Carsten's old one.'

'You don't mind second-hand?'

'No. Carsten's a strong, healthy boy.'

'Would it matter if he weren't?'

'A boy?'

'Strong and healthy.'

'I don't know.'

Petra gave her a comforting squeeze.

'And still no baby clothes allowed in the house before the birth?'

'Does it seem silly?'

'Very, but I want you to be happy.'

It was one of the things Jane had loved about Petra from the start, the directness verging on rudeness. She turned to face her, feeling the derelict building's stare on her back.

'You said everyone paid for sex sometimes.'

'Yes?' Petra's tone was cautious.

'Have you?'

She squeezed Jane's shoulders.

'Every day, baby.'

'Seriously.'

'Never.'

There was something there, a slight hesitation. Jane went to the window. Outside, the night was black and starless without even a passing plane to liven the sky. The backhouse was lost in the darkness. She asked, 'Shouldn't there be lights out there, in the back court?'

'Maybe a bulb needs changing. I'll phone the letting agency tomorrow.'

Jane could hear Petra relaxing at the change of subject. She turned to face her.

'Tell me about the time you paid.'

'There's nothing to tell.'

'But there is something.'

Petra looked away. 'I have to get up early.'

Jane put a hand on her arm, holding her there. Suddenly it seemed important to know the answer.

'If you go to bed now, I'll think the worst.'

'I thought there'd be an end of these late-night discussions when you stopped drinking.' Petra sighed. She sat on the bed. 'You promise not to get annoyed by something that happened years ago?'

Jane returned to the darkness outside the window. Her reflection stared back at her, mouth set, eyes level. The dream was still on her: Greta's body on the second floor.

'How can I promise when I don't know what it is?'

'Okay.' Petra took a deep breath and muttered, 'Where to start?' half under her breath. She paused for a moment, then said, 'You know some of this already, my misspent youth.' Her voice had a false jollity. 'When Tielo and I were teenagers we started taking the S-Bahn into Berlin and going to gay clubs together. I'd come out to Tielo, but our parents still didn't know. It was all very new and very, very exciting. You remember the scene back then.'

'I was probably still at primary school.'

'Yes.' Petra's tone was dry. 'Sometimes I forget. You missed out. It was a good time to be queer. Androgyny was in fashion; even the straight boys were wearing make-up and jewellery and dyeing their hair. I think part of Tielo wanted to be gay. Up until then we'd done everything together, but he'd always been the naughtier of the two of us, and I think it irritated him that I was suddenly the edgier, more fashionable one. He let himself get picked up by guys a couple of times, but it was obvious it wasn't his thing.' Petra laughed as if remembering something, then carried on. 'I thought we'd be able to meet girls together, but of course the kind of places I'd get lucky weren't the kind of places he'd get lucky.' She paused. 'Are you okay?'

'Of course,' Jane's back was sore and she felt like sitting down, but she kept her face to the window. 'It was a long time ago.'

'More than twenty years.' The realisation seemed to surprise Petra and she paused for a moment. 'I used to wear men's suits I found at flea markets; you could buy smart tailoring from the fifties for a few marks back then.'

Jane had seen photographs of the young Petra, hair slicked back, dressed in sharp checks and pinstripes, a trilby cocked at a jaunty angle, looking in turn like David Bowie in his Berlin phase and a young Al Pacino in *Scarface* mode.

'I wasn't interested in passing myself off as a man, but you know Tielo, always the joker. He found the idea of me snaring a straight girl hilarious, plus, of course, he wanted to snare straight girls too. So, after a while, we started going to straight clubs and I'd pretend to be his brother Peter.'

'They called their first child Peter.'

'After an uncle of Ute's.'

'Are you sure?'

'Of course I'm sure.' Petra's voice was indignant. 'I've met him.' She paused again, as if trying to conjure nightclubs crammed with boys in make-up and girls ripe for the picking. 'It worked. Most people don't look beyond what they expect to see. I was tall and boyish and dressed like a guy, so they took me for a guy.'

'Sounds like fun.'

'It was, at first, the thrill of getting away with it. I did all the usual things, but I was young so they seemed daring; the fake moustache, cigars and *Steins* of beer, the stuffed sock in my pants.' She laughed at the memory. 'Like I said, it was a gender-bending world back then. Most of the boys looked a little feminine, so I fitted in.'

'Girls must have flocked to you.'

'Yes, the girls were into me, but we were going to straight clubs, so I couldn't take it any further than kissing, and even that depended on my moustache glue.' Petra laughed. 'One false move and the whiskers might have been on her. Not a good look. Not safe for your health either. Androgyny was one thing, full-on gay another.'

'I bet Tielo wanted you to take it further.'

'Tielo thought it was a scream. It was ironic – there I was working up to coming out to our parents, and at the same time lying to every girl I met.'

'You were never a good liar. I bet all those girls you kissed knew and were as keen as Tielo for you to get them into bed.'

'If that's the case I missed a lot of fun.' Jane could hear Petra's smile in the dark. 'There weren't so many girls, but I started to feel a fraud. Finally I told Tielo, Peter was going to retire. He did his best to persuade me not to. "How would we have fun together? I looked wonderful in my suits. The girls in the straight clubs were so much prettier than the ones in the gay clubs; if anyone could turn them, it would be me", but I insisted.'

Jane turned and looked at Petra. She was dressed in striped cotton pyjamas, her elbows resting on her knees, her chin on her hands. In the dim light of the child's room it was easy to imagine her as the dashing Peter.

'I'm sure you could have turned plenty of girls if you'd wanted to.'

'Maybe.' It was typical of Petra not to demur. 'But I wasn't interested in those kind of conquests. I was young, I believed in love.' She looked up and her eyes met Jane's. 'Still do.'

'So Peter retired?'

'Yes.'

'But?'

Petra sighed.

'But before I packed the natty suits away, Tielo persuaded me to take Peter out for one last crazy night. We ended up in a bordello.'

It was the revelation that Jane had been waiting for, yet she was surprised by a rush, not of anger, but of curiosity. She waited a moment, then asked, 'What happened?'

'It was all very professional. I'm not sure if they thought I was a man or not, we were both pretty drunk by then, but if they realised I was a woman in drag it didn't seem to bother anyone. We were offered a choice of girl. Tielo made me choose first, then we went into a little room, more of a cubicle than a room really, and she offered me a massage. I told her I would pay, but that I didn't want to do anything, just sit there for however long it usually took. I got the feeling I wasn't the first person to request that. We sat there in silence and then she told me it was time to go. I waited for Tielo and we went home.' Petra looked up. 'Not sure it counts as paying for sex.'

'Did Tielo go through with it?'

'I never asked. Peter's clothes went in a box along with his moustache and his cock and we never mentioned it again.' Petra looked at her. 'So?'

Jane sat on the bed beside her.

'Do you still have Peter's clothes?'

'Maybe somewhere in storage with Mutti's stuff.' Petra smiled. 'But they might not fit me now.'

It was a blatant fish for a compliment. Jane trailed her fingers lightly down the inside of Petra's pyjamaed thigh.

'What about his cock?'

Petra caught Jane's hand in hers.

'Don't think badly of Tielo. He was young and wild. Once he met Ute he straightened out.'

Jane lied. 'I don't think badly of Tielo. Well, no more than usual.'

They laughed together, but when they were back, safe beneath the duvet in the darkness of their bedroom, Jane asked, 'Did Tielo ever try to get you into bed?'

'We slept in the same room when we were little. We were twins. He was the other part of me.'

'I mean when you were older.'

'Did he ever try to fuck me? No.' Petra's voice was harsh with shock. 'Of course not. How could you even ask that?'

'I'm sorry.' Jane rested her head on her lover's shoulder, convinced by the amazement in her voice. 'I didn't mean it.'

All the same, she wondered why Petra had been so surprised by the question.

Eleven

From where she lay on the couch Jane could just glimpse the treetops jiving with the wind. The branches were bare of leaves and it was easy to imagine the trees as dead things, skeletons of their former selves dancing into battle. The child would arrive before the trees started to bud. The thought filled her with half-pleasant dread.

Jane sat up and cradled her belly, trying to imagine the weight of it transferred to her arms. She could not believe in God, and had never really understood science. Sometimes, when it was still, the baby felt as abstract, and as unlikely, as the Big Bang or God and all his angels. Then it shifted, and she knew without a doubt that it was there, and that for good or for bad, she would see its face soon.

A door shut and she rose and went into the hallway, Petra's name on her lips. There was no one there, but Jane felt something, a disturbed current of air, as if someone had been standing in the hall a moment ago and had only just left. She opened the front door, but the corridor outside was empty and still.

The apartment's silence was broken by a hollow rhythm, like a horse crossing a cobbled stableyard. Jane went through to the child's room and stood by the window, hiding in the shadow of the curtains. Anna was clumping towards the backhouse in her ridiculously high heels, her red coat swaying. She watched the girl disappear into the darkness of the building, then, without stopping to consider, grabbed the half-full rubbish sack from the kitchen wastebin, pulled on her coat and made her way downstairs.

She loitered at the bin shelter, pretending to sort through the sack for recyclables, keeping her eyes fixed on the backhouse. Viewed from the ground, the building was dizzying. It seemed to fall towards her, out of synch with the tilt of the world.

She heard a sound behind her and turned towards it. Herr Becker was in his kitchen, tapping on the windowpane, his image ghostly behind the grimed glass. He shook his head slowly, like a man trying to send a warning across centuries, and Jane knew he was telling her to mind her own business. She raised a hand in greeting, saw him turn away as if in response to something in the apartment beyond, and guessed that his wife was trying to set out for school again, determined to teach children who had long since grown up. Jane dumped the rubbish sack in the bin, unsure of what to do next.

She had just resolved to follow Anna into the building, and to ask her if she would like to join her for cake and hot chocolate at Barcomi's, when she heard the ringing of high heels in the courtyard again. This was her cue. Petra was right: there was nothing more than overheard raised voices, and a bruise that might be as innocent as her own fading mark, to suggest that Alban Mann was anything other than a dutiful father, but Jane's instincts told her there was something wrong. Perhaps if the girl would talk to her, she could find out what it was.

Anna Mann had her hood up. Her eyes were lowered and she was carrying a sports bag Jane couldn't remember noticing when she'd entered the building. Her footsteps were quick and urgent, like someone who knew they would be in time, if they kept up the pace.

'Anna, *guten Tag.*' Jane stepped into her path.

The girl teetered on her heels and for a second Jane thought she might have startled her into twisting an ankle, but Anna regained her balance. She raised her face and Jane gave a quick intake of breath that tugged the girl's lips into a smile.

Anna's mouth was the same bright red as her coat, the stain drawn beyond her lips into a cupid's bow. Black pencilled eyebrows echoed the McDonald's arches of her upper lip. Any sign of her bruise was concealed beneath foundation several shades lighter than her natural skin tone.

Jane thought the effect ugly; a form of self-mutilation. If she had the power, she would make the girl strip and inspect her body for scars.

'Hi,' she faltered, under the fuck-you of Anna's stare. 'How are you doing?'

The girl opened her eyes wide, giving full effect to her mascara-crusted lashes.

'How am I doing?' Her accent was thick, her words hesitant. 'How are you?'

'I am well.' It was as if they were in the first moments of an elementary English class. 'How are you?'

'I am well too.' Jane heard herself replicating the girl's

awkward delivery. She pulled the red hair clasp from her pocket and held it out. 'Is this yours?'

The girl looked at it. 'Where did you get it?'

'The priest found it in the churchyard. He had it in his study.'

'No.' Anna shook her head. 'It isn't mine.'

'Are you sure?' The lie was so blatant that Jane couldn't help but smile. 'I thought I noticed you wearing something very like it.'

'Like it perhaps, but not so *billig*.'

'So *billig*?'

'So cheap.' Anna laughed. Her amusement seemed to improve her English. 'You should give it back to the priest. He can send it to the little children in Africa.' The girl shrugged. 'Or if you like you can keep it for yourself.'

She shouldered her bag and started to walk away.

Jane said, 'Anna, do you ever go into the backhouse late at night?'

For a moment she thought the girl was going to ignore her, but then Anna set her bag on the ground and looked Jane up and down, her eyes lingering for a moment on her belly.

'Let me ask *you* a question.' The girl's accent was less present now, her words sure. 'Who is the father of your baby?'

Jane's hands moved involuntarily to her stomach, but her voice was steady.

'I don't know.'

'Then I feel sorry for it.'

Anna picked up the sports bag and walked away. The sound of her heels was quickly killed by the slam of the building's door, and Jane was left alone, in the shadow of the backhouse.

She took the clasp from her pocket, snapped it in two and threw it into the bin. From now on Anna Mann was on her own. More girls than not were abused. It was the way of the world and there was nothing you could do about it. She heard creaking and looked up to see the backhouse's open window moving in the breeze, winking at her, as if letting Jane know that her decision had been observed and approved.

Twelve

Petra stretched a hand across the dining table towards her and said, 'I'm sorry. It's spectacularly bad timing, but I can't get out of it.'

Jane realised that she should have known Petra was going to tell her something she wouldn't want to hear when she had taken the already chilled bottle of Sancerre from her bag and insisted, 'One tiny glass won't affect the baby.'

Jane put her glass down. 'That means you won't be able to come to my next appointment with the obstetrician.'

Petra was still in the crisp white shirt and linen trousers she had worn to work that morning. The masculine tailoring was softened by a string of pearls and matching earrings, which brought out the pale-pink blush of her lipstick. She saw that Jane was not going to accept her hand and withdrew it. 'I know, and I'm devastated. If I could escape I would.' Her mouth turned down and her eyes widened with sincerity.

Jane wondered if that was the expression Petra wore when breaking news of badly performing investments to her clients and if she had remained in her work clothes, instead of changing as she normally did when she came home, in order to maintain some of her professional shell.

She shook her head. 'I don't believe you.'

'Don't believe what?'

'Don't believe you're devastated, don't believe you can't get out of it, don't believe you're telling me this.' Jane's voice was rising dangerously. 'You're delighted to be going to Vienna.' She pushed a strand of hair from her eyes and her sleeve brushed against her glass, knocking it over. White wine pooled across the dining-room table and started to trickle on to the floor. 'Shit.'

Petra got to her feet. 'I'll get a cloth.'

'No, I'll do it.' Jane pushed her chair back, but Petra had already lifted the fallen wineglass and left the room. She heard a tap running in the kitchen and then Petra was back with kitchen roll, anti-bacterial spray and a damp cloth.

Jane muttered, 'Typical German efficiency.'

Petra ripped some paper from the roll, soaked up the spilled wine, then sprayed the cloth and wiped the stickiness from the table. 'Thank you.' She took some fresh paper and dried where she'd wiped.

'That wasn't a compliment.'

'I know.' Petra left the room again and returned with a fresh glass of wine, filled to precisely the point the previous one had measured when Jane knocked it over. 'I truly am sorry. But you won't be on your own for the entire week. I phoned Tielo and he's promised to look in and make sure you're okay. He's even offered to go to the obstetrician with you.'

If she hadn't been so furious Jane would have laughed, but instead she pushed her glass away and walked out of the sitting room, slamming the door behind her.

* * *

92

It was after six in the evening, dark already and too cold for wandering the streets. Jane put her hand in her coat pocket and realised she had left her wallet in the apartment. She marched on anyway, fists clenched, hating Petra for reminding her of her own lost independence.

When they had lived together in London, Petra had often travelled for work. Jane had enjoyed the freedom her absences brought, the temporary slobbishness of living alone, the unwashed dishes and unmade bed, the micro-waved meals eaten in the glow of late-night TV reruns, smoking forbidden cigarettes at the kitchen window. None of it would have been any good without Petra's returns. The growing anticipation as she tidied their flat, as keen to remove all traces of self-indulgence as a teenager after an illicit party. She had visited their favourite delis, shopping for a welcome-home dinner that had sometimes gone ignored in favour of a shared bath, quickly followed by bed.

Petra was the same as ever. It was Jane who had changed. Motherhood had seemed a means of growing up, but the child had made her dependent before it was even born.

The cold was biting at her face and making her breath come in short gasps. A café glowed on the corner of Weinmeisterstrasse. Jane searched her pockets again, hoping for some forgotten euros, enough to buy her coffee and some warmth, but it was hopeless; not even a half-smoked cigarette. She walked blindly towards Weinmeisterstrasse U-Bahn. There were seats there and shelter of sorts.

The underground smelt of damp and tainted rubber. A man shambled over and offered her a cut-price train ticket; when she shook her head he asked for some change. Jane ignored him and made her way down the platform. A trio of youths were drinking from bottles of beer by one of the benches.

In London or Glasgow she would have been able to decode their hair and clothes and assess whether they were gang members, more interested in their rivals than in her, middle-class trustafarians, or potential muggers. But she didn't have the measure of Berlin street life yet.

Jane knew not to meet their gaze, but she gave them a quick glance, refusing to lower her eyes. They were older than she'd thought, or maybe drugs and rough sleeping had rendered them so. They were dressed in a combination of army surplus and punk gear, their hair shaved into Rocky Mohawks and skinheads. Their style looked dated and she wondered if they came from the East, or if punk was back in vogue. The uniformity of their outfits amused her. They were like the dark alter egos of the models in the clothing catalogues her mother had paid up every week, each one dressed in a variation of the same outfit; a change of pattern here, a different trim there; trivial adaptations designed to give an illusion of choice.

Jane took a seat at the other end of the platform, distant enough to be out of their range, but with a good enough view to know if something was about to kick off and it was time to move on.

A train rushed into the platform, the passengers' faces sharpening into focus as it slowed to a halt. The carriage doors breathed open, but no one got out. The doors shut and the faces blurred again as the train sped on to more popular stations. Beyond the tracks an animated advertising hoarding recommended the latest mobile phone, winter wear from H&M, an extravagant performance by the Blue Man Group, a film featuring stars Jane didn't recognise.

She had a sudden urge to go back to London. If she booked her ticket tonight she could be stepping on to the platform at St Pancras in two days' time.

The impossibility of it overwhelmed Jane. She would have to ask Petra for money for the fare, their flat had been rented to people she didn't know, she didn't have a job and, though there were friends she could stay with for a night or two, she couldn't think of anyone who would be keen to put up a pregnant woman for any length of time, let alone a woman with a new baby.

Her anger was fading. There was no one else but Petra that she wanted to live with. But the reminder of how dependent she had become bothered her. Petra wouldn't like it, but as soon as the child could be safely installed in some kind of day-care she would find a part-time job. There were plenty of English-language bookshops in Berlin; she could surely find somewhere willing to employ her for at least a couple of mornings a week. The resolution decided her. It was time to go home.

Another train hurtled into the station. Jane felt the blast of its slipstream warm against her skin. Did everyone worry about the urge to throw themselves on to the tracks? The carriage doors opened and the punks broke into a cheer. She looked up, checking the source of their excitement, wondering if she should take another exit to avoid them, and then saw the familiar high heels and red coat.

As she watched, Anna opened her arms wide and birled

amongst the men. One of them whooped and grabbed her. They kissed and then he pushed her towards his companions who each took their turn. Their kisses were deep and rough; the girl gave herself up to them, arching her body backwards in a parody of Hollywood passion, her laugh high-pitched and nervous. Jane thought the greeting was like a burlesque of the polite parties she and Petra were sometimes obliged to attend, the air-kisses from people you hardly knew, endured and returned for politeness' sake.

The taller of the men had his arm around Anna now and was leading her down the platform, in the opposite direction from where Jane sat. His hand gripped the girl's arm, fingers sinking into her sleeve, deep enough to bruise the flesh beneath. A beer bottle dangled from his other hand. Anna's gait was stiff and slightly jerky. She said something; he bent down to listen, and then laughed, repeating it loudly so that his compatriots could share the joke. The girl joined in, but there was an anxious edge to her laughter.

Jane got to her feet and walked smartly towards them. Her heels were loud against the tiled platform and she raised her voice to be sure of being heard. 'Anna.'

The man who had asked her for money had shuffled off, and there were only Jane, the men and Anna left in the station. The others turned to look at her and Jane smiled, as if there had been no altercation in the back court, and it were the most natural thing in the world to hail teenage girls and drunken skinheads.

'Anna, I'm walking home. Would you like to come with me?'

The girl's lip curled and she said something to her

companion. His laugh echoed off the walls, high and girlish. Anna leant against him, as if he were her protector and Jane the threat.

'No thank you.' The edge of stiffness in her body that had suggested resistance to the skinhead's embrace was gone; she was all softness and surrender now. Anna looked up into his eyes and smiled. 'I'm going to a party.'

Jane cursed silently. If she hadn't interfered, the girl might have extricated herself and headed home; now she'd been presented with an authority to resist. Jane turned her attention to the other two men. One sat sideways on the bench, his knees angled over the armrests designed to stop people sleeping on them. The third crouched on the headrest, in a pose that suggested a pent-up athleticism.

'Is it an exclusive party, or can anyone go?'

Anna snorted; her sullen expression made her look suddenly younger beneath her make-up.

'They don't speak English.'

'I speak good English.' The skinhead balanced on the back of the seat sounded offended. He sprang to the ground and Jane saw that he was the smallest of the trio. She smelled the beer on his breath, and saw the lines etched around his eyes and gouged into his cheekbones; a feral Peter Pan, drunk and not quite young any more. She remembered Frau Becker's warning about the Russians as she had touched Jane's belly: 'This wouldn't stop them.'

The old-young man said, 'You want to party?'

'Not really.' Jane kept her eyes on his. 'But Anna is only thirteen and her father worries about her going out late at night on her own.'

The skinhead repeated what she'd said in German for the benefit of the others and they *aaaah'd* as if she had told them a sentimental story.

Anna shouted, 'My father's a *Whoremeister*.' The skinhead with his arm around her sneered, 'Her daddy beats her.' And the aged Peter Pan said, 'Daddy sticks his cock in her.'

Jane looked at Anna. 'Is that true? If it is, I can help you find somewhere to go.'

The men laughed and Anna spat out a stream of invective. Ridiculously, Jane found herself looking at Peter Pan for an interpretation.

He raised his eyebrows. 'She says you are a pregnant lesbian bitch who wants to fuck her.' He leant forward, drawing open the front of her coat and revealing the bulge of her pregnancy. He placed a hand on her belly, put an arm around her shoulders and whispered, 'Is it true? Do you want to fuck her? I'm sure we could persuade her, if you really want to.'

His touch roused a swoop of fear in Jane's chest, but she stood her ground.

'No.' She elbowed his arm from her and was relieved when he put up no resistance. 'Her father is looking for her.'

There were tears at the back of her eyes, but she'd be damned before she let them fall.

'Maybe you want her daddy to fuck you?' He laughed. 'Someone's been up there. Or is this a little Frankenstein?'

His hands were on her again. Jane pushed him away.

'Fuck off.'

But he was more persistent this time, and she felt his cold fingers sneaking beneath her jumper and on to her skin.

'Why don't you try a man for a change?' It was a question

she'd been asked so many times she should have had a stinging retort ready, but she could only try to push his hands
away, muttering, 'I don't see any men here.'

'Why don't I show you then?' He pulled her closer, pressing his groin against her stomach. The man had looked
underfed, but she could feel the force of his muscles, his
superior strength.

The roar of an oncoming train filled the station. Jane
squeezed a hand up towards his face, twisted the skin
between his nose and upper lip and saw his eyes water. She
scraped the heel of her boot down the sensitive part of his
shin and then, like the self-defence instructor had shown
her back in college, let her body relax as she smacked the
inside of his elbows with all her strength before pushing
him hard in the solar plexus.

It helped that he was drunk. The man stumbled backwards
and for one sickening moment she thought he might fall
from the platform. Instead he ricocheted against the metal
bench and stumbled to the ground. The carriage doors
opened and Jane darted on to the train. She shouted for
Anna to follow her, but the girl stayed where she was, watching the doors slide shut. Jane sank into a free seat. The
window between them was scratched with names and
amateurish etchings, but she could see Anna leaning into the
tall skinhead's embrace, both of them laughing crazily at the
tumbled Peter Pan. The girl turned and kissed her new beau,
her eyes meeting Jane's as the train sped out of the station.

Thirteen

Jane got off at the next stop, her heart still beating fast in her chest, thankful that there had not been a ticket inspector on the train. Outside she took a wrong turning and walked for several blocks before realising and retracing her steps. By the time she reached their building she felt frozen through, but she went straight to Alban Mann's door and pressed the bell. It rang deep within the apartment, but though she waited, finger pressed to the button like a debt collector, there was no response.

The heat inside her own flat felt overpowering. Jane pulled off her coat and left it crumpled in the hall. Petra jumped up from the couch as she entered the sitting room.

'Where have you been?'

'I needed to clear my head.'

Alban's telephone number was scrawled on a scrap of paper she had slipped under the phone, almost as if she knew she would need it again. Jane dialled and listened to the electronic peal until Mann's smooth tones invited her to leave a message.

'This is Jane Logan from next door. Can you call me back when you get this? It's about Anna.'

Petra was at her shoulder. 'What's going on?'

Jane gave her an edited account of what had happened. It included Anna and the skinheads, if skinheads they were, but omitted her tussle on the platform.

'I shouldn't have interfered.' Jane sipped the camomile tea Petra had made her. The taste made her grimace. 'I just gave her something to kick against.'

'So learn your lesson.' It was a mark of Petra's distress that she still hadn't changed out of her office clothes. The collar of her shirt had lost its crisp edge, there was a splash of wine on her breast from when Jane had knocked over her glass earlier in the evening, and her hair was ruffled. 'Don't you remember what it's like to be a teenager? You tell lies, stay out past your curfew and hang around with unsuitable people. Most of us survive.' Petra ran a hand through her hair. 'This girl is nothing to do with us. Leave her to her father.'

'She called him a *Whoremeister*.'

'So what?' Petra rarely raised her voice, but she was raising it now. 'Teenagers call their parents all sorts of names.' She shook her head with exasperation. 'Christ, Jane, her job is to rebel, yours is to bring our child safely into the world.'

'You didn't see the way she was behaving; it was like she was setting herself up for a gang-bang. I'm not sure she'd even met these men before, but she was ready to waltz off with them to who-knows-where.' It had been a long night and the tears that had threatened earlier were trembling in her eyes now. 'It was like she didn't care what happened to her.'

Petra moved round to Jane's side of the table and put an arm around her. After the violent encounter on the station platform her touch was gentle and Jane felt a tear escape and roll down her cheek.

Petra wiped it away. 'You're making too much of this. I've seen the girl, remember? She's a little toughie. First sign of trouble she'll kick those boys in the balls.'

'There were three of them.'

'Shhh.' Petra put her mouth close to Jane's ear and whispered, 'I'm going to run you a nice warm bath. While you're having a soak, I will go to Dr Mann's door and see if he's home yet. If he is, I'll pass on your concerns.'

Jane pulled herself free. 'I don't trust him.'

'So why were you phoning?'

'I don't know.'

'Shall I tell you? You phoned Dr Mann because she is his daughter, and this is his responsibility.' Petra levelled her gaze and looked Jane in the eyes. 'It's none of our business.'

'You weren't there.'

'No, but I can tell Dr Mann what you've told me. And in the meantime you'll be getting ready for bed.' She pulled Jane back into an embrace, kissed her on the side of her face and whispered, 'Trust me.'

Jane soaped herself, feeling the child respond to the warmth of the water. Petra was right. Anna was Alban Mann's responsibility, and this child was hers. She washed the touch of the men's hands from her, but she couldn't rid herself of the feeling that she had betrayed Anna by running away. Where was the girl now? She slid beneath the suds, letting the warm water wash over her, trying to stop the movie running behind her eyes, a confusion of flesh and shadows.

Jane pushed herself back to the surface with a gasp, wiping her hair from her face, then running her hands over her stomach, remembering again Frau Becker's words as she had touched her: 'This wouldn't stop them.'

She dried and slathered her skin with body butter that promised to ward off stretch marks, wrapped herself in her oversized towelling dressing gown and blew out the candles Petra had lit. She stood for a moment in the darkened bathroom, wondering how the child felt inside her. Had it also experienced a blast of fear as the man grabbed her?

There were voices outside on the landing. Jane padded into the hallway and stood by the front door. Petra was talking to Alban Mann and she heard again the way their accents met and mirrored each other. Jane had expected stiff formality, perhaps even anger, but Petra's tones were light and relaxed; Mann's calm. She tried to make out what they were saying, but they were talking faster than her *Teach Yourself German* CDs and she could only catch disconnected words: her own name and Anna's . . . U-Bahn . . . *Jugend* . . . *schwanger . . . überreizt.* It was hopeless. She heard them laughing together and put her hand on the latch, ready to step from the flat, but then she heard Mann's door shut and Petra's key turning in their lock.

'What are you doing?' Petra looked startled.

'I was about to come out there and tell Mann it's no laughing matter.'

'He doesn't think it is.'

'Then why was he laughing?'

'Probably because he's embarrassed.' Petra had brushed her hair and changed into loose black trousers and a grey, silk jumper that fell in pleats to her hips. She looked chic and charming and capable. She put a hand around Jane's waist and led her down the hallway and into their bedroom. 'A good night's sleep will do you the world of good.'

Jane slid beneath the sheets, more tired than she had realised. She whispered, 'I hope we have a boy. Girls are too vulnerable.'

Petra stroked Jane's forehead. 'Girls are stronger than they look. You should know that.'

The curtains were open. Jane turned and caught one last look at the darkness beyond as Petra drew them closed. She asked, 'Will you come to bed soon?'

'In a while.' Petra switched off the lamp and they were left in the dim glow of light shining in from the hallway. 'I've got some work to finish.'

'Not trawling the Internet for lezbfun.com?'

It was an old joke between them and they laughed together.

Jane said, 'I'm more than a baby-pod to you, aren't I?'

'Of course.' Petra's voice was firm. 'Much, much more.'

They kissed and then Petra tiptoed silently to the door and closed it gently behind her, as if Jane were already asleep.

Jane lay in the dark waiting for oblivion, thinking about the way Anna had looked at her over the man's shoulder as the train had sped out of the station, and wondering at her own suspicion that Petra had lied, and that she and Alban Mann had been laughing together, at her.

Fourteen

She had stopped playing music and listened instead to the sounds of the building, the clicks and groans of the central heating, the slam of the heavy main door as the tenants came and went, the way the floorboards creaked when it rained. Most of all, Jane listened for sounds from the next apartment, but the Manns' place was silent as the grave, and even when she put her ear to the walls in the depths of the night, she heard nothing.

She thought someone in the street was calling her name, but when she ran through to the lounge and stood on the balcony she saw that it was a baby crying in a pram below. The ravens started to raise their voices and she worried that one might swoop down and peck the eyes from its head, but then the baby's mother appeared, a loaf of bread from the baker's shop in her hand, and fussed over it for a moment, before moving on.

Jane lingered on the balcony, hearing the child's cries fade, wondering how she could ever have heard her name in its bawling. The cemetery gate groaned and she saw the priest enter the graveyard and go into the church. He was dressed in black, his shoulders slightly bowed, steps slow, like a mourner following a cortège. If she hadn't known better, she would have thought him an old man.

It was two days since her encounter with Anna in the U-Bahn. Jane moved a chair into the child's room and sat by the window trying to read, but any sound in the courtyard caught her attention and when everything was silent there was the shadow of the derelict building darkening the room. Even when she looked away she could feel the backhouse's presence, brooding at the corner of her eye.

Petra's suitcase sat half-packed in their dressing room. Vienna was less than a day away by train. Jane had cut all her credit cards in half when she'd handed in her notice at work. But perhaps she could sneak one of Petra's from her bag and be waiting at the hotel when she arrived. The image was exciting but Jane knew the idea was hopeless. If Petra had wanted her company, she would already have bought her a ticket. It was a work trip, no partners allowed.

Jane set her book aside, reluctant to lie down in case sleep overtook her. But then her head started to droop and nod, the way her mother's had in front of the television in the evenings, and so she climbed on to the bed and pulled the coverlet up to her chin.

In fairy tales, mothers drew curses to their babies, sure as the sea drew the storm clouds. They would forget to invite a witch to a christening or mistakenly cheat a troll of its tithe, and their child would bear the punishment. Even to leave a baby alone in its cradle was to invite disaster. Stories were only stories, but they had their roots in reality. Tyrannical fathers and wicked stepmothers, abandoned children and murdered wives, they were the stuff of legend, but the stuff of life too.

The thought made her think of Anna again, and of Anna's mother. Could a woman simply walk away and never be found, never even be looked for?

She hugged her stomach. The mothers in these stories always invited the curse through some act of carelessness. That was true to life too. Turn your back for a moment and the worst might happen.

Jane slipped from between the sheets and went to the window. She felt an urge to cross the courtyard, climb the backhouse's precipitous stairs and explore the derelict rooms above.

It was stupid to listen to a poor old lady who was losing her mind. Herr Becker was no doubt right; Greta had gone to Hamburg or America, or somewhere else you could live off the radar. Jane pictured her: a woman with Anna's hair and build, dancing in a nightclub. Greta was dressed in the kind of clothes her own mother had worn for a night on the tiles, spike heels and shoulder pads, silky pastels and tight skirts that skimmed the knee. The image made her smile. It was out of fashion, but it had been a good look.

Jane went to the mirror and stared at her face. She was pale from winter and too much time indoors. She ran a hand through her curls. The baby books insisted your hair grew so much during pregnancy that your suddenly clogged hair-brush and moulted-on pillow were nothing to worry about but Jane was sure her hair was thinner than before.

She found a brush and tried to back-comb it into an

eighties bouffant. But her hair was too soft and it refused to hold. She had a sudden memory of her mother in front of the full-length mirror attached to her wardrobe door, spraying a stream of hair lacquer on to her upturned head. Jane could almost smell it; the over-perfumed scent that caught in the back of your throat. She sat on the end of the bed and saw for an instant her mother's face smiling at her in the wardrobe mirror.

No evening out would ever be as exciting as the nights Jane had imagined for her mother. She conjured up the smell of her return, smoke and drink, the sweet-sour scent of sweat. She remembered her relief at the sound of her mother's stumble as she took off her high heels in the hall, her mother's exhalation of pleasure as her feet were freed, her whispered thanks to the babysitter. Then the front door mortise lock was turned against the night, and shortly afterwards a sliver of light reached briefly into Jane's bedroom; her own private signal that it was safe to snuggle back under the covers and go to sleep.

Would her child crave her safe return as much as she had craved her mother's? She wondered if her mother had ever known how much Jane had feared for her.

Petra's key sounded in the door and then Petra was in the room, windswept and glowing from outdoors.

'What happened to your hair?'

'Nothing.' Jane ran the brush through it, smoothing the rats' nest she'd made of her curls into submission. 'I was just playing.'

Petra kissed her, but Jane had already seen a look of irritation flash across her face.

'I thought you'd be dressed.' Petra shrugged off her coat and scarf and draped them over Jane's chair.

'I will be by the time everyone arrives.'

Petra started straightening the unmade bed. 'The caterer is coming at half past. I was hoping we'd have everything ready for her.'

Too late Jane remembered that morning's promise to set the dining-room table with the new glasses, napkins and candlesticks Petra had bought and which were still bagged and boxed in the hallway. She had been dreading Petra's dinner party ever since she'd announced it.

'It'll be ready.'

'I still haven't finished packing for Wien.' The irritation was in Petra's voice now. She smoothed the coverlet, straightened up and looked at Jane. 'Why do you spend so much time in here?'

'I don't know.' Jane glanced instinctively at the window. The night was coming in. No bulbs had been replaced in the courtyard, or if they had, they too had burned out or been disabled, but she could still see the backhouse, a deeper shade of dark against the gloaming. 'I like it, I suppose.'

'When I took the lease I imagined you sitting in the lounge, or on the balcony, where it gets the light, not in here. It's gloomy; all right for sleeping in, but not for during the day.'

'Maybe it reminds me of home.' Jane smiled at the thought.

Petra looked out of the window. 'That building's an eyesore.'

'Do you think so?' Jane slid her arms around Petra's waist and kissed her neck. 'I'm getting rather fond of it.'

Petra returned her kiss, but their embrace was brief and hurried, and Jane could tell that her mind had already shifted to the evening ahead.

Fifteen

'It is kind of you to allow us to take Petra away from you for a week.'

Herr Hessler forked a piece of artichoke into his mouth. The candlelight gave a glassy sheen to his eyes. Jane thought she caught the glint of contact lenses and wondered if his eyes were really as blue as they seemed.

'I'm sure your wife would be just as accommodating.'

'I wouldn't bet on it.' Hessler laughed and gave a quick, compulsive glance at Jane's bosoms, fast as a camera shutter. 'Not when she was waiting for her first child.'

'There's a while to go yet.' Jane smiled what she hoped was a motherly smile. 'And I know that when it comes to work, there's no point arguing with Petra. I don't take on battles I've no chance of winning.'

There was something restful about playing the wife. Jane wondered if Petra's colleague really believed she was a long-suffering work widow, or if he could see right through her. Maybe it was just a willingness to play the game that was important. Petra would go to Vienna and leave her alone and pregnant in a country where she had no friends and was uncertain of the language, but she wouldn't make a fuss.

The thought was too self-pitying. She gave Herr Hessler another smile but he had turned to the person on the other side of him and was talking in fast, intense German.

Jane looked down the table to where Petra was deep in conversation with her new boss. Petra met her eyes and smiled and for an instant Jane saw the reckless girl she'd met six years ago, at another party loud with rich bankers. Jane recalled how she had noticed Petra's gaze flitting down the neck of her neat white waitressing blouse, and known. She'd offered Petra a glass of champagne from her tray, their eyes had met as Petra raised the glass to her lips, and they'd seen that each of them knew and laughed. She had left early in Petra's taxi, wanting nothing more than the thrill of an encounter. But later they had met again in the bookshop, and that, to the surprise of both of them, had been that.

Jane sipped her water. Petra was nodding now at something her boss was saying, her quick flash of wickedness put away for the night. Jane wondered if the other bankers also had this sharp, sexy side to them. She glanced at Herr Hessler. He was slathering chicken liver parfait on to a small triangle of toast, his blue eyes watering as he laughed at something his neighbour had said. It was hard to imagine him defecting with a filched bottle of champagne and a waitress from his firm's summer party, but who knew what people got up to when away from their spouses? The thought made her feel uneasy.

In the end, the woman from the catering company had set the table and it was a glimmer of crystal, stainless steel and candlelight. Occasionally a flash of diamonds or glint of gold caught the light, but the bankers and their partners were dressed with the kind of restraint that suggested real money. There were a dozen of them gathered round the white table in the sitting room, an almost even number of men and women, mainly around Petra's age. This was what the room had been styled for, Jane realised, impressing grown-ups, rather than nurturing a child.

Early in their relationship Petra had said, 'Glaswegians either dress like tramps or nouveau-riche Americans out to impress.' It had taken Jane a while to realise that she was included on the trampy side of the verdict, but Petra's habit of surprising her with outfits had given the game away. Tonight's new dress was an expensive blend of poly-fibres and silk that felt both natural and space-age. She would have preferred it in black, but Petra had chosen a soft blue which she said suited her complexion. Jane saw Herr Hessler's gaze skim her bosoms again and counted to ten before readjusting her neckline. She would rather be back in Weinmeisterstrasse U-Bahn, than here.

She thought about Anna. Was the girl sitting on the other side of the wall listening to the babble of voices and low music seeping through the plaster? She would find the scene bourgeois. It *was* bourgeois.

Anna had been carrying a bag when she had come out of the derelict building. Was that where she kept her treasures, in amongst the roosting birds and broken glass? Though she had never been there, Jane could see the ruined interior clearly in her mind's eye; the drifting feathers and splintered floorboards, the burnt scraps of tinfoil and cigarette butts smoked down to the stub. She should never have let Petra tell

Alban Mann about Anna and the skinheads. She had sided with her father and the girl would never trust her now.

The caterer was removing their starters. The man on Jane's right turned towards her, a little wearily, as if he realised it was his duty to pay her some attention but knew there was no advantage to be gained from the contact. Perhaps he had overheard some of her conversation with Herr Hessler, because he said in English, 'You are new to Berlin?'

'Yes.' There was no point in explaining the visits over the years, the toing and froing, the holidays with Tielo and Ute. 'I like it.'

The man shrugged. 'Too cold at this time of year, and sometimes too warm in summer, but it's a good place to live; a tolerant place.'

Jane wasn't sure why the word 'tolerant' irked her.

'Yes.' She met his eyes, smiling to hide her annoyance. 'Here the streetwalkers really do walk the streets.'

'Not all of them.' His gaze held hers. 'It wouldn't be much fun if everything for sale was on display.'

The caterer placed a large plate bearing a small, but artfully balanced, tower of steak, potatoes and vegetables in front of each of them. A smear of gravy circled the arrangement, like a ring road around a high-rise.

'No.' Jane lifted her knife and fork, welcoming the opportunity to look away. She had read about brothels where trafficked Asian and Eastern European women waited behind locked doors. It wasn't a topic that would impress Petra tonight. 'I guess it wouldn't be much fun.'

Perhaps the banker also thought the subject out of place because he asked, 'What do you like about the city?'

Jane repeated a description she had heard Petra give their London friends. 'It's cultured, but not exclusive.'

'No,' he laughed as if she had said something amusing. 'It's certainly not exclusive.'

Jane wondered if he was already a little drunk and if Petra had seated them together because it wouldn't matter if she were offended. She said, 'I like Berlin's consciousness of history. It's as if several parallel cities exist in the same place at the same time.'

'Yes.' His voice was slightly too loud. 'Foreigners are always fascinated by our history.'

Jane saw Petra glance down the table at them and gave her a reassuring smile.

'And your modern architecture is wonderful; so many iconic new designs.' It was a bore to have to coddle him like this. If they had been in a bar or at a real party she would have walked away, but now she met his eyes and tried to make her tone upbeat. 'Berlin is a forward-looking city.'

'Do you really think so?' He raised his eyebrows. 'In my opinion we're over-obsessed with the past.'

'Surely not in banking?'

'Probably not, though perhaps they should be, then they might learn from their mistakes.'

'You're not a banker?'

'A lawyer, Jurgen Tillman.' He nodded to Petra's boss, still deep in conversation at the top of the table. 'Johannes is my boyfriend.'

'I'm Petra's girlfriend.' Jane started to laugh. 'So that's why we were seated together.'

'Yes,' Jurgen smiled. 'Tonight neither of us is worth anything.'

If Jane hadn't been pregnant, Jurgen's polite contempt for the company might have tempted her into letting loose. Even though she stuck to water, she found his lack of regard infectious. When he nodded at her stomach and asked, 'How did this happen?' instead of being offended she gave an embarrassed laugh and said, 'I don't really know.'

'So we're not so different from the heterosexuals after all?'

This time Jurgen's raised eyebrows made him look devilish and Jane saw that he was handsome in a way Hollywood usually cast as dangerous.

'Perhaps not, except I wasn't allowed to get drunk first.'

'Ah no.' He glanced at Petra and Johannes. 'I imagine you were on a no-smoking, no-alcohol, no-trans-fats diet for months in advance?'

Jane followed his gaze and saw that sitting together, side by side, their partners looked like a long-married professional couple. She shrugged. 'I still am.'

Their portions were small, but Jurgen's plate remained untouched. He reached across the table and helped himself to more wine.

'Johannes and I have talked about it, having a child. It seems strange we can even have that conversation, but we can and so we do, and then we decide we prefer the life we have.' He shrugged. 'I like drinking and sailing more than I like the idea of a child.'

Jane sipped her water. 'Drinking and sailing; you'd better watch you don't drown.'

He chinked his glass against hers, as if he was toasting her.

'You, too, in a tide of diapers.'

It was meant as a joke and so she tried to smile but perhaps

Jurgen saw that his barb had hit home because he said more kindly, 'It must be difficult choosing a father?'

'I let Petra make all the arrangements.'

He was the first person she'd told.

'Why?' Jurgen turned his full attention on her and she felt the weight of his stare.

'Why not?'

He took a sip of his wine and shrugged his shoulders.

'No reason, except that it's your body. I thought feminists were keen on that, but perhaps you're not a feminist?'

'To my bones, but Petra's better at these kinds of things than I am.' She disliked the false breeziness in her voice. 'Anyway, I didn't like the idea of selecting a donor for their attributes. A child is a child, not a piece of designer furniture.'

Jane followed Jurgen's gaze as it travelled around the room, taking in the Hans Wenger armchairs, the Danish couch and Swedish credenza.

'Petra likes designer furniture.'

'Petra has good taste.'

'Better than yours?'

'Better than most people's.'

Jurgen gave her a wicked smile.

'I get the feeling that if it was left up to you, you would have gone to a nightclub and picked up a donor on the dance floor.'

She should have been offended, but instead she laughed and said, 'I don't know what I would have done if the technology hadn't existed. Snatched one from a pram perhaps?'

'I imagine that would have been cheaper.'

'Money wasn't an issue.'

'No, of course not.' Jurgen's smile was quick and apolo-getic, as if questioning her virtue was one thing, but doubting Petra's bank balance quite another. His eyes sparkled and Jane realised he was the kind of man whose charm allowed him to get away with a lot. As if to prove it, he said, 'Let's hope she's chosen well and it's not a little monster.'

'It can have two heads; Petra and I will still love it.'

'Mother-love.' He slipped a hand beneath the table and squeezed her thigh. 'A lucky child to have two mammas.'

'That's how we see it.'

Jane caught his hand and returned it to the table, thinking it was a shame that the first person she'd liked, since moving to Berlin, was such a dickhead.

The good thing about being pregnant was that you could escape almost anything simply by saying you were tired. Jane closed the door to the child's room and lay on the bed. She could hear the babble of talk drifting through from the lounge – strange how from a distance all gatherings sounded the same. They were on the coffees now; soon it would be liqueurs and goodnight. She lifted her book and started to read, but before long her eyes closed and sleep claimed her.

Jane woke abruptly, from a dream of twisting corridors and slamming doors, to the sudden knowledge that someone was in the room. She gasped and pulled herself upright on the bed.

Jurgen Tillman was standing at the window with his back towards her.

'I came to apologise for my rudeness at the table, but now I've woken you.' His voice was thick with drink. 'I guess that means I should apologise twice.' He turned to face her. 'It's dark out there.'

Jane swung her legs on to the floor, straightening her dress. The short sleep had refreshed her; she felt almost human.

'Petra rang the letting agency about getting the lights fixed.'

'She should ring them again. It's black as deep space, blacker, there are stars in outer space.'

She recalled the weight of his hand on her thigh and asked, 'Why are you here?'

Jurgen leant against the window, stretching his long legs in front of him.

'I'm bored and drunk.'

'I'm not sure I can cure either of these conditions.'

'The drunkenness is okay, but the boredom?' Jurgen gave an exaggerated shiver. 'I was hoping you'd save me.'

'Then you've backed the wrong horse.' Jane got to her feet, running a hand through her hair. 'Pregnant women are boring.' She joined him at the window. He was right; it was like looking out on the blackness of the universe. Anyone could be out there across the courtyard, watching them outlined in the window. She suppressed a shudder. 'The *Hinterhaus* is derelict. I think people use it at night.'

'For shelter?'

'For all the usual things people do after dark. Perhaps they disable the lights so no one will see them.'

Jurgen paused, as if imagining the things people could do in the dark.

'They have to go somewhere.'

'It's like a ghost building. It gives me the creeps.'

'It won't stay derelict for long. Before you know, it will be getting converted into luxury apartments. You'll be cursing the noise of the builders and wishing it was derelict again.'

Jurgen put a hand on her shoulder. It was warm and too large, like an unwelcome creature perched on her back. She tolerated his touch for a moment and then pulled away.

'Strange it hasn't been renovated sooner. I thought perhaps the title deeds might be in dispute.'

Jurgen shrugged. 'That happens, but less than it used to.' He rubbed his thumb and fingers together. 'People have realised they can make a lot of money if they come to a compromise.'

There was a new assurance in his voice and she said, 'Do you have experience of that kind of thing?'

He gave her a wry smile.

'I'm more boring than even a pregnant woman, I specialise in property law.'

There was a chatter of goodbyes and laughter in the hallway, the sound of the dinner party beginning to break up. Jane was aware of a small sense of deflation. Jurgen Tillman was a professional like the rest of Petra's guests, not an outlaw looking for an ally.

She smiled and said, 'It sounds like everyone's going home.'

Jurgen glanced at his watch, 'Ten to midnight. Earlier and it looks like they didn't have a good time, later and they worry their colleagues will think they're unprofessional.' He sighed. 'You only like girls?'

'Yes, only girls.'

He nodded at her belly.

'So this really was done without any touching?'

120

She smiled in spite of herself. 'In a way.'

Jurgen shook his head. 'Then perhaps you are the more boring one after all.' He touched her arm as if to assure her that he was joking. 'Don't worry about your ghost building. This city is full of ghosts, most of them harmless. It's the living you have to watch out for.'

It was almost dark in the room. It felt as if they too were suspended in space. Not dead, but disconnected from the living.

'A neighbour told me there's a woman buried beneath the backhouse's floorboards.'

Jurgen snorted with amusement. 'Then your neighbour should go to the police.'

'She's old and has some kind of dementia. They wouldn't believe her.'

'But you do?'

'Not really.' There was little point in telling him about Alban Mann's missing wife. 'But it looks like the kind of building that might have a body buried in it.'

Jurgen peered through the window, as if trying to make out the shape of the backhouse in the dark. He said, 'Builders used to bury a body in the foundations of new cathedrals to ensure that the spire stood tall. Maybe it worked.' He paused for effect. 'Cologne, St Paul's, everything around them blitzed, but the cathedrals left standing, like a miracle. This building though,' Jurgen pointed into the blackness outside. 'I imagine it's nothing special, not worth sacrificing a life for.'

'I don't think the suggestion was that it was done for the sake of the building.'

The noise in the hallway had died down and now there

were only two voices murmuring beyond the door. Jurgen glanced towards it.

'If I had a body to dispose of, I would weight it with concrete blocks and throw it in a river, or better still tip it into the foundations of some modern skyscraper or new motorway. Old buildings are too risky. The bones show through.' Beyond the door someone called his name. Jurgen rolled his eyes. 'Tonight Johannes is in charge.' He took her hand and squeezed it. 'Don't fear the dead, they've outnumbered us for a long time. If they wanted revenge they would have got it by now.'

Jane heard Petra and Johannes exclaiming as Jurgen joined them in the hallway. She hesitated by the bed, wondering if she should follow and add her goodbyes to Petra's. She was still standing there when the front door closed, and the flat sank back into silence.

Sixteen

Petra's suitcase was in the hallway, her coat buttoned and belted, but she was uncharacteristically slow to leave. She kissed Jane again and said, 'Tielo will call round to check you're okay.'

Jane had resolved to play the perfect wife again, but mention of Petra's twin irritated her.

'I might not be in.'

Petra had the grace not to ask her where she would be, but she smiled and kissed the tip of Jane's nose.

'I love you.' She cradled Jane's belly in her hands. 'It's only a week, and then I'll stay home until the baby comes, promise.'

Jane was surprised to see Petra's eyes sheen. She raised a hand, gently pressed Petra's lower eyelid, and caught a tear on her fingertip. She put the finger to her mouth.

'Salty.'

Out in the lobby a door slammed. Jane's gaze flickered towards the sound.

Petra's voice was suddenly serious. 'Promise me you'll have nothing to do with the Manns.'

'Why would I?'

'Because you have a tendency towards weird obsessions.'

'No I don't.'

'Yes you do, especially when you have time on your hands. The Manns aren't characters in a fairy tale. They're real life and none of your business.'

'Point taken.'

Petra's voice softened. 'I worry about you. You have a kind heart, but sometimes you act before you think.'

'I'm always thinking.'

'Maybe that's the trouble. You should switch your brain off occasionally. Watch television, put your feet up. Enjoy some leisure while you still can.'

Jane smiled, remembering how often Petra had told her she was wasting her intelligence working in a bookshop. She touched Petra's bottom and whispered, 'The Devil makes work for idle hands.'

'I'm serious.' Petra caught Jane's wrists and held them tight. 'Promise me you'll have nothing more to do with them.'

'I promise.'

Jane returned Petra's kiss. She leant over the banister, watching her carry her suitcase down the stairs, and then ran through to the balcony and waved her goodbye. Petra raised a hand before turning the corner towards the S-Bahn. The wheels of her suitcase rattled loudly against the cobbles and then faded. Petra was gone.

Jane stayed on the balcony, breathing in the cold air and sense of aloneness, until the cries of the rooks roused her and she realised she was shivering.

* * *

There was a slim, violet envelope propped against the kettle. Jane lifted it, felt the thickness within and knew immediately that it was money. She cursed, put the envelope in a drawer, then took it out again, slid the notes free and counted them: a thousand euros. Jane swore softly under her breath. Petra had never left her money when they were in London.

The week stretched ahead.

She made a pot of tea and found the baby book Petra had bought her. The infant on the cover was naked save for a pristine nappy. The child was plump as a drip-fed piglet and impossibly healthy, its photo superimposed on a white background. There was nothing in the image to provide scale and the baby might have been any size; as big as an elephant, big as a house.

Jane abandoned the book on the kitchen table, pulled on her coat and boots, shoved the envelope in her pocket and left the flat. She would buy some paint, a sunny yellow to brighten the child's room. If Tielo insisted on dropping by, he could do the upper bits. If he didn't appear, she would fasten the roller to a broom handle. The ceilings weren't so high, and if she stood on the lower rungs of the ladder, Jane was sure she could manage.

The decision cheered her and she hummed a tune softly under her breath as she went down the stairs. The song died on her lips halfway down the bottom flight. Anna Mann was coming out of the Beckers' apartment. Jane stepped into the shadows and watched as Karl Becker squeezed the girl's shoulder before shutting the door behind her.

The girl saw Jane and gave her a look of contempt. Then she slowly and deliberately raised her face to the light, like a silent movie star vogueing for the camera, and Jane saw that her left eye was blackened and swollen.

'Anna, what happened?'

The girl ignored her and started to climb the stairs to her apartment.

'Anna?' Jane changed her course and followed the girl up the staircase. 'I only want to help you.'

The girl looked back at Jane, her expression arch and amused.

'Help me with what?'

Jane was by her side now. She felt as if she were approaching a wild creature that might let her stroke it, but might just as easily attack. Jane reached out a tentative hand and pushed the girl's hair away from her face so she could examine the bruise. Anna had applied make-up but she hadn't been able to conceal the blue-and-yellow sunset radiating from her swollen eye and across her cheekbone. Jane let go of the girl's hair and it fell softly and perfectly back in place.

Anger clipped Jane's words. 'Did your father do this?'

The girl snorted, as if she had said something funny.

'Anna,' Jane grabbed a hold of her arm. 'No one has the right to hit you.'

'Let go of me.'

The girl tried to shake herself free, but Jane increased her grip. 'If you don't get help, it will only get worse. Have you any idea how many dead women accepted apology after apology from men who promised never to beat them again? Once they start they don't stop, no matter how many times they swear they will.'

'Let me go.'

Anna pulled at Jane's hand; one of her nails broke the skin, leaving a livid scratch from wrist to knuckle, but Jane held on.

'You mustn't let him do this to you.'

The girl gave a cry of frustration. She shoved out with her free hand and Jane lost her balance. For a dizzying moment she felt the weight of gravity, the nothingness between her and the ground, and knew how it would be to fall backwards down the staircase. Just in time she caught the banister and steadied herself.

'Anna.' She touched her stomach, scared again for the child within her. 'I only want to help.'

'Leave me and my father alone.'

Jane took a deep breath. Her heart pounded against her ribs.

'I know you feel loyalty to your father, but if he's hurting you, then he needs help too.'

Anna spat, 'You know nothing.'

'What happened to your mother, Anna?' The girl shook her head in disbelief but Jane went on, 'Did your father ever ask the police to look for her?'

The girl's voice was a whisper, but her words were a threat.

'Don't you ever speak of my mother.'

'Why not?'

Anna pushed her face close, so that their noses were almost touching. She smelt of bubblegum and sweat.

'Where is your girlfriend?'

Jane felt the warmth of Anna's breath against her skin. She took a careful tread backwards, on to a lower step.

'At work.'

127

'Are you sure?'

'Yes, of course.'

The girl sing-songed, 'I saw her on Friedrichstrasse last week.'

'That's no big surprise, her office is near by.'

Anna stepped closer, forcing her face close to Jane's again. The rhythm of her words was like a cruel nursery rhyme.

'She was kissing another woman, right there in the street. They looked good together, like they were in love.'

It was as if Jane went blind for an instant. Every atom of her was lost in Anna's accusation, and then just as suddenly, she was back on the staircase, facing the girl.

'You're lying.'

'Are you sure?' Anna smiled. The bruise above her eye was darker in the shadow of the stairwell. It gave her a piratical look. 'She's going to wait until your little bastard is born and then she will take it away from you and go and live with her other woman.'

Jane felt her hands tighten into fists. She said, 'There are agencies you can talk to. Come to my apartment and we can call one together.'

The girl shook her head in disbelief.

'My father loves me better than any mother would. That's why I feel so sorry for your baby.'

Jane felt the banister tremble at her back. She said, 'Lots of people don't know who their father is.'

But Anna was running up the stairs towards her apartment, and Jane's words were drowned by the clatter of her shoes.

* * *

Jane rang the Beckers' doorbell. Frau Becker's voice piped out a song, high and trembling from somewhere within. Jane pressed the bell again and rapped her knuckles hard against the wood but no one came to the door.

Outside it had started to rain. She stood in the shelter of the doorway, unsure of where to go next. A pop song blasted through her mind, not quite drowning out the sound of shouting as fists met flesh. She shut her eyes, remembering the way the punches took on the rhythm of the music. She had vowed that, no matter how thin the walls were, she would never turn the radio up when she heard the screaming start. It was her business, it was everyone's business, and pretending you didn't know what was going on didn't mean you weren't involved. To ignore abuse was to sanction it. She had made a pledge with her younger self never to know and not act, never to be one of those people who looked away when they met their neighbour on the stair because they had heard the screaming in the night and done nothing about it.

Jane pulled up the hood of her coat and lit a cigarette, her first in two days. Soon she would stop smoking altogether. She reached for her mobile, brought up Petra's number, hesitated, and then put it back in her pocket without dialling.

The church looked dark and remote today; a judgement in stone and spire. Only a couple of blocks away a busy intersection thronged with bikes and traffic, but the church, with its closed timber door and rain-stained walls, might have been at the centre of some blighted village. Jane crossed the road, opened the gate and walked into the graveyard, no longer concerned with what shade of yellow would wash the stain of the backhouse from the child's room.

It was gloomy inside the church. Jane glanced up towards the crucifix and felt her guts wrench as they had the first time she saw it. Jesus's wounds looked as if they had been freshly painted; they seemed redder than before, shining with a glossy wetness Jane didn't remember. She held on to the end of a pew, taking in his bleeding brow and gaping side. It was a good carving. Christ looked young and lithe and tortured, like an inmate of The Maze or Guantanamo Bay. The artist had excelled himself on the convenient folds of the loincloth, which clung precariously to the Saviour's groin, threatening to drop on to the altar below; a meditation on suffering and striptease.

The table at the back of the pews was still ranged with neat piles of pamphlets. Jane scanned photographs of smiling Africans drawing water from handy wells, badly sketched doves and a variety of crosses before she found the leaflet she'd noticed on her last visit. The image on its front was saccharine: an attractive, motherly woman with her arm around a sad, but equally photogenic, teenage girl. Some problems were too big to be solved overnight, the photograph seemed to say, but help was there if you were brave enough to seek it.

She was folding the pamphlet into her pocket, and trying to swallow her cynicism, when the heavy wooden door creaked open and a blast of wind and dead leaves blew down the aisle. A woman stood silhouetted in the doorway. For an instant Jane thought it was Anna, but then the woman walked into the *Kirche* and Jane saw that she was older, her hair a darker shade of black. Jane lifted a leaflet with the photo of a kindly nun ministering to a well-scrubbed old man on its cover; she stared down at its open pages as the woman genuflected before Christ, dipped her fingers in holy water and bobbed a curtsey to the altar before making her way down the aisle and into the priest's private sanctum.

Jane dropped the leaflet back on its pile and slipped from the building, out into a smirr of wind and rain. The treetops roared above, almost loud enough to drown the screaming rooks.

Jesus was the friend of prostitutes and sinners, so perhaps it was fitting that the woman who had just entered the priest's office was one of the street girls she and Petra had spotted Alban Mann talking to. All the same, it seemed strange that the woman hadn't felt the need to knock.

Jane let the gate swing shut behind her and walked away from their apartment block towards Hackescher Markt, where she remembered seeing a telephone box.

Seventeen

'Soon you'll be too big for me to kiss you.' Tielo kissed her three times on the cheek; left, right and left again. 'I'll have to stand on a ladder to reach over this.' He rubbed her tummy and then kissed her again. 'How's our baby?'

'Fine.' She could smell spirits on his breath. 'Kicking like a skinhead at a race riot.'

Tielo laughed and followed her through to the kitchen.

'You hate people touching you there, don't you?'

She filled the kettle, face turned to the sink so he wouldn't see the lie in her eyes.

'Not you, Tielo.'

He laughed again and Jane joined in. That was the joy, and the curse, of Tielo; he always brought you round.

'You do. Ute did too.' Tielo sat at the kitchen table and regarded his own rounded belly. 'Personally, I think I would enjoy it.' He stuck his stomach out. 'Come on, give it a rub.'

'No thanks.'

'Go on, get your revenge.'

Jane ignored him and set two mugs of tea on the table. Tielo looked at them with dismay and she asked, 'Are you driving?'

'Ute says I have to lose weight. I came by bike.'

Jane mussed his hair; it had been raining earlier and she could feel the dampness still clinging to it. She went to the cupboard and took out the bottle of malt she had bought at duty-free in Heathrow, the shop assistant's stare hard and disapproving, as if she thought Jane was about to open the bottle and down it in the departure lounge. She poured a small measure into a glass and handed it to Tielo.

'A low-calorie whisky?'

'As I cycled here I think I'm entitled to a full-calorie measure.'

Tielo held his glass out. He reminded her of a greedy nestling, always demanding more.

'Only if you promise to push your bike home.'

Tielo gave a non-committal snort. Jane topped up his glass, filled the milk jug with water and set it on the table. Tielo added a touch to the whisky, as she'd taught him to. He lifted the glass to his nose and breathed in.

'The water of life. Here.' He held the glass towards her. 'Would you like a sniff?'

'No thanks. It makes me queasy.'

'Nature.' Tielo took a sip. 'Amazing. It knows what a habitual drinker you are and so it takes away the urge.'

'Yes, amazing.'

Jane thought of the cigarette she had smoked that afternoon on the balcony and wondered if the scent of it still clung to her. They sat together in silence for a moment, Jane warming her hands on her mug, Tielo regarding the malt in his glass as if it held the secret to some vital conundrum.

'Ute sends her love. She would have come too, but bedtime,

bath-time, you know how it is. Well,' his laugh sounded forced, 'you soon will. You should call round some afternoon. You could keep each other company.'

'Yes.'

Jane couldn't imagine an afternoon alone with sweet Ute.

It was as if Tielo had read her mind. He said, 'You'll have lots in common when the baby comes.'

'You mean we'll both be mothers.'

'Members of the same sisterhood. Speaking of sisters, how are you coping, without Petra?'

'Okay. It's only for a week.'

'She said the people next door were disturbing you.'

'No,' Jane lied. 'They're no bother.'

'A man and his daughter.'

'Like I said, no bother. I hardly see them.'

'It must be hard, bringing up a daughter without her mother.'

'I suppose so.'

'Tell me if they become a problem. I'll go and speak to them.'

'Do you think you'd be more intimidating than Petra?'

'Probably not.' He shook his head. 'My sister won every fight we ever fought.' Tielo emptied his glass, got to his feet and poured another measure from the bottle Jane had left on the draining board. He brought the bottle back to the table with him. 'Do you mind if I help myself?'

'Too late if I did.'

Tielo gave her a weary smile. He was still in his work clothes, his tie slightly askew, shirt rumpled. He was forty-two, and though she could still see traces of the naughty schoolboy Tielo had once been, he looked older than Petra, as if life were treating him less kindly. Perhaps it was simply what happened when you had children. Broken sleep could make you age at the same rate as a premier whose country was at war.

'Ute says I drink too much.'

'Do you?'

Tielo raised his glass, as if toasting her.

'I think I drink exactly the right amount.' He took a slug from his glass. 'You know, I will be a father to your child when it needs one.'

Jane kept her voice neutral. 'Be an uncle to it, that'll be enough.'

'Even if it's a boy?'

'What difference would that make?'

Tielo took another sip of his whisky.

'Boys need role models. They need someone to show them how to become a man.'

She gave the same answer she'd given Anna. 'Lots of people never know their fathers.'

'Yes, and so it's hard for those people to know how important a father is.' Tielo stretched a hand across the table. She moved her own hand away, but he was too quick for her and grasped her fingers in his own. His skin felt clean and soft, pen-pusher's hands. 'Maybe Ute's right, I drink too much. I just want you to know I'll be there when it needs me.'

Tielo stared at her, his face creased and stubbled. She gave his hand a squeeze and said, 'You're a good man, Tielo.'

He grinned bravely. 'You only ever say that when you're feeling sorry for me.'

'It's Ute I feel sorry for.' She'd meant it as a joke, but Tielo winced. Jane topped up his glass and asked, 'Is everything okay between you two?'

Tielo rolled the whisky around in the glass, watching the way the viscous amber clung to its sides.

'Yes, everything is okay.' He took her hand again and this time she didn't resist. 'It should be me who asks you that question. How are things for you?'

'Fine.'

Jane extricated herself from his clasp. When was the last time she had been alone with Tielo? She couldn't remember. He looked towards the kitchen window and Jane followed his gaze. The sky was the same grey it had been yesterday. She couldn't see the backhouse from where she sat, but if she were to rise and go to the window, she would glimpse its far corner, a dark square a shade deeper than the night. She thought about what Anna had told her on the stairs. It was preposterous, Petra was too honest to ever be unfaithful.

Tielo asked, 'Do you ever wonder about the child's father?'

'No, why should I?'

His eyes met hers. 'No reason, I suppose. But he's a part of it too.'

'A biological element, necessary to the process, but no more significant than the midwife who'll deliver me. Petra and I will be the ones who love and rear this child. We're its parents.'

'You don't think the father matters?'

'You're a great father, Tielo, Carsten and Peter need you. But our child will have two parents. They'll just happen to be the same sex.'

136

'You sound like my sister.'

'That's hardly surprising. I love her.'

'So do I, but sometimes I think we should be careful of her.' Tielo's expression was rueful. 'She has a talent for persuading people to do what she wants.'

'I want this child just as much as Petra does.'

'It took you a long time to agree.'

'I needed to be sure.'

He nodded. 'Ute thought you were going to split up. She was upset.'

Jane knew Tielo's habit of expressing his own feelings through the filter of Ute, but she asked, 'And you?'

'I wondered.'

'Would you have been upset?'

'No.' He rose and pulled her into a squeeze, kissing her hard and wet on her cheek. 'It would have been my one chance to make you my mistress.'

Jane pushed him away, slapping his hands when they threatened to draw her back into a clinch.

'I wish you'd be serious.'

'The world is too serious, Jane, and we're too soon dead not to laugh at it a little.' Tielo took a deep breath. 'Okay, I'll be serious for a moment. Please know that you are a part of our family, and that this baby is very precious to all of us. It's precious to Ute, to Peter and to Carsten, but especially to me.'

'Thanks, Tielo.' Jane wondered how much he'd had to drink before he arrived. He never used to drink so much. She leant over and kissed him on the cheek, feeling the burn of stubble against her lips. He pulled her to him again, and this time she was aware of the emotion in his embrace. 'Tielo, is there something wrong?'

'No.'

He stroked her hair, still holding her close. Jane smelt the fabric softener Ute had washed his jumper with and beneath that, the slightly sour scent of a day at the office. She stifled the urge to pull away and asked, 'Do you want to tell me something?'

'No.' He let her go. 'There is nothing you need to know.'

'Okay.'

Jane held his gaze for a moment, wondering what Tielo was leaving unsaid, and if she should push him further. But he was Petra's brother, not hers. She would be home in less than a week. He could confide in her then, and add this new affair, or whatever it was, to the stock of secrets the twins shared.

She was in the hall, helping Tielo on with his jacket and trying to persuade him to push his bike home, when the banging started, as loud and sudden as the jackboots that stamped through her dreams.

Jane clutched his arm. 'What is it?'

'Next door. Shhh.'

Tielo raised a finger to his lips and tiptoed down the hallway, light despite his bulk. He put an eye to the spyhole and then placed an ear against the door.

There was no need for the manoeuvre. Jane could hear the voices now; two strangers, loud and official, and Alban Mann, confident in his fury.

She beckoned Tielo to her and whispered, 'What's going on?'

He kept his voice low.

'Some people from Child Protection. They say there has been an accusation that he is ill-treating his daughter. They want to see her.'

'Good.'

Tielo held a hand up, signalling for quiet. Mann was talking again. A jolt of nausea shot through Jane at the smooth insistence in her neighbour's voice. She whispered, 'What's he saying?'

Tielo cocked an ear towards the door, listening intently.

'He's saying she does have a bruise on her face, a black eye in fact. She got it at a basketball game, and they are welcome to call the girl's coach, if they would like verification.'

Jane hissed, 'He's lying. She's not the kind of girl who plays basketball.'

Tielo looked at her, his eyebrows raised. Jane whispered, 'What's Alban saying now?' And he turned his attention back to the locked door and the voices beyond. 'Alban is asking who gave them this information. They're saying it's confidential and that they must speak to the child.' Tielo paused. 'He's inviting them inside.' The sound of voices faded. Tielo turned to her, his coat still half on, half off, and asked, 'Do you know who might have reported him?'

'No.'

Jane turned her back on him and walked through to the silent chill of the child's room. Tielo followed.

'It's a serious allegation.'

Was Anna home, or hiding in her den, somewhere in the backhouse?

139

'I'm sure whoever did it had good reason.'

Tielo turned on the light. He had shrugged off his coat and held it clutched messily in one hand.

Jane said, 'Please, I prefer it dark.'

He switched the light off again, plunging them into invisibility and gloom. Had Anna caught a sudden glimpse of her standing at the window? Part of Jane liked to think of the girl looking out through the window of the backhouse and knowing she was there.

Tielo put a hand on her shoulder. 'You don't know who this informant might be?'

'I told you. I've no idea.'

'Whoever they are, I hope they're careful. If someone reported me to Child Protection I might be tempted to kill them.'

She turned to look at him, the pressure of the backhouse's stare a weight between her shoulder blades.

'You're a good father. That will never happen.'

'You're so certain he's guilty?'

'It's nothing to do with me, Tielo.'

'Sure?'

She had seen him cry twice, at the funerals of each of his parents, but otherwise Jane didn't think she had ever seen him look so serious.

'Positive.'

For a moment she thought Tielo was going to challenge her into telling the truth, but then he raised his hands in resignation. 'Okay.' He sighed. 'They sound like a problem family. You're right to keep out of their way. Concentrate on your own baby.'

'I'll do that.'

Their eyes met and Jane saw that Tielo believed her, as much as she had believed him when he'd said there was nothing he wanted to tell her.

Eighteen

Jane set the telephone receiver back on its cradle, trying not to mind that Petra's call had been so brief it made her feel like another item on a long list of tasks. She switched the CD player back on and the calm voice of her German lesson resumed.

Für mich ist ein Einschreibebrief da.

She repeated the sentence, trying to mimic the teacher's crisp accent.

'*Für mich ist ein Einschreibebrief da.*'

Wie heißen Sie bitte?

'*Wie heißen Sie bitte?*'

Brigitte Hoffmann.

'Jane Logan.'

She had lit the lamps against the dark and the sitting room glowed white in the carefully calibrated light, so sterile it might have belonged to the clinic of some celebrated plastic surgeon. It was easy to imagine a trolley being wheeled into the almost bare expanse by masked surgeons, ready to carve out some beauty. She saw them for a moment, gloved hands moving deep in blood. The image was too suggestive of the forthcoming birth and she pushed it away.

Ja, hier ist ein Einschreibebrief für Sie. Zeigen Sie mir, bitte, Ihren Ausweis.

'*Ja, hier ist ein Einschreibebrief für Sie . . .*'

She had lost track of the conversation. Jane lifted the book that had come with the CD and tried to find the right page.

Hier, bitte . . .

. . . und unterschreiben Sie hier.

It was useless; she should have gone to classes at the Goethe Institute, as Petra had suggested.

Geben Sie mir vier Briefmarken für . . .

Jane turned off the CD player and placed her pack of cigarettes on the coffee table. There were three left. After that she would give up for good, or at least until after the child was born. The dilemma was whether to smoke one now, or save it for morning. She stared at the box, meditating on its logo, the familiar block capitals she used to think were stylish. Morning was when she felt the craving most, but evenings came a close second; just in front of the afternoons.

Jane had half-dreaded Petra's call, worried that she might have spoken to Tielo first and would blame her for the social workers' visit, but Petra had put her on speakerphone while she dressed for dinner and only asked about the child. Was he moving a lot? *He*, it was always he. Had Jane been playing him music? Was she sticking to the diet they'd agreed?

Jane took the pack from the table and tipped a cigarette loose.

'Okay, soldier,' she whispered, 'time to do your duty.'

The phone burred back into life. She crossed the room and snatched it to her ear. It was typical of Petra to get distracted by work and typical of her to phone back to apologise.

143

'Hey, baby girl,' she put on the American drawl she sometimes used in love-play. 'In the mood for some sexy phone fun?'

'That's the best offer I've had all day.' The voice was male, with an accent she couldn't quite identify.

A warm blush blazed across Jane's chest and up her neck.

'I'm sorry, who is this?'

'Jurgen Tillman, Johannes's boyfriend. We met a few nights ago, at your dinner party.'

'Oh, yes.' She couldn't think why he would call her. 'How are you?'

'In good health. And you?'

'I'm well.'

She had had a headache ever since Tielo had left; the sound of the social workers banging on Alban's door still echoing in her head.

'You're wondering why I'm phoning.'

'No.' She laughed. 'Well, perhaps.'

A white orchid stood in a pot, next to the phone. One of its petals was browning at the edges. Jane started to gently peel away the decay with her fingernails.

Jurgen said, 'Firstly, to apologise for my drunkenness.'

The tear she had made caught in one of the flower's veins, ripping half the length of it. She suppressed a curse.

'Were you drunk? I didn't notice.'

'Then pregnancy has made you blind.'

Jane laughed again, hating the sound of her own voice, false and tinny in her ears. She nipped the remaining shred of petal from the orchid, leaving the flower with a lopsided look that made her think of Anna's black eye.

'And the second reason?' She tried to focus on Jurgen's call.

'I felt I owed you more than an apology, so I did a search on your backhouse. You dislike it so much I thought you might like to know if there are any plans for it.'

He had her full attention now. It was odd to think of strangers deliberating over the building's fate. Jane wasn't sure she liked it.

'That was kind of you.'

She could almost hear the casual shrug of his shoulders.

'It might be a good opportunity for someone.'

'For you?'

'I'm not sure.' Jurgen paused. Jane felt a question in the silence and wondered what he was about to ask her to do. He said, 'The building belongs to your landlord.'

'I guess that could make sense.'

'Do you know him?'

'No, Petra dealt with the lease. She went through a letting agency.'

'Ah, I see.' Jurgen sounded disappointed and Jane wondered if he was going to make a reference to how much of her life she left to Petra's care, but he asked, 'So the name, Dr Alban Mann, doesn't mean anything to you?'

'Alban Mann owns this place?'

'You do know him?' The enthusiasm was back in his voice.

Jane held the receiver to her chest. She had imagined Anna haunting the backhouse, but now it seemed as if the building had been looking at her with Alban's eyes.

She put the phone to her ear again and heard Jurgen say, 'Hello?'

'I'm sorry, I got distracted. Dr Mann is our next-door

neighbour. We nod to each other when we meet on the doorstep, but I don't really know him.'

'Do you think you could get to know him?'

'I doubt it. He's a busy man and I'm a seven-and-a-half-month-pregnant lesbian.'

Jurgen laughed. 'I guess I sounded like a pimp.'

'A little.'

'Dr Mann owns a lot of property in Berlin – some he leases, some he sells at a profit. He's been sitting on this particular building for quite a while.'

'Longer than you would expect?'

'More than ten years. A long time, but then I don't know what he has in mind.'

'Maybe he likes it the way it is.'

Jurgen snorted. 'That seems unlikely. I imagine he's just not found the right person to move it on to. It's a large building, in poor condition. There's potential there, but it would take a lot of investment to realise it. Could be there's a lucrative deal hovering, maybe a series of lucrative deals that haven't come off. One falls through, another beckons, and before you know it you've held on to a property longer than you should have. It happens.'

'Could he have held on to it for sentimental reasons?'

'Anything's possible. I still own the first apartment I ever bought, a one-bedroom flat in Neukölln. It no longer fits with my portfolio, but it reminds me of where I came from, and where I might end up if I'm not careful.' Jurgen paused, and Jane imagined him trying to calculate the kind of sentiments that might lead a man to snub a profit. The equation eluded him. 'No, it would be too much money to tie up in nostalgia.'

'How much money?'

'Impossible to say. It depends on what he paid for it and whether he would renovate the apartments himself or sell the whole building in its present condition to a developer. The state it's in at the moment, maybe three-quarters of a million euros, if he got lucky.' Jurgen hesitated, as if considering whether to divulge valuable business information. 'Derelict properties with that kind of potential are getting harder to find, so he could well get lucky.'

'How much would Mann raise if he renovated and sold them as individual apartments?'

This time the answer came immediately.

'A friend of mine recently sold a similar property for two and a half million.'

Jane whistled softly under her breath.

'A close friend?'

She heard the smile in his voice.

'Close as it's possible to be. Get to know your landlord, Jane. I can make business enquiries but nothing beats a personal introduction. Put us across a table from each other with a drink in our hands and I'll make sure you get a generous finder's fee.'

Jane laughed. 'I'm sorry, Jurgen, but I really don't think I can help you.'

'Don't underestimate yourself, Frau Logan. I've done some research. Mann isn't just any kind of doctor, he's a gynaecologist. No man does that job unless he likes women. Try being friendly; even in Berlin we occasionally invite our neighbours round for an aperitif.' Now that he had set her her task,

Jurgen was in a hurry. 'You should do it soon, before the baby arrives and takes over your life.'

Jane slept in the child's room that night. She woke suddenly in the dark with the certainty that someone was standing over her bed. She screwed her eyes shut and kept her breathing regular, feeling the force of their presence glowering above her. She lay like that for a long time, not daring to move and then, even though the terror was still upon her, slipped back into a deep and dreamless sleep.

The memory of her night-time horrors was still with Jane when she woke the following morning. She walked through the apartment looking for signs of an intruder, but everything was as she remembered: the half-read paperback splayed on the floor beside the bed, the rumpled couch cushions, her few dishes stacked on the draining board.

Still, the impression that someone had been there lingered. Jane thought about phoning Tielo, and then of getting in touch with Jurgen Tillman. Tielo would insist she stayed with him and Ute, and the thought of fitting herself into the chaos of their household was exhausting. She wasn't sure what Jurgen would suggest, but it was enough to imagine his eyes gleaming.

The rucksack Petra took with her on hikes was hanging in the cloakroom. Jane searched its pockets until she found the hunting knife that had once belonged to Petra and Tielo's grandfather. The twins had fought over it after their own father's death, Tielo insistent that it should pass down the male line, Petra furious at the suggestion.

Jane slid the blade from its sheath and touched its cutting edge. She could feel the sharpness lurking there. Petra's father's eyes had shone as he had told her how the hunters gutted the deer they had shot before bringing them home; blood and entrails and sinew. The memory of his description made her stomach do a quick flip, but Jane slipped the knife under her mattress.

She washed and dressed, wondering what had happened between Mann and the social workers the previous evening. Had Anna been taken to some foster home? The thought disquieted her, but surely it was better to be placed with vetted carers than a father who beat you.

Nothing was certain, least of all people.

Jane pulled on her coat, wrapped a scarf around her neck and slid her fingers into her gloves. She felt in her pocket for the envelope of money Petra had left her. It was gone.

Jane had been careful to keep the flat how Petra would like it. Now she tore the place apart, searching everywhere the money might conceivably have ended up; rifling through her clothes, emptying the bin, tearing the sheets from the bed.

After that, she searched places where she knew the envelope couldn't be: on top of kitchen cabinets, under the rug in the sitting room, inside books she was yet to read. She had sent Petra an email the night before and now, even though she was certain she hadn't taken the money into Petra's office, Jane slipped in and scanned her desk, lifting up the computer keyboard and running her fingers beneath the monitor.

There was something there. A piece of paper too insubstantial to be the euro-stuffed envelope, but she lifted the monitor anyway, slid her hand beneath and pulled it free.

For an instant Jane thought that she was the woman in the photograph, with her arm around Petra, but then she saw that although the woman had the same dark curls and pale complexion, she was someone else, someone Jane had never met. She turned the image over, hoping Petra had written a name on the reverse, but it was blank. Perhaps people only labelled things they were in danger of forgetting. Jane ripped the photo in half and slid it back where she had found it.

Her hands trembled as she filled a glass with water from the kitchen tap. Apart from a few brief weekend visits, Petra had been in Berlin for three months on her own while Jane wound up their London life. Of course she had made new friends. The girl had placed her arm around Petra simply for the photo; it was an innocent pose, nothing more.

Anna's words came back to her: 'I saw your girfriend on Friedrichstrasse last week. She was kissing another woman, right there in the street. They looked good together, like they were in love.'

It was a lie, a cheap shot aimed at upsetting her. Jane made a conscious effort to push the photo from her mind, and saw again the way Petra had answered the mystery girl's smile with her own wide grin, the way Petra had reached up and clasped the hand the girl had placed on her shoulder.

The child hit out and the tumbler of water slipped from Jane's grasp, exploding against the tiled floor. A splinter of glass ricocheted into her face, cutting the skin just below her eye.

'*Fuck.*'

She let the mess lie where it was and went through to the

bathroom, shaking her head at the stupidity of it all. The wound was tiny, barely more than a scratch, but it was as if all the blood in her body was determined to drain from it. She drenched a towel in cold water and dabbed at the puncture, but it refused to stop bleeding.

'*Fuck, fuck, fuck.*'

Her reflection swore back at her, eyes puffy from misery and lack of sleep. Jane washed her face, then pulled on her coat and stepped out of the apartment, holding a piece of toilet paper to her face to staunch the flow.

She was worried that the sound of her front door slamming would bring Alban Mann into the hallway, so it was a moment before she saw the red gloss splashed across the doormat. Jane stared at it, knowing it wasn't blood, but unsure of what it was. It was only when she looked up and saw the words 'LESBEN RAUS!' daubed in large clumsy letters across their front door, that she realised it was paint.

Nineteen

She bought turpentine, sandpaper, heavy-duty rubber gloves and a small tin of paint in a hardware store near Hackescher Markt, handing over the money with trembling hands. Each brushstroke had screamed fury. Had Anna been waiting behind the door of her father's apartment, an eye to the spyhole, watching to see what Jane would do? She imagined her, sweet face distorted by loathing, smiling as Jane reached out and touched the still wet letters.

It was market day and the pavements around the U-Bahn were a crush of stalls and shoppers. Jane weaved her way through the crowd, her canvas bag an unwelcome weight on her shoulder. Did Alban Mann know what his daughter had done? Anna had been in his sole care since she was a baby, and even now, when she must realise that what he did to her was wrong, the girl adored him. She was like a desperate hostage falling in love with her jailer.

Jane stopped for a moment, resting her heavy bag on the ground. She would persuade Petra to break their lease and move flats. Mann would be glad to see them go, and then he and Anna could play out their lives in the way they would have done if she had never encountered them.

The thought of Petra made her feel sick. Jane shouldered her burden again, wondering if it might be she who moved on alone. Was her baby's childhood destined to be a rerun of her own? Jane didn't believe in Fate, but sometimes it seemed impossible to escape the life you'd been elected to.

She had spent the last of her cash on the turpentine. Now she went to an autobank, used her debit card to withdraw the rest of her balance and bought some bread, cheese and fruit at a stall. There was enough money left to last her until Petra came back, if she was careful. Jane turned for home, her bag weighing on her back like a penance.

The voices boomed around the stairwell from the landing above, deep and male and unfamiliar, but with an unmistakably official edge. These were men with some authority behind them, men happy to announce their visit to the entire tenement, a free warning of what might happen if you disobeyed the rules.

Jane stood in the building's lobby, wondering if they had heard the door slam behind her, or if she could still sneak away without being noticed. She took a deep breath and gathered up her bags. It was cold, but she was wearing the snug new coat Petra had bought her. She could sit in the graveyard opposite and watch them leave. She wondered if they had come for Anna or her father. The thought of Anna being led away like a witch to the pyre was horrible, but there would be some satisfaction in seeing Alban Mann in handcuffs.

'Frau Logan?'

She looked up and saw a young policeman leaning over the banister above.

'Yes?'

His boots thudded against the stairs as he jogged down them and Jane thought of Frau Becker in the ground-floor apartment, convinced that the Russians were invading. She put a hand on her tummy.

The policeman was younger than his voice had sounded; tall with sandy hair, freckles and an open smile. His uniform jacket and trousers were ill-fitting and crumpled, but the shabbiness of his clothes added to his air of masculinity, as if he were too busy catching criminals to worry about grooming. He met her eyes and said, 'Let me carry that for you.'

Jane saw him glance quickly at the turpentine and paint inside her canvas bag as he lifted it.

'Thank you.'

She had no option but to follow him up the stairs to her landing, where his colleague, older and broader, wearing an equally creased green uniform, was waiting.

The slogan looked even redder than it had that morning. The paint had been splashed against the door with all the energy of a young Jackson Pollock, and drips descended from the letters, like a reminder that there were sharper weapons than words, whatever the poets might say.

The young policeman asked, 'When did this happen?'

'I don't know. Last night I suppose. It wasn't there when my partner's brother visited yesterday evening. I discovered it this morning.'

The older man said something in German to her and Jane said, 'I'm sorry, I don't understand.'

'Your hands are red.'

His accent was thicker than his young colleague's.

Jane looked at her palms and saw the stain across them.

'I touched the door to see if it was still wet. Look.' She pointed to where one of the letters was smudged. 'You can see my handprint there.'

He gave the door a cursory glance and returned his attention to her.

'This is a crime in Berlin.' It sounded like an accusation. 'Do you wish to report it?'

'No, it's okay.' Jane smiled stupidly. 'I mean, it's not okay, but I don't want to report it. I can take this now.' She turned to relieve the young policeman of her bag but he ignored her and his colleague said, 'May we come in?'

She had learnt early that it was best not to show weakness in front of authority, but it was an effort to meet the eyes below the visor.

'Perhaps you can tell me what this is about first.'

The older policeman's face was unreadable.

'We can talk out here, but I think you might prefer it if we went indoors.'

Jane thought of Petra a plane journey away in Vienna, and her head swam. The younger policeman grasped her elbow.

'Are you all right?'

'Yes, thank you.'

He kept his hand on her arm, whether from fear that she would fall or try to escape she wasn't sure.

'You've cut your face.'

'I dropped a glass, it's nothing.'

'You were lucky it missed your eye.'

155

Jane pulled herself free, took her keys from her coat pocket and let them into the flat.

As soon as they entered Jane knew she had made a mistake. The evidence of her frantic search for the money was everywhere. She led them through to the sitting room where the mess was only tumbled cushions and drawers emptied of papers, but she had left the doors to the other rooms open, and they could see the chaos as they passed through the hall.

The young policeman said, 'Let me get you a glass of water,' and went into the kitchen before Jane could stop him. She heard his boots crunch against the broken glass and remembered with shame the blood spattered cabinets, the upturned bin, its contents strewn across the floor.

The older policeman helped her put a bolster back on the couch. He restored the cushions to one of the armchairs and took a seat. Jane watched him cast a quick glance around the room and saw what he saw: the upscale apartment reduced to the level of a dosshouse.

'Have you been burgled?'

His tone was so casual he might have been asking if she'd been on holiday yet.

For a mad second Jane was tempted to lie and file a report, but she said, 'No, I was looking for something.'

'It must have been something important.'

'Yes.'

'Did you find it?'

'No.'

His colleague came through and put a glass of water on the coffee table in front of her. Jane saw the young policeman exchanging a look with his partner as he put the final easy chair back in its place and sat down.

The older man asked, 'Do you know why we're here?'

Jane reached out for her water but found that her hand was trembling too much to lift it to her lips.

'I assume you've come about my neighbour, Dr Alban Mann. I heard Child Protection officers at his door last night.'

'Dr Mann has filed a complaint about you.'

'About me?'

'You're surprised?'

'Of course.' She faltered. 'I don't know. Maybe it makes sense. Attack's meant to be the best form of defence.'

The young policeman leant forward, his open face full of sympathy.

'Why would Dr Mann feel the need to defend himself against you?'

'Not against me particularly, against society. He obviously wants to deflect attention from the charges against him.'

The older man's voice was firm.

'There are no charges against Dr Mann, only an anonymous accusation. Dr Mann says it was you who made that accusation and has asked us to charge you with harassment.'

'Charge me?' She laughed although there was nothing funny about it. 'On what evidence?'

The policeman shrugged.

'Dr Mann claims you've troubled his daughter many times. He has given us a list.'

'Can I have a copy of this list, please?'

'No.'

'I see.' Jane met the policeman's eyes, like an innocent person with nothing to hide. 'I've seen Dr Mann's daughter Anna several times with bruises on her face and stopped to ask if she's okay. I also asked her if she needed my help when she was having a fight with her father on the landing.'

'A physical fight?'

'No, but he was shouting at her so loudly, I could hear him in my apartment.'

The older man leant forward and bared his teeth in what she hoped was a smile.

'I'm glad you don't live next door to me, Frau Logan. I have two teenage daughters. Sometimes people three kilometres away can hear me shouting.'

'And how often do they see your daughters with bruised faces?'

The policeman kept his voice low and calm.

'We interviewed Anna Mann; she told us she had been accidentally hit in the eye by a team-mate during basketball practice. Her coach confirmed that this was what happened.'

'And did someone go and see this coach or did they talk to them over the phone?' Jane tried to keep her voice neutral, but anger seeped into her words, turning her question into an accusation.

'I spoke to her myself.'

Jane asked, 'On the telephone?' and the policeman broke eye contact. She shook her head. 'Who gave you this coach's number? Doctor Mann?'

'Berlin is a busy city. We don't have time to interview every minor witness in person.'

'And yet you're here.'

'We take allegations of harassment seriously.'

'But a girl gets beaten up, and you allow the person who beat her to arrange a phone alibi?'

'Frau Logan, did you make the call to the social services department?'

Jane hesitated. She had promised Petra she wouldn't get involved, but here she was with graffiti splattered over their front door and the police in their flat. She looked at the young policeman.

'If I said it was me, would you investigate further?'

The older policeman's voice was as final as a closed case.

'We've investigated as much as the evidence allowed.'

'I'm a witness. You haven't interviewed me yet.'

His young colleague met her eyes. 'You're the object of a complaint from Dr Mann. Your opinion can't be treated as unbiased.'

'Which is a good reason for him to make a complaint.' Jane heard her voice rising and stopped for a moment, breathing deeply, trying to calm herself. She saw the policemen exchange a worried look and wondered if they thought she was about to go into labour. 'I'm all right.' She took a sip of water. 'I've heard him through the wall shouting abuse at her. They had an argument in the hallway, right in front of my apartment. I have seen the bruises on her face and watched the way she tries to protect him. She's disappeared overnight at least once. Anna is a disturbed young woman.'

The young policeman leant towards her, his hand on his knees. The dusting of freckles across his nose made him look fresh and outdoorsy.

'Are you a psychologist, Frau Logan?'

159

'No.'

'An educationalist perhaps, someone who is used to working with young people?'

'No.'

'A social worker or probation officer?'

'I managed a bookshop in London.'

'A bookshop.' The policeman nodded as if he could see the neatly stocked shelves, the easy chairs and quiet browsers. 'That must have been nice.'

'It was.'

'I see you still read a lot.' He nudged a tumbled stack of books on the floor beside his feet with the toe of his boot. 'Reading is good for the imagination.' He looked up and she saw how little he believed in her. 'I'm interested in your qualifications for diagnosing Anna Mann as disturbed.'

Jane took a deep breath and closed her eyes for a moment. When she opened them, the policemen were still there.

'I've known girls who have been abused. The way that Anna behaves; her defensiveness, her provocative clothing, her attitude towards her father, hating him one moment, protective of him the next, it's the way these girls acted.'

'I see.'

The older policeman nodded as if considering what she had just said, but he was a poor actor and the gesture looked hollow.

Jane asked, 'So will you do something about it?'

'What would you like me to do?'

Jane wondered if he was gay, and if he resented her for not reporting the graffiti splashed across her door.

'I'd like you to investigate Alban Mann.'

She saw him cast a quick glance at his companion.

'It's like my colleague said. We've investigated as much as the evidence we have allows us to. But everything you've told us will go on file.'

'That'll come in handy if he murders her.'

The older policeman shook his head.

'Please remember there is a serious accusation against you, which will also stay on file. All phone calls to the Child Protection hotline are recorded. You have a distinctive accent, Frau Logan, it wouldn't take an expert to identify it.'

He stood up, the radio at his belt squawking as if on cue. The young policeman followed his example and rose from his chair, and the living room shrank a little at their combined bulk.

Jane hauled herself to her feet. She looked from one to the other, staring each of them in the eye in turn, and said, 'Go ahead.'

Twenty

It was strange being out at night on her own, the rush of lights and people disorientating after the white silence of the apartment. This must be how it felt to be released from jail, or set ashore after a long sea voyage; a blast of noise and colour that quickened the blood with nervous expectation.

Jane had dressed as if she was going to an expensive restaurant with Petra, spending time on her make-up, teasing her curls into an artful mess and choosing one of the empire-line dresses she had brought with her from London. She thought she might have grown bigger in the past week. Her tummy led the way, proudly tenting the folds of the cleverly cut coat Petra had found her.

A stag party was congregated outside one of the bars on Oranienburger Strasse, wearing T-shirts that proclaimed them, *Dave's Pussy Posse*. A couple of the street girls were on the edge of the group and gusts of manly laughter followed whatever suggestions they were making. It was still early in the evening and the banter seemed leisurely and good-natured. The stags were cockneys; a mixture of wiry men who sucked their leanness from cigarettes, and broad-chested, bullet-headed blokes who looked like they had swaggered out of an English Defence League poster. Dave sat at their centre, king of the weekend, sweet-faced beneath his razor-cut, bemused in his booziness.

Jane wondered if the street girls were using the Englishmen to help them get into character for the long night ahead, or if they had already spotted likely punters and hard-edged calculations lay behind every smile. She considered taking a seat beneath one of the halogen heaters, ordering a mineral water and listening in. Trying to spot who would sheer off from the group later, when the night had moved on and more drinks had been downed, and Dave put to bed, drunk in self-defence. But time was short and her wallet slim. She walked on, hearing one of the men say, 'Her indoors would kill me, love,' in the kind of tones that invited more persuasion. Jane stared at the girls' faces, just to make sure, but she already knew that neither of them was the woman she was looking for.

She had spent the afternoon putting the flat to rights, the policemen's visit acid in her chest. Three times she lifted the phone to call Alban, and twice she left the flat and stood in front of his door, daring him to come out and face her. But in the end she didn't telephone or ring his doorbell.

She had also resisted the urge to slip into Petra's office and retrieve the torn photograph, and when Petra phoned had managed to keep her voice the right side of breezy, inventing a walk through Galleria department store that she knew would be approved of.

The child was still moving, but something else had hardened within her, a determination to see things through. She'd assumed it was Anna who had defaced their door, but what if it was Alban, determined to make sure that Jane moved out and left his daughter alone?

Jane pulled her scarf over her mouth, protecting her face from the cold. She'd borrowed it from Petra's drawer and could smell her perfume, complex and zesty, masking the scent of roasting meat from the restaurants that lined the street. She wondered what Petra was doing now. Dining with colleagues while they discussed the finer points of the audit or out somewhere with the girl in the photo, Jane's not quite Doppelgänger? The thought made her feel miserable.

She passed the Friedrichstrasse Theater, an electric riot of pink and purple neon. There was a cabaret on that evening, and well-dressed couples were filtering up the building's steps and through its doors. She stopped and watched them, thinking how many different worlds existed on this street alone: the respectable couples dressed for a night of titillation, Dave and his stags gearing up for lost days on the lash, and the world she was seeking out.

Jane had been sitting on the balcony, two cigarettes into a fresh pack, when she'd heard the rooks' machine-gun cries and spied a flash of red disappearing amongst the gravestones. She had hunched down in her chair, though there was no way Anna could see her, a smudge of black on grey, from that distance.

The paint she had bought still sat by the door, but Jane had resisted starting work. The words would still be there even if she applied a fresh coat of gloss; she wanted the ugliness of them seared on the memories of the Manns the way they were seared on hers.

Any anger Jane had felt towards the girl over the graffiti was gone. If it was Anna who had defaced the door, then she'd done it out of desperation and fear of what Jane's suspicions might mean for her father. If it were Mann, then he too was desperate and frightened. The thought bothered her.

The gate had creaked open and the streetwalker she had seen talking to Alban and then, later, entering the minister's inner sanctum, hurried into the churchyard. Jane had fetched a quilt, wrapped it around herself and waited, but although she stayed out on the balcony for over an hour, resisting the urge for another cigarette, her face stiffening in the cold, she had caught no more glimpses of Anna or of the other woman.

Night-time was no longer her realm. Jane felt tired, the weight of the child more than she had realised. She had left the lights burning in the apartment, but couldn't help wondering if Mann had heard her going out and was even now wandering through the empty rooms, exploring their lives and deciding how to wreck them. She wanted to hail a taxi and head home, the lights of the city speeding by, but trudged on, trying not to mind that her feet were aching. The child was still and she imagined it curled inside her, rocked to sleep by the rhythm of her walk.

'Little troll, little goblin,' she whispered.

Two streetwalkers strolled towards her, arms entwined like sixth-formers in a boarding-school novel, their personalities smoothed away for the night, concealed beneath make-up as thick as Anna's. One of the women met Jane's eyes and winked, letting Jane know that she'd seen her. Jane looked away and the girls laughed, loud and careless, showing the world they didn't give a damn. She envied them their camaraderie. It was easier to be defiant when you had an ally.

She had never seen Anna with a friend. Alban Mann schooled the girl himself and, except for when she'd met the men on the station platform, she was always alone. No wonder Anna defended Mann. He wasn't simply her father; he was the only person she was allowed to get close to. The girl was ready to break free, Jane was sure of it; she just needed some help.

A bicycle bell pinged. Jane realised she had drifted into the pavement's cycle lane and stepped swiftly out of the way, her heart a hammer in her chest. A passer-by bumped her shoulder and was gone, leaving a muttered swear word in the air, before she had time even to register whether they were male or female. Jane quickened her pace and walked on. This was the city at night, a fellowship of strangers, united by the knowledge that nobody really gave a damn about anyone but themselves.

She had almost given up when she saw her quarry. The woman was standing in a doorway, beside the same girl she'd been with on the evening Jane and Petra had spotted them from the taxi, laughing with Alban on the corner of Sophienstrasse. They were wearing the same high heels and close-fitting corsets as before, their long black hair pulled up into elaborate bouffants. The effect was tough and tightly efficient.

Jane walked round the block twice, rehearsing what she wanted to say, but when she passed a third time, the woman's

166

companion was alone, tapping something into her mobile phone.

'Excuse me.' Nerves and frosty air sucked the breath from her and Jane's voice sounded hoarse. 'Where did your friend go?'

The woman kept her attention on the telephone keypad, her features illuminated by the glow of the phone. Close up, her face had a witchy look sharpened by suspicion. Jane saw herself, smartly dressed against the cold, her pregnancy obvious beneath her cashmere coat, and wondered if the woman thought her some wronged wife come to make trouble.

She forced a smile. 'I have some money for her.'

The woman pushed her hands deep into the pockets of her short, fur-trimmed jacket. She stared at Jane without speaking and it wasn't clear if she had heard or not, but then she said, 'I'm her sister. You can give it to me.'

Her voice was deeper than her small frame implied, her English lilting to the cadence of a different language.

'I promised to hand it directly to her.'

The girl shrugged. She pulled her mobile back out of her pocket and started to tap at it again.

'Then you must wait.'

'How long will she be?'

It was a stupid question and the woman didn't bother to answer. She pointed across the road.

'Wait there, and if any men ask you to take a walk with them, send them over here. You don't want your baby damaged before it's even born.'

Jane nodded and did as she was told.

No men propositioned either of them in the fifteen

minutes she waited and Jane's feet lost their last residue of feeling. She had never thought the sex industry an easy way to make money, but she'd never imagined that it would be boring. Prostitution was turning out to be like all the slacker schemes of her youth, more work than a real job. Jane wondered if the girls had a pimp, and if he was concealed in another doorway, watching her and waiting to see what she was up to. She took out her phone and checked the time, shielding the screen with her hand, keen to keep her face in the shadows. There was a message from Petra:

I love you. Sleep tight and keep our baby safe.

She snapped the phone shut, looked up and saw a slight figure watching her from the pavement.

'Hello?' Jane's voice was soft and tentative, carried on a fog of frosty air.

'Hello.' The woman she'd been searching for stepped into the doorway, standing so close that the plumes of their breath met and mingled. She said, 'I heard you had some money for me?'

Twenty-One

Her name was Maria; she had two children, a girl and a boy, and came over the border from Poland most weekends. She talked in machine-gun rattles, as fast as the rooks that haunted the graveyard. Her English was good, though her German was better. She also spoke Russian and a little Czech, though not so well. She offered all of these details unasked, quick and flirty, keen to put Jane at her ease. Her story was clichéd enough to be lies and simple enough to be true: two children, a husband killed in an industrial accident, and a determination not to beg. Jane trusted the woman as much as she trusted her own flawed judgement, but found herself warming to her. She wondered if Maria had glimpsed her loneliness and was charming her, as she must charm the men she serviced.

They sat at the back of a brightly lit café that smelt of hamburger grease, boiled sausage and that special odour that only comes from regular congregations of unwashed bodies. A skinny man in a stained apron planted coffees in front of them, slopping a little on to each of their saucers, so evenly that it might have been a novel attempt at presentation. His smile was too wide for his face and directed as much at the scratched tables, unwashed floor and greasy walls as at the two women.

Apart from an old man keeping a worried eye on a Norma carrier bag filled with empty beer bottles he'd collected for their *Pfand*, the two women were the only customers.

'Look at this place.' Maria's words sounded loud and shrill in the small space. 'It's us who keep this dump open. We pay their wages and not even a "thank you" when we order.'

Jane took a sip of her coffee. It had a bitter aftertaste she couldn't identify. She added a spoonful of sugar and said, 'You should go somewhere else.'

'Where?' Maria's long hair was piled on top of her head in a dark cascade. It quivered as if in irritation at the stupidity of the question. 'You want to be sitting in some high-class bar with your husband when a gang of prostitutes come in?'

'I don't have a husband.'

'Your boyfriend, whatever.' The woman's eyes were so dark they were almost black. 'You want to be there when a bunch of good-looking girls who rent their bodies come by? No. You're a good-looking girl, but perhaps there are things he don't like to ask you to do, he respects you too much. He sees us and gets to thinking, "I could ask these pretty girls to do that bad thing with me."' She raised her eyes to the heavens, playing the part of the thoughtful boyfriend, and then snapped out of character and leant across the table, restored to her shrill self again. 'Or maybe there are girls who are not so good-looking, nice to talk to, and their husbands they love them – who knows, maybe the husband is not so good-looking either, it happens. He sees us and he thinks, "I love my ugly wife, but just this

170

once I'd like to stick it to a pretty girl."' Maria laughed at the picture she had painted. 'I understand why they don't want us in bars that make good money. We upset all those other women and street girls don't drink enough to make up for that kind of lost business. Some of them don't behave so well either. But this place,' she held out her hands as if she could seize the whole dingy café in her palms. 'Who's going to worry if you don't behave well here? Who will care if you run off with their husband?' She looked at Jane, suddenly serious. 'You have some money for me?'

'Yes.'

'How much?'

'It depends.'

'Okay, so tell me what you want me to do and I will tell you the price.'

'I want to ask you about someone, a man I know.' She took out her phone and found the photograph she had snapped from her balcony of Alban Mann walking towards their apartment block. Mann's head was tilted away from the camera, his expression lost in shadows, but she had captured the awkward jut of his hip, the contrast between his cane and trendy hairdo. Jane slid the phone in front of Maria. 'Do you know him?'

Maria traced a finger around Mann's hair and along his jawline.

'Why do you ask?'

Jane had thought about how to answer this question during her walk and had tried to settle on a tack that would work regardless of whether the woman liked or hated Mann. She said, 'I think he might be in some trouble.' Maria kept

171

her dark eyes on the photograph; Jane found it hard to read her expression. She asked, 'Do you know him?'

'Perhaps. I see a lot of men. Maybe I saw him before. I don't know.' Maria handed it back to her. 'What kind of trouble?'

'I'm worried about his daughter, Anna.'

Maria's eyes blinked, but her face remained expressionless.

'What is she to you?'

'Nothing. A distant relative.'

'Are you her mother?' Maria's eyes widened and then she laughed. 'No, I think you're too English to be her mother.'

'You know her?'

'She talked to me, the way you are now.'

'What about?'

Maria sipped her coffee. She put the cup down and said, 'I will have to get back to work soon. My little boy needs new shoes and my daughter needs so many new things for school. I want her to do well at school so she doesn't end up on the streets like her mummy.'

'How much?'

'Two hundred euros.'

Maria leant back in her chair, a slight smile on her face. It was hard to know how old she was. It wasn't just that her make-up was thick, or that turning day into night had given her eyes a strained appearance. It was something in her expression that said what she knew about the world had put her beyond the reach of workaday folk. She looked as if she could wait all day, but when she left, would leave without a backward glance.

Jane said, 'It sounds like you have a lot to tell me.'

172

'That depends on what you already know.'

'Enough to spot a lie.'

Maria grinned, showing her teeth. 'I'm a good liar, but I promise not to lie to you.'

Jane smiled to show she had got the joke. If Petra were here she would negotiate, but it was impossible to imagine Petra on this mission. She said, 'I only have a hundred and seventy-five on me.'

It was everything she had.

'Okay, a hundred and seventy-five, and I promise to leave nothing out.' Maria's smile stretched even wider and Jane was sure she could have got whatever the woman had to tell her for less.

'Half now, half when you finish.'

Jane took her purse from her bag and Maria said, 'No, pass it to me under the table. I don't want him seeing.'

She nodded towards the back of the café where the waiter was lolling against the counter, his eyes not quite on that day's edition of *Bild* splayed out in front of him. Jane counted out ninety euros and slid them into Maria's waiting hand. The woman leant back in her chair and took another sip of her coffee, wincing at its taste.

'I don't know what they make this from. Perhaps they go to the Zoo and the keeper sells them some elephant dung.'

Passing over the money had subtly altered the atmosphere between them. This was how the men must feel, Jane thought, entitled to ask for what they wanted because they had paid good cash. She kept her eyes on Maria's, as if by holding her gaze she could keep her to the truth. She saw her own reflection in the woman's pupils, a distant pale figure; a gleam in an eye.

'How do you know Anna?'

'She's a strange girl. Maybe she's like her mother, but I never met her. I heard of her, though, all the girls have heard of her. It's a romantic story, like a fairy tale.'

Jane could feel the facts slipping away from her.

'Please,' she held up a hand. 'You've heard of Anna's mother?'

'All the girls have.'

'Start with Anna's mother. Why is it a romantic story?'

'Because she was a street girl like me and she married a doctor, just like Julia Roberts in *Pretty Woman*. Life is not usually romantic, but it can be.'

'Anna's mother was a streetwalker?'

Maria's smile was teasing. 'See, already I told you something you didn't know.'

'How did they meet?'

The woman shrugged. 'Maybe the usual way, maybe at the clinic. I don't care so much about how they met. I like that they fell in love, got married and had a little baby girl, like in a fairy story.'

'What clinic might they have met at?'

'You don't know?' Jane shook her head and Maria said, 'You must be a very faraway relative to know so little. Dr Mann works at a women's clinic, a place for girls like me. We go there and get checked, or else our licence is not renewed.'

'Your licence to work?'

Maria nodded. 'They want to know we're not going to spread any dirty diseases.'

Jane had expected Mann to work somewhere more prestigious. Had he been someone else, she might have credited him with compassionate tendencies, but now she wondered if the doctor had done something to tarnish his reputation, or if he was drawn towards sex workers for some other reason. She asked, 'Has he treated you?'

'What?'

'Have you gone to see him at the clinic?'

'Yes.'

'What's he like?'

'Okay. He does his job.'

'Nothing more?'

Maria might have been a sulky schoolgirl asked to recite a text she had learnt for detention.

'He smiles; he asks if we're okay. He doesn't ask to have sex on the operating table or for a free blow job. He treats us with respect.'

'Doctor Mann doesn't live with his wife any more. Do you know what happened to her?'

Suddenly she had the other woman's attention.

'Now you ask the same question she asked.'

'Anna?'

'Yes.' Maria leant forward as if they were two friends used to sharing confidences. 'At first I think she wants to join us. You notice her style?'

'She likes to dress up.'

'It's street-girl style. Okay, she doesn't wear the clothes.' She indicated her own tight top, cut low to show the curve of her breasts, and frowned in the same way that a girl at a supermarket checkout might frown at an unflattering overall she was forced to wear. 'But I think she would like to. Her make-up, those high heels she loves; all things that prostitutes would wear.'

'Lots of girls dress like that.'

'We set fashion.' Maria laughed, plumping her chest like a comedy tart. 'Us and the blacks and the gays.'

Their eyes met. Jane wondered if Maria had sussed her sexuality and was playing with her.

'Did she ask to join you?'

'No.' Marie's voice dropped to a dramatic whisper. 'She asked about her mother. She had some old photo of her and she starts approaching street girls, asking, does anyone know this woman or where she might be? I can see beneath her tough detective act and I know that under the lipstick and foundation is a little girl who is going to end up alone in a room with some men she don't want to meet. I have a little girl at home and maybe what goes around comes around. So I say, "Yes, I know her," before anyone else can. Then I take Anna for a walk and I tell her, the girls she is asking are too young to know her mother. I am too young to know her mother. There is no one here who knew her, though perhaps we know her story. She met the doctor, she had a baby and then she moved on. That is all.'

'Is it?'

Maria shrugged her shoulders, opening her empty palms in a 'who knows?' gesture.

'It's all I can tell you.'

'What do you think happened to Anna's mother?'

'I think she got bored. This life isn't easy, but it isn't easy to leave either. Stuck at home with a baby while your respectable husband goes out to work and when you step out of your apartment the neighbours look at you like you're still a whore. Before you know it, you're meeting the girls on the corner to pass the time. One day one of them asks you to do her a favour, one thing leads to another, and suddenly the fairy story is over. '

'You never heard that anything bad happened to her?'

'Like he kill her?'

'Yes.'

'That's what people always say. A woman disappears and everyone whispers her husband shot her, or he cut her throat, or drowned her in the bathtub. Sometimes the husband says it himself to save his pride.'

'You don't believe men murder their wives?'

'I am not stupid.' Maria gave her a withering look. 'But more often the wife gets sick of him and runs away before he gets the chance.'

'I saw Dr Mann talking to you and your friend in the street. Does he use your professional services?'

'My what?' Maria raised her eyebrows and Jane asked, 'Does he pay to sleep with you, or any of the other girls you know?'

'I don't sleep with no one.'

Jane closed her eyes. The café's harsh fluorescence glowed bright behind her eyelids. It was none of her business, but she opened her eyes and asked, 'Have you had sex with him?'

'Why do you want to know that?'

'I want to find out what kind of man he is.'

Maria's laugh was bitter. 'Asking about sex will tell you that? Not all of the men who go with us are bad.'

'So is Mann one of the good ones?'

'I don't know if he's good or not.' Maria's mouth had regained its sulky cast. 'He recognises us from the clinic and sometimes he stops to talk, that's all I know.'

Jane sensed the invisible meter edging to zero and realised their conversation would soon draw to an end.

'What does Anna think of her father?'

She smiled, trying to regain the comradely atmosphere of earlier, but Maria stared at her as if she were the enemy.

'She thinks he's a prince, she thinks he's a bastard. How do I know what she thinks? I only met her once, when she ask about her mother.'

'What did she ask?'

'I told you. Did I know her? Did I know anyone who knows her? Had I heard where she went?' Maria's voice was rising. 'I told her, the same as I told you, I know nothing.'

There was a clinking of bottles as the old man gathered his carrier bags and shuffled out into the street. Neither of them had had the stomach to finish their coffees, but Jane looked up, wondering if she could somehow hold the woman there with another cup of the stuff. The counter was empty; the waiter had disappeared, leaving them alone together. It occurred to her that no one knew where she was. It was time to hand over the balance of the money they had agreed, but Jane went on, 'You've met Anna more than once?'

'No, I told you, only once. We talked on the street and I warned her to stop asking questions.'

'I saw you together in the graveyard of St Sebastian's Church.'

'That's a lie, you never saw us together.'

Maria's face flushed and Jane realised that the woman was right. She said, 'Okay, not together, but I saw you follow Anna into the churchyard.'

'I never followed no one. I take care of my health and

mind my own business.' Maria took her jacket from the back of her chair and pulled it on. 'Now you know everything I know.'

'I'm sorry; I didn't mean to offend you.' Jane reached for her bag and paused with her hand on its clasp. If she wanted to, the woman could take it from her and disappear into the night, but Jane pressed on. 'Can you think of any reason Anna might go to the church?'

'Maybe she went there for the same reason I did, to pray.' She looked pointedly at Jane's bag. 'I need to go now.'

Jane took the rest of the money from her purse and folded it into the palm of her hand, keeping her actions under the table even though they appeared to be alone in the café. She looked Maria in the eyes as she passed over the money.

'I'm only here because I'm worried about her.'

The notes bristled between Maria's fingers as she counted them. She folded the money away and leant towards Jane.

'You say her father harms this girl, but I never saw it.' Her voice was hard. 'All I see is you sticking your nose into something that is none of your business. Maybe it is you she should be careful of.'

The street outside was as empty as the café, but only a block away Oranienburger Strasse still thronged with people. Soon the dancers would be taking their bows at the Friedrichstrasse Theater and not long afterwards the audience would spill down its steps, the crowd held together for a moment by the shared experience of light and music. Then they would disperse, atomising into couples and individuals as they were absorbed into Berlin.

It was a mistake to think you were anonymous merely

because the city was big and full of strangers. Prostitutes and their associates were everywhere. If Maria put the word out that Jane was some kind of lesbian predator with a penchant for teenage girls, life in Berlin could become impossible. Jane leant back, showing she had nothing to fear, and spread her hands across her middle, as if her pregnancy offered some guarantee of purity.

'Anna's young and heading for trouble. I know how dangerous life can get for a young woman. I think you know how bad it can get too. I only want to help her.'

'You're like the young priest, right? Trying to help fallen women?' Maria rolled her eyes, but the aggression was gone from her voice. 'You're right to be worried. I've seen girls like her before; they think they are in a book or a movie and that nothing bad will happen to them because they are the star.' She lowered her voice. 'Do know who she reminds me of?'

'No.' Jane leant across the table. The other woman took her hand in hers and whispered, 'You.' She looked at Jane's belly and her mood altered again. 'There are men who have a thing about pregnant women.' She laughed. 'You think of anything, there is a man somewhere who has a thing about it, but a pregnant woman can make good money. I can put you in touch with someone if you want.'

Jane shook her head. 'I'll pass, thank you.'

'How long do you have?'

'Six weeks.'

'You could buy some nice things for your baby. You wouldn't have to do much, just let a man I know take some photographs.'

'I'll let you know if I change my mind.'

'Do that.' Maria patted Jane's hand, friends again, and got to her feet. 'Maybe the girl went there to try and find out more about her mother. The young priest thinks "fallen women" are his mission. It's a tradition at St Sebastian's. The old one who was there before him used to try and fuck some believing into us, but this new one is different, he just wants to pray.' Maria laughed. 'So far, he just wants to pray.'

Twenty-Two

Before she went to bed Jane took one of the kitchen chairs and angled it under the front door, the way she had seen people do in the movies. She wasn't convinced it would keep anyone out, but the sound of it falling would wake her.

She dreamt that there was another room in the apartment, concealed behind a door that she hadn't noticed before at the end of the hallway. She was walking through the empty space, amazed at the strangeness of her discovery and wondering if Petra knew it was there, when she suddenly realised she was no longer pregnant and that somewhere a baby was crying.

She woke to the sound of the telephone bleating in her ear.

'Hello.' The clock beside the bed showed 10.05. She'd slept for almost eight hours without waking. 'Hello?' The other end of the line was silent. Jane asked, 'Who is this?' and Alban Mann said, 'I'd like to talk to you.'

She sat up, bleary with sleep, her heart still beating to the rhythm of the child crying in her dreams.

'Why?'

'Perhaps if we talk face to face we can resolve our differences.'

'It's a little late for that. You sent the police to my door.'

'And you sent social workers to mine. I think we're even.' Jane didn't bother to contradict him. 'Please, Frau Logan, at least give me a chance.'

She rubbed her face, realising a meeting might be to her advantage. 'Okay.'

There was a second's hesitation, as if Mann couldn't quite believe she'd agreed, and then he said, 'Shall I come over now?'

'No.' She couldn't bear to have him in their apartment. 'Give me twenty minutes and I'll come to you.'

'Fine.' She heard the smile in his voice. 'I'll prepare some coffee.'

She had slept in the child's room again. Now she dressed in there, the shadow of the backhouse reaching in through the window, staining her skin. The same shadow would fall in Alban's rooms, she realised. She wondered if it felt like his dead wife stretching out a hand to touch him. No, Jane reminded herself, there was no proof that his wife was dead, no corpse, just an absence.

She ate some cereal and cold water, standing by the sink resolving to forage through Petra's pockets and handbags for some change to buy milk. There were four cigarettes left in her pack. Her mother had once told her that she had been advised to smoke more during pregnancy, to encourage a small baby and an easier birth. Jane snapped the cigarettes in half one by one and tossed them in the bin. She wondered if she should phone someone, or leave a note to say she was going to Mann's flat, but didn't. The child was her charm against badness, her talisman.

Alban Mann opened the door, stepping to one side to let her enter. The hallway was the mirror image of theirs, but its dark walls and white ceiling seemed to telescope it into a long and shrinking corridor. The effect was reminiscent of her dream, the extra room hidden in full view.

Mann said, 'I'm glad you decided to come.'

Jane glanced down the hall, hoping for a glimpse of Anna, but the doors beyond were closed and sunk in shadow.

'I can't stay long.'

'No, of course.'

He ushered her into the lounge and she felt the atmosphere of her dream once again. It was the sitting room she shared with Petra, reflected through an earlier time. The clean angles and light tones of the Scandinavian furniture Petra had chosen, replaced by dark mahoganies carved with curves and curlicues. Mann's desk stood to the left of the window, a bureau piled with papers. It was too small for his needs and behind it a large circular dining table had been colonised by stacks of books and papers. A bookcase the Beckers would have envied filled most of the back wall. Jane strained to make out the titles on the spines, but Mann ushered her towards a dark-green three-piece suite. The room was functional and masculine, with little concession to style. Jane would never have guessed that a teenage girl also lived there. She wondered which room was Anna's. Had Mann given her the master bedroom, or did she sleep in the child's room?

She asked, 'How long have you lived here?'

'Since I was born. The apartment belonged to my parents.'

'And your grandparents?'

'No.' Mann smiled. 'My grandparents didn't live here.'

He indicated an armchair and Jane sat. Coffee, milk and an array of small biscuits were laid out on a low table in front of her. How many trips had it taken him to carry everything through, encumbered with his stick? She knew she didn't want to eat anything he had touched, but she had skipped dinner the night before and the lack of a proper breakfast gnawed at her. Was the child hungry too? She had to find the mislaid euros or phone Tielo and borrow some money for groceries.

Mann asked, 'How are you feeling?'

'Fine.'

'Everything goes well with the baby?'

'Yes.'

She kept to monosyllables, letting him know that she hadn't come there to discuss her health.

'Good.' Mann poured the coffee, asking if she took cream and sugar. He offered Jane the biscuits, smiling when hunger got the better of her and she took two, hating herself. 'It's good for the baby that you eat well.'

He was wearing a white linen shirt and faded jeans. The top two buttons of the shirt were unfastened and she could see tendrils of dark chest hair creeping towards his throat. She raised her cup to her lips. The coffee was superior to the sludge she and Maria had shared the night before, but there was an unfamiliar bitter tinge to it. She took another sip, trying to identify the flavour, but it eluded her.

'You said you wanted to talk to me.'

'Yes.' Alban Mann leant back, legs splayed. Jane sat on the edge of her chair, her hands cradling her bump. In the dream it had been gone and she had been restored to her lean self. Mann said, 'I saw the mess on your door and wanted you to know it had nothing to do with Anna or with me.'

'You expect me to believe that?'

'It's the truth.'

She shook her head. 'You must think I'm stupid.'

She raised the coffee to her lips again. Mann watched her drink.

'Anna is often difficult, but she isn't prejudiced. It would not occur to her to write such a thing. Nevertheless I questioned her about it and she confirmed what I already knew. She is not responsible. Neither am I. You and I have got off to a hard beginning, perhaps we will never be friends, but I would like us to put our differences aside and be cordial neighbours.'

'That's very tolerant of you.'

'It is better to be civilised.'

She put her cup back on the table.

'I'm afraid I'm not very civilised, Dr Mann.'

Alban Mann rubbed his face. She heard the rasp of his stubble against the rough skin of his hands and looked away. It was too intimate, sitting opposite him like this, drinking his coffee, eating his biscuits. She let her gaze take in the rest of the room. The pictures were the kind of views that graced hotels, dreary punctuations on bare walls, which revealed nothing about their owner. She guessed that everything was as it had been in his parents' time: the dark furniture, heavy curtains and few ornaments. Mann's desk and the disordered dining table gave the only suggestion of his personality. Jane's eyes travelled down the stacks of papers and piles of books, then up again to where a slim violet envelope poked out from one of the volumes. Her head felt a trifle woozy, as if sleep was trying to reclaim her.

The doctor asked, 'Frau Logan, what happened in your life to make you so suspicious?'

Jane smothered the urge to throw her coffee in his face. She ignored his question. 'Can I have a glass of water, please?'

Mann put his hand on his cane and pulled himself to his feet.

'Yes, of course.'

She waited until she heard the kitchen tap running, then moved as quickly as she could to Mann's desk. A thick green hardback embossed in gold was positioned halfway down one of the piles of books. Normally she would have tried to decipher its title, but it was the violet envelope she had noticed peeking from between its pages that she wanted. The envelope was unmarked and empty. Jane ran a hand across the broken seal, noting its chic blue-and-white lining. She remembered how she had ripped the envelope of euros carelessly across the top, and tried to recall the exact shape the tear had made. The memory eluded her but the envelope was the same distinctive brand that Petra used. She slid it back where she had found it and managed to settle herself in her seat just before Mann returned carrying a glass of water.

Jane raised the water to her lips. It was a small ration, in keeping with the dark walls and outmoded furniture. She hid her expression behind the glass, trying to calm herself.

Alban Mann was their landlord. Did he have a key to their flat? Had he stood by the bed, watching her as she slept? Jane drank half of the water and set the glass back on the table.

Her eyes met Mann's and she caught a glimpse of his professional self, a doctor who knew the secret workings of women's bodies, a man who could take you apart. As if to confirm her thought he said, 'You're pale. Are you feeling unwell?'

'A little tired, it's normal at this stage.'

'Not necessarily. Perhaps you should let me take your blood pressure.'

She ignored the suggestion, pulling the cuffs of her shirt down over her wrists. 'How is Anna?'

'Challenging.' He met her eyes with all the candour of a talk-show host. 'I hope you never have to learn how hard it is to raise a child by yourself.'

Jane had learnt the demands of single parenting at her mother's knee, but she merely said, 'How long has it been just the two of you?'

'Since she was two years old.'

'And Anna's mother?'

'She left.'

He submitted to her questions with the resignation of an interview candidate who knew he wasn't going to get the job, but would go through the motions anyway.

'Does she still live in Berlin?'

'I don't think so, but I can't be sure.'

Jane hesitated, not wanting to give away how much she already knew.

'You lost touch?'

188

She half expected Mann to tell her to mind her own business, but he sighed and said, 'When my wife left, she left for good. She didn't want to be found.'

'Didn't you worry she'd had an accident or been abducted? It might sound unlikely, but these things happen.'

'She'd warned me often that one day she would go. I thought family life would be good for her, that as soon as we had a child she would realise it was what she wanted.' He shook his head. 'It was what I wanted.'

'You never tried to find her?'

'The first few years I travelled to places where I thought she might be; Hamburg, Amsterdam, London. I became an expert on red-light districts.'

His frankness surprised her. It must have shown on her face because Mann said, 'My wife was a prostitute, Frau Logan. I knew that when I married her.'

He held Jane's eyes in his until she looked away. She took another sip of coffee, welcoming the harshness of it, raw and slightly sour against her tongue.

'And the police? Did they turn up any traces of her?'

'Greta was not someone who would welcome the involvement of the police. She knew where we were. In the end I had to be satisfied with that.'

Jane recalled stories of selkies, seal women captured by fishermen who fell in love with them and made them their wives. The women would seem content for a while, keeping house and having babies, but in the end the lure of the sea was always too strong, and they retrieved their sealskins, regained their old form and dived back into its depths. At night you could hear the selkie women, torn between sea and shore, crying for their lost children. Sometimes they returned with skins for their sons and daughters, and they joined their mothers in the waves, leaving their mortal fathers abandoned on the shore.

She asked, 'Does Anna look like her?'

'Yes.' Mann smiled. 'Anna looks so like Greta, she could almost be her. Sometimes it takes my breath away. You think I am over protective of my daughter.' It was the opposite of what she thought, but Jane didn't interrupt and Mann continued, 'Perhaps you are right. Searching for Greta was like stepping into one of the circles of Hell. I talked to men who buy and sell women as if they were cattle, men who would kill you without a thought, if the price was right.'

'Couldn't you report them to the authorities?'

Mann shook his head. 'The world that you and I inhabit, the world of taxes and licences and governments, seems solid, but that's an illusion. If you have the courage to look, you find that just beneath its surface is another reality, a place where money is the only authority.'

Jane felt the room slipping away from her. She gripped the armrest of the chair and kept her eyes on Mann. His coffee sat untouched on the table and it was as if he could see the lower depths stretching out before his eyes.

'I met women I wanted to save and couldn't. Sometimes I still have nightmares about them.'

Jane lifted her coffee cup to her mouth. She despised him and yet she wanted to reach out and touch Alban's face.

'Were you attracted to them?'

The question slid from her mind to her lips before she had time to censor it, but Alban smiled and said, 'Sometimes.

They were good-looking women, many of them very intelligent. But I had learnt my lesson, Frau Logan.'

'Do you think your wife is still alive?'

He paused, as if considering her question, and she found herself looking at the gap between his shirt and his shoulder, the line of his collarbone.

'Sometimes I hope she is. Other times, I think it would be simpler if I knew for certain she was never going to return. Mostly I try not to think of her.'

Now was the moment to tell Mann that his daughter was scraping away the fragile world of order and venturing into the realms that haunted his nightmares, but she merely said, 'You've been through an ordeal.'

'Yes.' He stared into the middle distance for a moment, his leonine head looking serious and noble, and then he turned to face her and smiled. 'In the end it had some good consequences.' Mann added some sugar to his untouched cup and stirred, though the coffee was cold now. 'I was disturbed by how often women who work in the sex industry are exploited and so I established a clinic where they can get check-ups, treatments if they need them.' He glanced at her stomach, straining the buttons of her shirt. 'Including abortions. It's not much, but it's something.'

'It must be very demanding?'

'In the beginning it took up most of my time, I was driven. But then Anna started having difficulties at school and I realised she was suffering for my principles. Eventually I decided to work part-time and now I teach her myself, at home.'

'That's all very commendable.'

You didn't have to lock your daughter in a cellar to isolate

191

her. Anna already had no mother, and Alban Mann had ensured that she had no school friends. Jane felt her head swim again. For a moment the room looked soft and insubstantial, and then she recovered herself.

Mann said, 'I tell you all of this not because I want your praise, or even because I think it's any of your business, but in order to let you see that I am not an abuser of women. I am devoted to Anna.'

The proprietorial tone in Alban Mann's voice when he said his daughter's name reminded Jane too much of other voices she had known. She took another sip of coffee. Her words seemed to come from somewhere outside of herself.

'I heard you shouting at Anna, calling her names.'

Mann touched his cold coffee to his lips and then set it back on the table.

'Did you never fight with your father when you were a teenager?'

She would tell him nothing about herself.

'No.'

'Your mother?'

'My mother and I never argued.'

Jane pushed aside the memory of the long silences that had stretched between them towards the end.

'You must have been saints. Most families argue.'

'Perhaps, but most fathers don't call their daughters whores.'

Mann's face flushed. When he spoke next, it was as if his words were being relayed to her by four different loudspeakers, one in each corner of the room, each one playing out of synch with the others.

'I would never

never

I would never call

never call my daughter names

call *my daughter names*

least of all

least of all

least of all

all

all

all

least of all

never call my daughter names,

least of all

least of all

that.'

Jane tried to decipher what he was saying. It was important, the key to the whole thing, but it was too difficult and
she sank back in her chair, feeling the words bouncing around
the room.

Mann asked, 'Are you okay?

Are you okay?

O-

Kay?'

And Jane realised she was going to pass out. She pulled
herself to her feet, the floor rocking like a North Sea ferry on
an amber weather alert that was shifting to red. She wanted
to tell him that she was going back to her own apartment,
but the words tumbled together before she could get them
out. Mann rose to his feet and took her arm. She smelled his

cologne and leant into him, surprised at the firmness of his body.

'No,' she said, 'I'm fine.'

For some reason she was smiling; a big grin that belied the panic in her chest.

Mann said, 'I think you should lie down.'

'At home.' Jane looked up and felt a strange desire to put her lips to his. She said, 'Did you drug me?' and he laughed. 'Frau Logan, you have some strange ideas.'

'Is this how you killed your wife?'

'Please, I think you should have a rest.' Mann's voice was stern now. Jane shoved against him but her blows were weak. He hooked an arm around her back and half carried her from the living room, strong and nimble despite his cane. The hallway was long and dark and spinning. Mann steered her towards the unknown rooms at the back of the apartment.

'No, I want to go home.' His strength was too much for her. Jane put a hand to her stomach. 'Will what you gave me hurt my baby?'

He ignored her and asked, 'Is there anyone waiting for you?'

'Petra.'

Mann's grip tightened on her arm.

'Why are you lying to me? I met her on her way to the station. She's gone away on business until next Wednesday. You're unwell, Frau Logan. I can't allow you to go home alone.'

'Please.' She seemed to be sinking further into a world of cotton and cashmere, soft as the jumpers Petra favoured in winter.

'Don't you care about your child?'

Jane wanted to raise her hand and punch him, but it was important to conserve her energy. She was drifting away. He would put her under the floorboards in the backhouse next to Greta. From somewhere outside – or was it in her head? – Jane heard the sound of banging.

'Hello,' she shouted. 'I'm here.'

But her voice was weak, and she didn't think anyone would hear her.

Twenty-Three

It was like coming out of a three-day drunk. First there was the dream of being awake; the light behind her eyelids and the urge to surface. Then the tow of sleep pulled her back down into its depths. She kicked out again, heading for the world of light and texture, only to be sucked back down into the dark. Then fragments of jumbled thoughts began to break into the deadness. Jane moved beneath the sheets, regaining the knowledge that she had a body. She opened her eyes, relieved to find herself alone in the bed she shared with Petra. Her head felt the way it did before a thunderstorm, heavy with the pressure of what was to come.

She lay there for a while, then pulled herself up and sat on the edge of the bed. Someone had removed her shoes and socks, but she was still wearing the leggings and tartan shirt she had put on to visit Mann. Jane wondered if he had put her to bed and if he was still lurking somewhere in the flat. She got to her feet, steadying herself against the wall, the bedside mat rough against her bare soles.

Whatever he had given her was wearing off, but the world still looked strange; brighter and with sharper edges, the room and its contents resoundingly present in all their detail.

The child moved and she touched her stomach lightly, as someone might touch the elbow of a close friend they valued, but didn't want to talk to right then.

Jane slipped into the ensuite, peed, and washed her face with cold water, drinking a little from the tap. There were headache tablets in the medicine cabinet but she ignored them, worried about how they might react with the drug Mann had spiked her coffee with. She wondered if it was still in her system and if she should go to the hospital for blood tests. If they found something, would they believe it was the doctor who had drugged her, or accuse Jane, and arrange for the child to be taken into custody once it was born?

Footsteps sounded in the bedroom beyond. Jane shrank against the shower cubicle, wishing she had slipped Petra's hunting knife from beneath the mattress. She remembered a bottle of drain cleaner under the basin and hunkered down to look for it.

'Jane?' The familiar voice sounded strained.

She got to her feet and pushed the door open a crack. Tielo was standing on the other side, too close for her to open it further. His face was puckered with worry, the way it had been, back when Ute had threatened to leave him. 'I didn't hear you get up.'

She held on to the door handle, ready to close it, and asked, 'Who else is here?'

'No one, just me.'

'Mann?'

'He left.'

Tielo pulled the door wide and took her arm, but Jane was tired of people touching her and shook him free. She wrapped her dressing gown around her, on top of her crumpled clothes, and sat on the edge of the unmade bed. The shame that comes after a drinking binge was on her like a weight. She tried to recall what had happened, but could only remember trying to resist Mann's strength as he pulled her into the hallway, towards the receding corridor of doors.

Tielo said, 'Should I call a doctor?'

'No.'

'Doctor Mann said he would come back if we needed him.'

'Fuck Mann.' Jane put her head in her hands and squeezed her skull, trying to relieve the pressure inside. 'Did you phone Petra?'

'Of course.'

She looked up.

'Christ, Tielo, what did she say?'

'Nothing, her mobile was switched off. I left a message asking her to call me back.'

'Nothing else?'

'What did you expect me to do, Jane?'

'Fuck-all without your sister's permission.'

He stared at her, as if seeing her for the first time.

'You're difficult, do you know that?'

'And you're a walk in the park.'

'Bloody hell.' The British curse sounded strange on Tielo's lips and she wondered if he had picked it up from her. He sat on the bed and put an arm around her. His voice was gentle, but she could tell it was an effort. 'What happened?'

'Mann drugged me.'

Tielo swore under his breath. 'Don't be preposterous.'

'Your English vocabulary is better than I thought.'

'And you are stupider than I thought.' He removed his arm from her shoulder and turned to face her. 'If it weren't for that man, you might have lost your baby. What if you'd fainted in here, with no one to help you? You could have banged your head, really hurt yourself.'

'I've never fainted in my life.'

'You've never been pregnant before. I looked in your fridge, Jane, there's hardly anything there; half a block of butter and some jam.'

'I'm happy with bread and jam.'

'There's no bread, I checked. Doctor Mann said the faint might have been brought on by lack of food.'

'It was brought on by Dr Mann.'

Tielo shook his head. 'Petra shouldn't have gone to Wien. It's not fair of her to abandon you like this, pregnant and alone in a country where you don't even speak the language.'

'My German's getting better.' She looked up at him, holding his gaze in hers. 'I'm not delusional, Tielo, the coffee tasted funny. I was fine until I drank it.'

'So you had a caffeine rush and it was too much for you. It can happen on an empty stomach.' Tielo got up. He ignored the tangled piles of clothes on the floor and opened the wardrobe. 'I'm going to pack you a bag. You tell me what you need, you know I'm no good at that, then I'll call a cab and we will go to my house. Ute and the boys will be pleased to see you.'

'Mann didn't touch his coffee. I thought it was because he was too busy talking, but he'd poured it from the same pot as the cup he gave me. He was only bluffing when he pretended to pour one for himself.' The full horror of it dawned on her. 'If you hadn't come along I might have died.'

'Don't be ridiculous.' Tielo had found a holdall and was flicking through the clothes on the hangers. 'What shall I pack?'

'How did you find me?'

Tielo opened Petra's underwear drawer, saw the jumble of lace and satin and closed it again.

'I dropped by to check if there was anything you needed and saw the filth painted on your door. When you didn't answer I decided to speak to Mann. Petra had warned me you'd had an argument, so I assumed the graffiti had something to do with him. Are you going to tell me what to bring?'

'Did he answer straight away?'

'He was struggling to get you into bed.' Tielo laughed. 'Sorry, that came out wrong. You'd fainted and he was trying to hold you up. Of course he didn't answer immediately.'

'I'm amazed he answered at all.'

'I was rather an insistent caller. I could hear sounds and knew he was there, so I battered on the door with my fist, shouting that I was the police and if he didn't open up immediately I would knock the door down. I don't know what I was going to do when he did open the door, punch him, I suppose. Then I saw you and all of a sudden we were carrying you together, across the landing and into this apartment. He seems like a nice guy. I don't know who did that to your door, but it wasn't him.' Tielo levelled his gaze at her, his face set in the solemn expression he used to convey that the joke was over and he was being serious now. 'He didn't poison you, Jane, he's a doctor.'

'So was Crippen.'

'Who?'

'Never mind. Means, motive and opportunity, Tielo, that's what the police look for. He's a doctor so he has access to drugs, that's the means. I know he's been abusing his daughter, there's the motive . . .'

'And you gave him the opportunity by going round for coffee.'

'Exactly.'

'It hangs together perfectly, except for the fact that you're beginning to look pretty lively. If he wanted to feed you some kind of overdose he didn't make a very good job of it. Tell me what I'm meant to pack.'

'I don't imagine he was going to kill me right there. He knocked me out so he could make it look like some kind of accident.' She got to her feet, full of the awfulness of it. 'Mann knows I'm not going to give up on Anna, so he wants me out of the way. His wife went missing without a trace. He says she abandoned him, but Frau Becker on the ground floor is certain he murdered her.'

Tielo lifted a handful of dresses from the wardrobe and bundled them into the bag, hangers and all.

'For fuck's sake. You sound like a mad woman.'

Jane was pacing the floor now. Her head was still sore, but her mind was racing and the words tumbled out of her.

'I admit he's plausible, he comes across as a pillar of society; a good man raising his difficult daughter alone, a doctor who works with the disadvantaged. And people believe him because it's not entirely an act. Alban Mann loves his daughter, even though he's abusing her. He'd do anything to keep Anna with him, including getting rid of me.'

Tielo held up a hand.

'You've convinced me.'

Jane sat on the bed, her sudden energy leaching out of her with the relief of being believed.

'You're convinced he drugged me?'

'No, I'm convinced things are getting too much for you. You're not in your right mind.' Tielo pulled at the holdall's zip, cursing under his breath when it refused to fasten. 'This has ceased to be a discussion. I'm not taking no for an answer.'

'Then you better be stronger than you look because you'll be carrying me down those stairs and into the cab, and when we get there I'll tell the driver I don't want to go.'

'Christ Almighty.' He let go of the bag and it landed on the floor with a thump. 'What is wrong with you?'

'Nothing.' A tear leaked from Jane's eye and trailed down her cheek. She brushed it away impatiently and made an attempt at a smile. 'It's been a long day.'

'That's one way of putting it.' Tielo gentled his voice. 'You're alone and vulnerable. No one is trying to hurt you, Jane. We just want to help.' He kissed the top of her head and released her. 'Will you at least have something to eat while we argue this out?'

She realised she was starving.

'If you promise not to call Petra again.'

'I can't make that promise.'

'Then promise not to do it behind my back.'

'Okay.' Tielo reached out a hand and helped her to her feet. 'If you let me make you something to eat, I promise not to phone Petra again without telling you first.'

* * *

The kitchen table was still crowded with the contents of the room's fitted cupboards, pulled out in her search for Petra's euros. Tielo ignored the jumble of crockery, spices, herbal teas, the half-empty bags of dried pulses, and zoned, like a hawk plucking a mouse from a field, on the pack of cigarettes. He turned it over in his hands, reading the health warning on the back, flipping open its lid and tugging gently at the tinfoil lining, examining it as if it were a rare curio.

'Did you think you could survive purely on smoke?'

'I threw the cigarettes in the bin. You can check if you don't believe me.'

'All twenty of them?' He looked around and spotted the almost-full whisky bottle on the floor next to the cleaning products Jane had dragged from beneath the sink. 'This place is a mess. Do you want me to ask Ute to come round and help you tidy up before Petra gets back?'

'No. I'll fix it.'

'What happened?'

'I was looking for something.'

'Inner peace?'

He brought the bottle of whisky to the table, selected a glass from the array spread across the worktop and poured himself a shot. 'You're lucky Ute asked me to do some shopping on the way home.' He shifted a bundle of newspapers from a chair, set a canvas bag bulging with groceries in their place, and started to rummage through it. 'What about that great English delicacy, beans on toast?'

He rattled around in the cutlery drawer, found a tin opener and started to peel the lid from the can. It was restful watching Tielo's bulk negotiating the kitchen. He scanned the contents of the table, exclaiming with pleasure when he found a bottle of Worcester sauce.

'I haven't had this since the last time I was in London.' Tielo emptied the beans into a pan and added a dash of Worcester. He cut thick wedges of bread from a crusty loaf, placed them under the grill, delved back into the canvas bag and pulled out some tomatoes. He sliced them thinly and set them to cook beside the bread. 'A nice piece of English Cheddar would make this perfect, but I'm afraid our luck only stretches so far.'

He took a carton of orange juice from the bag and poured her a glass. The acidity would give her indigestion, but Jane took a sip and said, 'I hope Ute doesn't mind us using up her shopping.'

'She won't.' Tielo turned over the toast, swearing softly as it singed his fingers. He found a knife, used its edge to flip the tomatoes and then drizzled a generous dose of olive oil over the lot. 'It's in a good cause and there's a stack of stuff in the freezer she can give the boys.' Tielo set the toast on two plates, poured on the beans and added tomatoes on top. He looked at the arrangement with satisfaction. 'I should have been a TV chef.'

He set a plate in front of Jane and took the other for himself.

'*Guten Appetit.*'

'*Guten Appetit*, it looks like haute cuisine. What would you call your show?'

'I don't know.' He forked some toast and beans into his mouth. 'One hundred and one ways with a can opener, something like that.'

'I'd watch.'

Jane sliced into her toast and began to eat. It was an effort not to wolf it down.

Tielo said, 'It might improve your cooking.' She smiled at him and he asked, 'Why don't you want to come back with me? Ute will take good care of you and I promise to keep the boys out of your way.'

'I don't know why not. Maybe I'm nesting.'

Tielo looked around at the chaos Jane had made of the kitchen and laughed. She got a sudden view of the contents of his mouth, the half-masticated beans on toast. Her stomach rolled over and she felt nauseous.

'I'm sorry, Jane, but the flat doesn't look very nested in.'

She got up and poured herself a glass of water.

'Not all nests are tidy.'

'Maybe not.' Tielo cut into his toast. Chewed and swallowed, chewed and swallowed again. 'Aren't you eating?'

Jane sat back down at the table. The food had taken on a congealed look that withered her appetite, but she cut herself a square of toast and put it in her mouth.

'I'm settled here.'

'I can't force you to come with me, but you know I'll have to tell Petra what happened.'

'I'd rather you didn't.'

'Why?'

'I don't want to worry her.'

It was the easy answer, but only half true, she realised. If Petra came back now, all of Jane's freedoms would be curtailed in the interests of the baby's health, and with them would go any chance of rescuing Anna.

Tielo finished his own supper and pulled her barely touched plate in front of himself.

'So come to our place and let Ute look after you. That way, no one needs to worry, including me.'

'I can't.' The child would be fine. It was a survivor like her.

Tielo pushed the beans on toast to one side and fished his mobile from his pocket.

'You're leaving me no option.'

'I'll be okay.'

'I'm not willing to take that risk.' Tielo began to punch his sister's name into his phone, looking for her number. 'Maybe Petra can talk some sense into you.'

Jane put her hand on his wrist and said, 'Remember my friend Meghan?'

Tielo laid his phone on the table and looked at her in amazement. He said carefully, 'That was a long time ago.'

Jane nodded, surprised by her own calm.

'Three years to be precise.'

'Ute and I were separated.'

'She won't mind then.'

He shook his head in wonder. 'Why would you do this?'

'I need my independence.'

'This isn't you, Jane. You're not well. You have another life to think of.'

She looked him straight in the eye, showing how sane she was. Was this what it felt like to be ruthless?

'I'll tell Ute about the weekend you spent with Meghan in Brighton and then I will email Meghan and ask her to send me those happy snaps she took of the two of you on the beach together. She's a terrible hoarder, she'll still have them.'

'I'll email Meghan first and tell her not to. She knew it wasn't serious. I was depressed and lonely and she was sweet and kind to me. I said from the start that I wanted Ute to take me back.'

'Do you have her email address?'

'I'll find her on Facebook.'

For a moment she thought he had trumped her, but then Tielo glanced away and she said, 'You don't even remember her last name, do you?'

'I'll find her through your page.'

'Good idea, except that there are too many people in my past I never want to see again for me to join Facebook.'

Tielo slammed a fist on the table and shouted, 'How dare you judge me?'

Jane wondered if Alban and Anna could hear him through the wall.

'I'm not judging you.' She kept her voice calm. 'I know you were just looking for some comfort with Meghan. But you're trying to force me into a corner.'

'I'm trying to look after you. And for that you would break up my marriage? What next? You call Child Protection and advise them to take my children away?'

Tielo cleared the plates and cutlery from the table and threw them into the sink, remnants of beans, toast and all. A plate smashed against the tap. 'Fuck.' He looked at the mess he'd made and shook his head, but made no effort to clear it up. He turned to face Jane and all of his bonhomie was gone. 'Let me tell you about the last time I was in London. I had dinner with my sister, your other half, the great manipulator. Do you know what she asked me?'

'No.' Jane's voice was small.

Tielo's face was scarlet with fury.

'To become a sperm donor.'

'I don't believe you.'

'Then we're equal, because I don't believe you, but let me assure you, what I'm saying is true. I'd proved my fertility and Petra liked the idea that you might have a child with some of her family genes. Even more than that, she liked the idea that the baby might look a bit like her. You know my sister, she tries to hide it, but she's always been vain.'

'Did you do it?'

Tielo pulled on his jacket.

'Ask her.'

She said, 'Tielo, please don't go like this.'

But he barrelled out of the kitchen and from the flat, slamming the front door behind him. Jane put her head in her hands and closed her eyes.

Twenty-Four

Alban Mann had sworn he would never call his daughter names, 'least of all that', but Jane had heard him on the other side of the wall screaming at Anna that she was a whore. It was unusable evidence, Jane's word against his, nothing that would stand up to the scrutiny of a court, but she knew now, without a doubt, that Mann was a liar, and that she must do all she could to stop him hurting his daughter.

Jane sat on the bed in the child's room, wrapped in the cashmere shawl Petra had given her when the pregnancy had been confirmed. The baby was moving inside her, as if trying to get her attention. She stroked her stomach absently; it was still a part of her, a separate being, but without autonomy. When it was born it would become a person, someone she might not like, but right now it was completely hers. She was glad she hadn't given in to Petra's urgings to find out its gender in advance. Not knowing made her and the child more equal. They would meet for the first time at the birth. She hoped she could love it.

Petra had phoned around nine o'clock that evening, full of apologies for calling so late. Jane heard the slightly slurred edges to her words and knew that Petra had been drinking, not a lot, probably just a couple of glasses of wine with dinner, but enough to bring out the edge of recklessness usually concealed beneath her elegant façade. They often had their best sex when she was in that mood.

Jane had said nothing about Tielo's visit, the defaced door or the incident with Mann, but perhaps the strain had sounded in her voice because Petra asked, 'Is everything okay?'

'Yes, I just want it to be over soon.'

'The birth?'

The noise of a restaurant or hotel lobby sounded down the line; music too distant to identify, a wave of laughter building and receding as someone somewhere shared a joke. Jane imagined Petra glancing at her watch, taking a sip of white wine, reluctantly getting to her feet and excusing herself from her companions (companion?) with a quip about 'having to phone the wife'.

'Yes.' Impatience made her curt. 'What else would I be keen to get over?'

'I don't know.' Petra sounded bored. 'Life?' Jane's hand had trembled with the urge to hang up, but Petra asked, 'Have you seen my idiot brother?'

'Briefly, he called round earlier.' Jane tried to keep her voice neutral. 'Have you spoken to him?'

'No, but he called in some kind of a flap and left a message on my voicemail.' Petra laughed. 'All he said was to phone him, but I knew he was panicking about something, money probably.'

Jane said, 'He mentioned some crisis, but I think Ute sorted it.'

'Good old Ute.' Petra put her hand over the mouthpiece of the phone and had a quick, muffled exchange with someone at the other end of the line. 'Sorry, baby, we're moving on somewhere. I'm going to have to go.'

Jane wanted to hold her there.

'The lights in the back court are still out.'

'I promise to call the letting agency again when I get back.'

'Do you know who the landlord is? Maybe I could get in touch with him or her direct.'

'I've no idea who they are. That's why people pay a percentage to agencies. They don't want their tenants getting in touch.'

'I just thought you might have noticed their name when you signed the lease.'

'Don't worry about it. It's not like you'll be going out there after dark anyway.' Far away in Vienna someone said something witty in German and Petra laughed. 'Sorry,' the laugh was still in her voice. 'I really have to go or they'll leave me behind. I'll fix it when I get back. Look after our baby and sleep well.'

Petra had hung up before Jane could tell her that their landlord was Alban Mann and that she was afraid he might have a key to their apartment. She had hung up without saying that she loved her.

Jane got up from the bed, went to the window and unlatched it, letting the chill night air touch her face. There was a light shining on the second floor of the backhouse, flickering like a distant promise. She felt its call, but had no intention of answering. That was for another time.

Whatever her child would turn out to be, she felt sure that right now it was brave. It would need courage to embark on the journey it was about to endure. But maybe that was nonsense. After all, no one chose to be born; just how they would live once they were in the world.

No, Jane closed the window and clicked the latch home; very few people decided how they would live. Life was a series of calms and storms, tossing you this way and that, and most people only just managed to keep their heads above water.

Jane thought again about what Tielo had told her, and wondered when she would have the courage to ask Petra about it. Her phone was on the bedside table. She opened the camera function and scrolled through her photos, not stopping to look at the ones she had taken of Petra, as she normally would, spooling past pictures of the flat, the grave-yard, the backhouse, and realising how confined her world had become.

The headshot of Tielo with his two boys had been taken on the evening she and Petra had first visited his new apart-ment in the *Wasserturm*. Jane remembered the way Tielo had scooped the boys up, one under each arm, and deposited them, giggling, either side of him on the couch. The boys' faces were flushed with excitement, their father's with the three glasses of wine he had drunk during dinner. They both had his sandy colouring, but Carsten's face was slim and feline, Peter's eyes almond-shaped like his mother's. Neither of them looked particularly like Tielo.

She felt sure the child wasn't his. Even if Petra had asked him to be a donor (surely she hadn't) Tielo would have said no. Ute would hate the idea and he wouldn't dare jeopardise his marriage, even to please his sister.

Jane propped the kitchen chair against the front door, as she did every night now, then she undressed, pulled on her nightie and climbed into bed. If she knew that Tielo were the child's father she would be compelled to let it know. How would it feel, living with its aunt and its mother while its half-brothers lived with their dad? She cared for the little beast, whoever its biological father was. Her only option would be to move away from Berlin, to somewhere too far away for Tielo to play the parent.

She was making plans as if Tielo had been telling the truth. But he had been angry, maybe he had simply hit her with what he thought would hurt most. Petra would be furious if she found out what he'd said.

Jane rolled over in bed, trying to get comfortable. She should never have relinquished control so utterly to Petra, blindly signing any forms placed in front of her, with the recklessness of a teenager on their first acid trip.

She pulled a pillow from Petra's side of the bed and wrapped an arm around it. Petra would never have allowed Tielo to father their child; the thought was ridiculous. She remembered the *Wasserturm*, the people tortured to death in its basement, right below where Tielo, Ute and the boys lived. The memory returned her mind to the backhouse, the light shining in the window on the second floor.

Her last thought was of Tielo. Was part of him growing inside her? She had wanted the child to belong entirely to her and Petra, to be all of their own.

Twenty-Five

It was strange to think she had ever found St Sebastian's churchyard charming. The iron railings were still ornately wrought, the gravestones still quaintly listing, but the weeping angel looked as if she might suddenly pull herself up against her cross and laugh in mourners' faces, and the ivy, twisting thick and arabesque across the graves, seemed horribly succulent. Jane could not look at it without thinking of what lay beneath. It had been a frosty night, but now the damp had set in, bringing fog in its wake, and the air around the graveyard seemed wreathed in decay. Jane walked up the gravel pathway towards the *Kirche*, her scarf wound tightly around her face, the sound of her footsteps deadened by cold.

Two rooks crouched in the centre of the path before her, tearing at the belly of a pigeon. She saw the open wound, the way they clutched it with one claw, steadying the body so they could draw out the entrails with their beaks, and her stomach lurched.

'Fuck off.' Jane clapped her hands. 'Away with yous.'

But the birds barely raised their heads from their feast. Maybe her woollen gloves had muffled the sound of her hands, but one of the birds glanced up as she skirted the banquet, and its black button eyes seemed to gleam with the promise that she'd be next.

Jane had checked the hours of service on the Internet and had timed her visit for fifteen minutes into morning mass. She had watched people entering the churchyard from her spot high up on the balcony. Back home they were converting churches into pubs and luxury apartments, but St Sebastian's had managed to pull in more than a dozen worshippers.

Jane felt the eyes of the congregation on her as she entered the church and slid into a pew near the front, where the priest could get a clear view of her. He was standing behind the altar, doing a fine job of making the old routine look sincere. Jane wondered if he was a good actor, or if he believed in the smoke and mirrors he used to gull the congregation.

The altar boy was in his sixties, dressed smartly in a dark suit and tie. He swung the censer from side to side, slow as a hypnotist's pocket watch. The priest placed a cloth over the chalice and all eyes fixed on him as he prepared to transform sweet wine into the blood of Christ. Above him, the man himself raised his eyes to the heavens from his place on the cross, looking as if he wanted to curse the father that had nailed him there.

There was a sound of shuffling feet and closing hymn-books as people started to rise from their seats and file into a queue for communion. Jane stayed where she was, fighting the urge to bow her head. The incense felt like it was creeping down her throat and she coughed against the taste of it. She imagined vomiting a tiny devil on to the aisle, the ugly creature wriggling helpless against the flagstones.

Maria wasn't among the queue of communicants, but a couple of young, well-groomed women stood out from the elderly people lowering themselves painfully to their knees. They were both dressed with care, their long hair pinned discreetly back, but their dye jobs were flashy, their make-up expertly applied.

There were many different worlds, Jane thought, but they didn't exist on different planes: one slotted on top of the other, as Alban Mann had implied. They overlapped, like Venn diagrams, and you could be at the intersection of several realities without even knowing it.

The organ hummed into life and the child kicked out, hitting hard against Jane's ribcage, winding her. She wondered if it was a leap of joy or distress and if babies in the womb ever broke their mothers' ribs. A child who could do that would surely be a survivor.

The congregation were beginning to file down the aisle and into the churchyard. Jane noticed a few curious glances in her direction. One of the young women aimed her fingers at her in the sign of the evil eye, holding her hand low at her side so that no one else would notice. Her companion spotted what she was doing and slapped her arm. The girl pulled away, pouting like a school bully who had been thwarted at playtime but knew her intended victim's route home. Jane wondered if Maria had put the word out about her quest, and what it would mean if she had. She was surprised to find her hands clutching her belly.

'Come along, little monster,' she whispered. 'Let's go and see what the priest has to say.'

She had expected him to be standing in the doorway, bidding his congregation goodbye, but she must have lingered inside longer than she'd intended because when she came out the churchyard was empty except for a trio of elderly women dawdling by the gate. One of them glanced at her and called out, '*Suchen Sie den Priesster? Er befindet sich in der Sakristei.*'

There was something strange about the way the old woman looked Jane up and down, pausing for a moment on her bulging coat as if it were an element to be factored into other calculations.

Jane smiled and asked, '*Bitte?*'

The woman repeated what she had said, stabbing her index finger impatiently back towards the church.

'*Danke.*'

The *Kaffeeklatsch* re-formed, heads nodding as the lady who had pointed the way held forth. Jane considered join-ing them and asking if they remembered Greta Mann, a pretty girl who used to be on the streets but married a doctor and then disappeared, leaving a small child, the only trace of her that remained. The rooks' chorus started up, harsh and piercing, metal on metal. The women raised their heads towards the treetops, then turned as one and headed out through the unoiled gate and into the street. Jane watched them go, thinking that even though they were dressed in the bright colours favoured by elderly ladies in winter, the trio resembled the rooks. It was something about the way they moved, their heads bobbing in rhythm to their talk. Jane turned and went back into the dim shadows of the church.

Twenty-Six

Father Walter stood alone by the altar. He looked up as Jane entered and she wondered if he had been expecting her, but he didn't say anything, not even when she drew level and stood by his side. Jane had never been so close to a churchman in full regalia before. She realised that she felt shy. The priest appeared more present in his vestments, as if for him civilian clothes were some kind of fancy dress.

Jane asked, 'Do you have time to talk?'

'Some time, yes.'

He spoke without looking at her. Jane wondered if she had interrupted a prayer and if he was even now winding it up with an apology to the Big Man.

'Would you like me to wait somewhere else?'

'Where?' Father Walter turned to face her. The same anxious expression as before creased his features. Whatever magic he'd possessed during the mass had vanished. He looked younger than she remembered but faintly troubled, as if he had witnessed some ordeal and not yet managed to come to terms with it.

'I thought I might be interrupting you.'

'No, mass is over.'

This time the priest didn't ask her into his private room. He indicated the front pew, and once she was seated, settled himself an arm's length away and sat silently, waiting for her to speak. Now that the church was empty it felt larger and colder. The stone pillars and vaulted roof resembled a ribcage; it was as if they were alone together in the fossilised belly of some long-dead beast. Jane drew her coat closer, glad of its warmth.

'I wanted to talk to you about a young neighbour of mine. I think you may know her already, Anna Mann.'

Jane watched the priest's face as she said Anna's name and was sure she detected the ghost of a flinch. He nodded, but didn't say anything. She let the silence ride and after a long pause Father Walter asked, 'Tell me what's worrying you.'

'I think Anna's father may be abusing her.' The blood rose to the priest's face and his eyes fluttered, like the remnant of an old stammer. Jane paused but he said nothing and she continued, 'I live next door to Anna and her father. I've seen her with bruises on her face and heard her father shouting at her. He calls her horrible names.'

'Her father is a doctor.'

Jane wanted to tell him how Alban had drugged her, but remembered Tielo's scepticism and said, 'Do you know him?'

'Our paths have crossed on committees, we nod at each other in the street, but I don't know him well. He's spoken of highly.'

The scent of incense still hung in the air, but the church was silent. A bank of freshly lit candles flickered their brief remembrance, but no other trace remained of the mass that had so recently taken place.

Jane said, 'People are not always so respectable behind their own front doors.'

'Do you have evidence that Dr Mann is ill-treating his daughter?' Father Walter's voice was so low it was almost a whisper, but Jane thought she could detect a note of hostility in the question.

'I've seen the bruises with my own eyes and heard the shouting with my own ears.'

The priest murmured, 'I have seen bruises too.' He raised his head and his eyes met hers for the first time. 'Has Anna told you that her father is harming her?'

'Anna wants to protect him. She refuses to speak to me. I've talked to the police, but they're on his side. They warned me I could get into trouble for even accusing him.'

'The police were right to warn you. It is a serious allegation to make without proof.'

'You said you'd seen bruises too. What did you mean?'

The priest looked away. 'Everywhere there is pain.'

The dark was creeping in, the shadows of the trees outside in the churchyard reaching through the stained-glass windows and lengthening across the flagstones. She would have to walk home between the graves alone in the dark. Jane glanced up at the cross and then back to the priest sitting hunched on the bench beside her.

'Have you noticed Anna's pain in particular? Her bruises?'

Father Walter looked at his feet.

'Anna is nothing to do with you, Frau Logan. Leave her care to those who know her.'

'Would that include you?'

'Anna comes here sometimes. She's lived in the apartment

across the street all her life. The graveyard used to be her playground; she still likes to sit there and read.'

'You knew Anna as a young child?'

He shook his head. 'I've only been here six months. Father Engler told me, my predecessor.'

Maria had claimed that the old priest had tried to fuck Christianity into the street girls. Jane said, 'Then perhaps I should speak to your predecessor.'

They were keeping their voices low, but their words seemed to find an echo in the stone walls. Jane glanced down the aisle, almost expecting to see someone standing there taking in their conversation, but the church was empty except for the plaster saints, stoic in their suffering.

The priest said, 'That's no longer possible. Father Engler was in his seventies. He was called to Italy, to Assisi. He passed away soon after, God rest his soul.' He raised his eyes to the crucifix above the altar. His lips moved wordlessly and Jane looked away, allowing his prayer some privacy. The priest crossed himself swiftly. 'Father Engler told me that when she was small, Anna Mann adopted a grave and said it was her mother's. She would cut the grass around it and decorate it with flowers.'

Jane glanced at a statue of the Virgin, high up in a niche. The statue's eyes were demurely lowered, staring down at her hands. Jane turned her attention back to the priest, trying to rid herself of the feeling that the Virgin would raise her head and glare as soon as no one was looking.

'Is her mother dead?'

'I heard not, but what I am trying to tell you is that Anna has been coming to St Sebastian's since she was a child. If she wanted help she would turn to the church.'

He looked at Jane, as if waiting to see whether she would contradict him.

'What else did Father Engler tell you about Anna?'

'Nothing that I can recall.' The impatience was in Father Walter's voice now.

'Did he mention her father, the way he is with her?'

'You know that if he had, I would not be permitted to discuss it with you.' The blood was still in the priest's cheeks as if some emotion, anger or embarrassment, was raging within him. 'I will pray for her and for her father.' His eyes met hers. 'And for you.' He got to his feet and stood with his back to the altar, giving her a cue to go.

'You tell your parishioners they should believe in God as an act of faith, but when I tell you I know that a girl is being abused by her father, you refuse to do anything.'

'You have offered me no real evidence, Frau Logan.'

'Isn't the fact that I know it to be true enough?'

The priest's voice took on some of the cadence and authority it had held during the mass. The gilded cross on the altar table behind him caught the light, like an intimation of a halo.

'I know our Saviour exists. I do not know Dr Mann has done anything to harm his daughter.'

Jane pulled herself up from the pew and stood in front of him. On a far wall, St George was getting the best of a dragon, his lance piercing its chest, red gore gushing down its scaly front. If you could believe in God, it was probably no bother to believe in dragons. Why couldn't she make the priest see that there were other monsters left to fight? Jane forced some meekness into her voice.

223

'The Catholic Church has become a byword for paedo-philes. Help restore people's trust in it by saving a young girl who is being exploited.'

Father Walter was a full head taller than her, but he took a step backwards.

'The Church is changing. We recognise that abuses happen and try to deal with them.'

'Was that why Father Engler was sent back to Italy?'

'He was old. It was time for him to retire.'

'Saint Sebastian's is popular with street girls.'

'Our Saviour was a friend to all of the oppressed.'

'I heard Father Engler wasn't much of a friend. Young women came here looking for spiritual comfort and found someone ready to misuse them.'

Father Walter took another step back. One more and he would be pressed against the altar.

'The biggest prize the Devil can win is the soul of a good man.'

'So the women he had sex with were merely instruments of Satan?'

'Father Engler was old and weak. I light a candle for him every day.'

'Did he seem especially fond of Anna?'

'No.' Father Walter shook his head, as if trying to dislodge an image Jane's words had fixed there. 'Father Engler didn't like Anna spending time in the churchyard. He warned me about her.'

'She's only a child. Why would he warn you?'

'He said she had the Devil inside her.'

Jane wanted to take a lighted torch to the church and

watch it burn, plaster saints, wooden crosses, pews and all. She would warm her hands by the flames and sing.

The priest was staring at her, his eyes dark and troubled in his white face. Jane asked, 'Did you believe him?'

'I couldn't believe him. But it shows he had no interest in Anna. He didn't approve of her.'

'Perhaps Father Engler thought she had tempted him into doing something he knew was wrong. Once girls have been mistreated it's as if they're wearing a badge or carrying a flag. Abusers seem to know they're vulnerable and are drawn to them, then they blame the girls for their own weaknesses.'

'Father Engler died a lonely man.'

'Good. If I believed in Hell, I'd hope he was burning there.'

'There's no sympathy, without sympathy for the damned. Some people would say you've condemned your child to damnation.' The priest glanced again at her stomach. 'They would tell you that the means by which it was conceived, and your way of life, commits it to an eternity in Hell.'

'And what about men who batter children or abuse them sexually while preaching love and respectability? Where do they end up?'

'They end up in Hell, too, in this life and the next. Did you doubt it?' Father Walter had regained some of his composure. He looked Jane in the eye, but she noticed that his left hand was trembling. The priest saw her glance at it and stilled it with his right. He asked, 'What do you want from me, Frau Logan?'

'I told you. I want you to help me to help Anna. Speak to her and persuade her to tell the police what's been going on.

If she won't, then go to the police and ask them to investigate her father. I've tried, but they won't listen to me.'

'Anna is a young woman. She must make her own decisions.'

'So you're happy to sweep everything under the altar table?'

'Even if I believed what you're saying was true, and you must realise that nothing you have said has convinced me, I couldn't force Anna to go to the authorities.'

'She's only thirteen years old, still a child. She can't escape her father without help.'

The priest shook his head. 'You're mistaken. Anna is a young woman; she will be eighteen on her next birthday.'

'No, *you* are mistaken, Father Walter. Dr Mann told me her age himself, and in that at least I believe him.'

The priest stared at the altar and Jane saw again how pale he was.

'Thirteen?'

'Children younger than that are abused.' Jane saw uncertainty flicker across his face and pressed her advantage home. 'Surely you must be able to see that beneath all the make-up Anna's just a vulnerable little girl. You have the power to help her.'

Father Walter whispered, '"Whoever shall offend one of these little ones who believe in me, it were better for him that a millstone were hanged about his neck, and that he were drowned in the depth of the sea."' The priest looked hard and white and brittle, as if he were all bone and no flesh. 'You have remarkable instincts, Frau Logan. The Church should employ you as a divining rod for corruption.'

'You believe me?'

'I believe the child has been polluted by someone who should have been trusted to keep her safe.'

The priest looked beyond her, towards the door of the church. Jane felt a draught at her back, as if the graveyard outside suddenly also believed her and the dead were rising up, ready to join in her revenge. Father Walter held his right hand up in the air and was restored back into the conjurer who had mesmerised the congregation into thinking their god was amongst them.

Jane turned her head and followed Father Walter's gaze. Anna was standing at the end of the aisle.

The priest lifted his voice towards the rafters and his words rang through the church.

'Remember you are a child of God, more sinned against than sinning. He will not punish anything you have done in your innocence. All of His vengeance will rest on those who have harmed you.'

Even from that distance Jane could see the hate blazing in Anna's eyes. The girl took a few tentative steps forward, like someone learning how to walk, and then stopped. Her words seemed to shatter against the stone floor.

'No one has harmed me.'

Jane started to speak, 'Anna . . .' but the priest's voice was louder. It echoed over and beyond her words.

'Love is a gift from God. It cannot exist where He would not allow it.' There were tears in the priest's eyes. He looked fierce and sorrowful, like some muscular saint refusing to escape torture by renouncing his beliefs. 'Sometimes the Devil creeps into men's souls and tempts them into sins that cannot be redeemed.'

Anna said, 'Don't listen to her, she's mad.'

But the priest had turned his back on them both. He sank

to his knees before the altar and started to mutter a prayer. Jane could hear the low drone of its rhythm, the words running together, too fast and fervent for her to make them out. She said, 'Anna, no one blames you . . .'

The girl screamed and she looked for a moment like a woman glimpsed on a news report, weeping over the rubble of her home. She pointed at Jane.

'I'm going to kill you, you and your little bastard, even if I have to cut it out of your belly.'

Anna swept the bank of candles on to the stone floor, and turned and ran, her high heels clattering down the aisle. She heaved open the heavy door and fled. It swung slowly closed behind her, shutting out the view of the graveyard beyond, fading into the dusk.

Twenty-Seven

Frau Becker was sitting on the stairway outside her apartment, singing. Jane lowered herself carefully down on to the step beside her. The old lady continued with her song for a while, then she looked at Jane and said, 'So they caught you then?'

'Yes,' Jane said. 'They caught me.'

A paper rose nodded among Frau Becker's sparse curls and strings of mismatched beads were tangled on her chest. She was wearing a chiffon tea gown today, on top of a long-sleeved woollen dress. The effect was eccentric, but surprisingly stylish.

'My mother hid us in the cellar, but they caught her too. She said not to move, and so I didn't. I lay under a pile of sacks in the coal hole and stuffed my hands into my ears.' She patted Jane's hand. 'Will you keep the baby?'

'Yes,' she said. 'I'll keep it.'

'Give it a good German name. That way, people will forget where it came from.'

'That's a clever idea.'

Frau Becker set her head on one side, like a cheeky sparrow soliciting for crumbs at a pavement café. She stared at Jane.

'Are you going to have your baby right now?'

'No.' Jane put her hand on her tummy. 'Not yet.'

'That's good.'

The old woman started to sing again. She reached out and held Jane's hand, tapping it gently in time to the song. The sensation was soothing and Jane tried to give herself over to it, but the memory of all that had just happened was too strong.

'You're a pretty girl,' Frau Becker said. 'Some man may still want to marry you. Just teach your baby to be quiet. Men find it hard to live with children who aren't their own.'

Jane patted the old lady's hand, tempted to tell her she already knew the kind of things that could happen when some men found themselves living with children who weren't their own. Instead she smiled and said, 'I'm going to teach my child to speak out. If anyone hurts it, I want to know.'

She had found an ally of a sort in the priest. She wondered what Anna had heard of her conversation with him and if she would pass any of it on to her father. What would he do next if she did? Her neck tingled. There was no proof that he had strangled his wife, nothing to suggest it at all except for Greta's absence and Frau Becker's ramblings.

She kissed the old lady's hand and said, 'Tell me again about Greta Mann.'

'Who?'

Frau Becker's voice was sharp; she was annoyed at the interruption to her song.

'Greta Mann, Alban Mann's wife, the pretty girl from the top floor.'

'I used to love Greta.'

Frau Becker lifted her legs in the air and kicked them up and down in pleasure at the memory.

'What was she like?'

'Greta was fun. My boys are grown up and gone. Karl and I were starting to get old, but Greta brought youth back into our home. She liked to sing and dance and drink. I like to sing and dance and drink too, but I never knew it until I met Greta. People shook their heads, a doctor marrying a girl like that, but I liked her. My mother used to say, "Let a whore into your house and soon you won't have a husband."' Frau Becker was still holding Jane's hand. Now she squeezed it, with a surprisingly strong grip. 'My mother lost any kindness she had during the war.' She lowered her voice to a whisper. 'The Russians caught her.'

'That must have been awful.'

'Worse than you could know. I thought she was being mean, my mother was a mean woman, but I never blamed her. I blamed myself for staying hidden under those sacks when I should have jumped out and strangled a Russian.'

'How old were you?'

'Ten.'

'Too little to strangle a Russian.'

'How big do you need to be to kill a man who is hurting your mother?'

'Bigger than you were, Frau Becker.'

'Sometimes I forget I'm a Frau.' Her voice became high and excited. 'I look back and think I'm a little girl again. We used to play out in the street until late at night, Lotte, Hilde and me. Mother said we ran wild, but we didn't care.'

'Tell me about Greta,' Jane coaxed her.

'Who?'

'Greta Mann, the pretty girl who married Dr Mann. They live on the top floor.'

Frau Becker screwed up her features with the effort of remembering. The wrinkles creased her guileless face, making her look young and old at the same time, an ancient child. Jane prompted, 'Greta's good fun. She likes to drink and dance and have a party.'

Frau Becker shook her head sadly. 'Karl doesn't like me to talk about Greta. Greta Mann's a whore. Let a whore into your house and she'll steal your husband.' She leant in close to Jane and whispered, 'I'm waiting for her. When she comes down these stairs I'm going to trip her up and push her eyes into the back of her skull.'

The old lady started to tremble, with cold or fury, Jane wasn't sure which. She wrapped an arm around her and felt the other woman's bones, brittle beneath her layers of clothing. Jane gave her a gentle squeeze and began to rock her slowly to and fro, as she might to comfort a troubled infant. 'I thought you liked her.'

'I used to like her, that's true. But I was glad when she was gone and buried.'

'I heard she went away, to Hamburg or America.'

'No, he got rid of her.'

'Who? Dr Mann?'

'Karl told me not to say.'

Jane caught a glimpse of herself, wheedling slander from a confused old lady.

'Your husband's right, it's bad to gossip. I think you and I should get into the warm.'

But Frau Becker ignored her.

'He put his hands around her throat and pressed tight until she was dead. I hope she was dead, because he buried her beneath the floorboards in the backhouse. No one wants to be buried alive. When I go, I'll tell Karl to make the undertaker slash my wrists, one – two.' She made a cutting gesture with her hands. 'To make sure.'

The baby was moving, kicking out as if it wanted all of her attention focussed on it. Petra would have phoned by now and would be worrying why she hadn't answered the landline or her mobile. The thought of another night alone in the apartment, listening out for sounds of Mann and Anna on the other side of the wall, appalled her. Jane said, 'There's no need to think of that right now.'

'I went there once to look. It was dark, the stairs creaked and there were rustling sounds. I knew they were birds, or maybe rats, but I was frightened it was Greta Mann and that she would find me and pull me down there with her.'

'Down beneath the floorboards?'

'No.' The old woman looked up, her eyes a pale-blue wash, forget-me-nots bleached by the sun. 'Down into Hell.'

It was the second time that day Hell had been mentioned. Jane said, 'Hell doesn't exist.'

'I used to have nightmares about the Russians and then I had nightmares about Greta Mann dragging me down to a party with the Devil. Sometimes the dreams would get mixed up and the Russians would be there with Greta, waiting for me.'

Jane rested her head on Frau Becker's shoulder.

'Do you still dream about her?'

'I saw her with my husband yesterday. My mother was right; I should never have let a whore into my home. I thought she was fun, we would drink and dance and sing together, but all the time she was making eyes at Karl. Late at night he sneaks out of our bed and goes to meet her in the backhouse. They think I don't know, but I do.'

It was hard to imagine Herr Becker creeping out of bed to meet a lover, but Jane recalled the way he had stood close to her in the hallway and wondered if the old lady was remembering true. Perhaps Greta had started to ply her trade close to home and that was what had prompted Mann to violence. Jane pushed her doubts from her voice and said, 'I'm sure you're wrong, Frau Becker. Your husband's a good man. He's probably out looking for you right now.' She helped the old lady to her feet. 'Do you have a key to your apartment?'

'He thinks I don't, but I do.' Frau Becker reached into a secret pocket, somewhere beneath the folds of her clothing, rooted around for a moment and drew out a key, which she held triumphantly in the air. 'Have you ever had another woman go after your man? No.' Frau Becker stared at Jane in a sudden burst of clarity. 'You don't have a husband, you have a wife. Have you ever had another woman go after your wife?'

Jane thought of the photo she had found in Petra's office. 'I'm not sure.'

Frau Becker slapped her knee. 'That means yes. So you know what it is to feel jealous.'

'I suppose I do.'

'Could you kill her?'

'Petra or the other woman?'

'Either of them, both of them. Two for the price of one.' Frau Becker started to laugh. 'The French call it a crime of passion.'

Jane started to guide Frau Becker towards her front door.

'I might shout at them, hit out at them perhaps, but I know I couldn't kill anyone.'

'Greta deserved all she got. She kissed me once. She was a good kisser. I kissed her back, but all the time she was sneaking out to the backhouse with Karl. She turned his head just for the fun of it.' The old lady shook her head sadly. 'A man old enough to be her father, her grandfather. I saw her today.'

'No, Frau Becker.' Jane took the key from the other woman's hand and slid it into the lock. 'Don't upset yourself, Greta's long gone.'

'I saw her. She ran up the stairs just before you arrived. I tried to trip her up but she jumped over my foot.' The old lady lifted the hem of her skirt and blew her nose noisily into it. 'Her hair was tangled, there were leaves in it, as if she'd just crawled out of the grave, and she was crying. Maybe she was a ghost.'

Jane opened the door to the Beckers' flat and smelled again the scent of dampness, unwashed bedclothes and stale cat litter. Frau Becker looked up, sudden realisation brightening her face. 'Do you think my husband sneaks out at night to meet a ghost?'

'No, I don't.' Jane pictured leaves tangled in Anna's hair as she ran up the stairs to her apartment. Had she tripped and fallen in the graveyard? Jane steered Frau Becker into the sitting room and on to an easy chair. 'I shouldn't have let you sit out there, you're freezing.'

She took off her gloves and started to rub the old woman's hands with her own, trying to chafe some heat into them. The parchment skin was loose on its bones. Frau Becker refused to be diverted. 'If he was meeting a ghost, surely I would know. I'd feel it, wouldn't I? The coldness of her grave entering into me.'

'I suspect you might.' Jane wanted nothing more than to climb into the Beckers' unmade bed fully dressed and draw the grubby sheets over her, but she smiled and said, 'Let's have a cup of tea.'

'No.' Frau Becker got to her feet. 'Let's have some Schnapps. It'll be good for the little one.'

The child moved as if in agreement and for the first time that day Jane laughed.

'Tea first.' She filled the kettle and set it on the stove. 'And then perhaps a Schnapps later.'

There was the sound of a key in the front door and Herr Becker shouted, '*Hallo, ich bin da.*'

The old man made the small bed-sitting room seem even smaller. He was dressed for outdoors in a woollen hat and scarf and a thick overcoat which was still smart, but old enough to qualify as vintage. 'Frau Logan.' He put his hand on his wife's shoulder, keeping his eyes on Jane, as if he were unsure about letting her out of his sight. 'Did something happen?'

Jane saw a splash of red on his coat sleeve. A distant thought tugged at her brain and was gone.

'Nothing to worry about.' She set the mugs she'd been

236

rinsing back on the draining board. 'I met Frau Becker in the lobby and we decided to have a cup of tea together.'

'How did you get out, Heike?'

Frau Becker pursed her lips, suddenly becoming the schoolteacher she once was.

'I'm not a prisoner.'

'We go out together, remember we agreed.'

She looked up at her husband but his stare was still fixed on Jane.

'You went out alone, and so I decided to go out alone too. I saw Greta Mann.'

Herr Becker glanced at his wife and then back to Jane. *'Wir sprechen nicht über Greta Mann, erinnerst du dich nicht mehr an unsere Absprache.'*

Frau Becker looked suddenly sly.

'I remember more than you think, Karl. Much more.'

Karl Becker let go of his wife's shoulder and turned towards Jane. Something lurking behind the sadness in his eyes made Jane wish she was standing in the doorway, instead of with her back to the draining board, but his voice was mild.

'Thank you for looking after my wife. I try not to leave her alone, but sometimes I have to go out and she cannot always be with me.'

'I understand.'

'He goes to meet his ghost girl, his lover,' the old lady chirped cheerfully from her armchair. 'He doesn't want me with him then.'

'I should get going.'

Jane took Frau Becker's hands in hers and gave them a squeeze. The woman stage-whispered, 'Watch out for my husband. Don't accept any invitations to go to the backhouse with him.'

Jane smiled apologetically at Herr Becker.

'I'll remember that.'

He followed her out into the hallway.

'She doesn't know what she's saying.'

'Of course not.'

His thin lips were dry and cracked, turned white by the cold, but his mouth was still wide and clownish, and it was easy to imagine him haunting a ghost cavalcade.

'My wife has never been strong. She had a hard war, it made her vulnerable.'

'Yes, I'm sorry.'

Jane wasn't sure if she was apologising for the war or commiserating with him over Frau Becker's fragile grasp on the world.

'She had good years when we were younger, but then our boys grew up and left home, and the war seemed to come back to her.' Herr Becker touched Jane's arm. 'I need to talk to you.'

She wanted to be gone, but managed to summon a weak smile.

'Maybe I could visit Frau Becker later in the week and we can chat then? I'm tired, and your wife needs you.'

Jane put her hand to the latch but Herr Becker seized her wrist and pulled her roughly towards him. He turned Jane back into the hallway and placed himself in front of the door. It was a rough move, a hooligan dance step, which caught her by surprise.

Herr Becker sighed, as if regretting the necessity of what he was about to say.

'Anna Mann told me you've been bothering her.'

Jane rubbed her wrist, too dazed to ask the old man what he thought he was playing at.

'She visits here sometimes, doesn't she? I saw her coming out of your flat.'

'So it's true what she says, you follow her?'

'No.' Jane felt herself floundering. A wave of exhaustion washed over her, threatening to drag her under. 'We live next door to each other, sometimes our paths cross.'

'Anna tells me it's more than that.'

Herr Becker's eyes were small and hooded, his pupils sunk a long way back in his skull. Jane realised how old he was and wondered what it was like to know you were going to die soon. Did the world seem sweeter, or was everything tainted by the knowledge that life would go on without you? There was no point in burdening the old man with something that didn't concern him.

'No.' Jane shook her head. 'Nothing more.'

'I don't believe you. I've watched the way you look at her, like a vampire.'

Herr Becker was an old man. Jane knew she could push past him and out on to the landing, but she stayed where she was, fascinated by what he was saying.

'Perhaps you and your girlfriend should think about moving somewhere else. Berlin is a big city; there are plenty of nice apartments.' His voice was gentle. 'This place doesn't suit everyone.'

'Like Greta.'

'No.' Herr Becker dragged a hand across his face. 'It didn't suit Greta.'

Jane noticed the splash of red on his coat sleeve again and realised what it was.

'Did you paint those words on my front door?'

'Please, Frau Logan.' Herr Becker's voice was apologetic. 'Stop bothering Anna Mann.'

'Karl.' Frau Becker's voice sounded, loud and shrill from the front room.

'*Einen Moment bitte*, Heike,' he shouted, without moving.

Jane said, 'You did, didn't you? Why? What is Anna to you?'

He looked away. 'Anna is precious. When her mother died, I promised myself I would do all I could to help her.'

'Including threatening pregnant women?'

'It was a warning, nothing more. You think you're in love with her; love can make people act foolishly.'

'Anna is a child and I have a *Lebenspartner*. We've been together for six years. We're having a baby together.'

The old man made an impatient sound.

'People can be together for twenty years, thirty, have brought several children up together, and all of a sudden a thunderbolt hits them, a tsunami, and they are in love with someone else.'

'Someone like Greta?'

The old man gave a sad smile. 'Alban Mann should never have married her.'

'Maybe she was impossible to resist.'

'Maybe.'

Herr Becker would have been in his late sixties when Greta died. Uncertainty coloured Jane's voice.

'You were in love with her?'

'I've said all I have to say, Frau Logan. Please remember what I told you. Leave Anna alone.'

'Or else?'

He sighed. 'Please don't test me. Old age makes some people reckless. They have nothing to lose.'

'And every chance of happiness could be their last.'

He touched her face and his hands were soft and cool against her flushed cheek.

'That's true of the young, too. The only difference is they don't know it.'

Herr Becker opened the door and pushed Jane gently out into the lobby.

Twenty-Eight

She was dreaming about Anna. They were alone in the dark, the girl's soft hair drifting over Jane's face. She thought they were in bed together and started to panic; this wasn't what she wanted, it was all wrong. The girl's lips met hers and then they were kissing, Anna's tongue thrilling and insistent. Jane realised again what she was doing and tried to push her away but some other, stronger force pressed them together. She felt the weight of the girl's body, the softness of her breasts, and twisted loose of her, desperate to escape, but whichever direction Jane moved, she was trapped. She shoved Anna with all her might, but it was no good, they were locked together, and then all of a sudden Jane realised what was holding them there. They were sealed, one on top of the other, beneath the floorboards in the backhouse.

It was 2.30 a.m. Jane pulled on her dressing gown, went to the bathroom and then drank some water straight from the kitchen tap, not bothering to find a glass. There was a bruise on her wrist where Herr Becker had gripped her. She wondered when Frau Becker had discovered his love for Greta and how she had managed to stay married to him once she knew. Maybe she had needed her husband to help her feel safe from marauding Russians, or perhaps the knowledge of his infidelity had helped shatter her fragile sanity.

Jane walked along the hallway to the child's room. The flat was pitched in darkness, but she didn't turn on a light. The kitchen chair was still propped against the front door, but there was an unfamiliar sound coming from somewhere in the apartment; no, not in the apartment, from somewhere outside. She followed the noise into the sitting room and out on to the balcony.

There was no moon and only the North Star was out, marking the way home. It was cold and there was a damp quality to the air that told her it would rain soon. The Fernsehturm was half hidden behind mist or clouds, it was too dark for Jane to tell, but the street below was lit up like the Friedrichstrasse Theater. An ambulance and two police cars were parked askew in front of the *Kirche*, throwing their flashing lights across the churchyard, staining the tumbled graves blue.

It took Jane less than five minutes to pull on some clothes, get down the stairs and out into the street. A line of police tape cordoned off the graveyard. She walked towards it, still not quite free of her dream. A tired-looking policeman blocked her path and she asked, 'Can you tell me what has happened, please?' He muttered something under his breath and she said, 'Sorry, I couldn't hear you.'

This time the policeman replied in English, 'I told you to go away.' She stared at him, still not understanding, and he barked, 'Have you no respect for the dead?'

The forgotten, familiar taste of burnt ashes was in her mouth.

'Who's dead?'

He looked at her with naked contempt.

'Go away or you'll be giving birth in prison.'

His words hit her like a slap. She raised a hand to her cheek and walked slowly to where a small crowd of tourists and late-night drinkers had gathered on the pavement. She asked, 'Does anyone know what's going on?'

A trendy-looking young American, wearing a natty sports jacket and black-framed spectacles, said, 'Someone was taking a shortcut and found a body in the graveyard.'

His girlfriend was slim and pale; her blonde hair fastened around her head in a long plait, the way Heidi had worn it on the cover of a book Jane had often borrowed from the library as a child. Her voice was soft with the surprise of it all.

'A priest. They found him in the graveyard with his wrists slashed.'

'Are you sure?'

'I heard the police talking. Apparently it often happens that way. Someone cuts their wrists and then thinks better of it. I guess he crawled out there looking for help, but it was too late.' She shook her head. 'Horrible.'

Her boyfriend put an arm around her and Jane could see he had been drinking.

'I guess that'll be an elevator straight down to the basement for him.'

He laughed, but no one else joined in.

Jane moved to the edge of the small group. She could feel their anticipation; they were like a theatre audience waiting for the star of the show. A small frisson of excitement coursed through the spectators as the stretcher was loaded into the back of the ambulance.

'He might still be alive.'

'No chance,' the American boy said. 'If he was, they'd be moving faster than that, trust me.'

And as if to prove his point the ambulance's flashing lights died, its engine growled into life and it drove slowly out of the street.

It was starting to rain, a soft smirr, like spray from a speeding boat, and the crowd was already breaking up. Jane stuck her hands deep into the pockets of her coat and walked slowly back to her building. There was a light glowing behind the lace curtains in the Beckers' sitting-room window. The curtains moved, as someone straightened their folds and stepped away, but Jane could still see their silhouette, dark and indistinct, watching her from the other side of the glass.

The hall light cut out when she was only halfway up the second flight of stairs. Jane cursed under her breath and gripped the banister, slowing her pace even further as she let her eyes adjust to the dark. The priest was dead. She thought of his lips moving quietly in prayer; the way his hands shook, one grasped in the other, as he'd knelt before the altar. What had possessed him? Suicide was a venal sin, a one-way ticket to Hell, or so Father Walter had presumably believed.

She reached the second floor landing and saw him waiting there, a shadow darker than the surrounding blackness, his robes hanging still and straight around his thin body. She gasped, the light came on and she saw Alban Mann, standing outside his front door, wrapped in a grey towelling dressing gown. His hair was tousled, his eyes bleary with sleep. He asked, 'What's going on?'

Jane hesitated on the top step. She hadn't seen Mann since the episode in his flat and wasn't sure whether she could bring herself to push past him. She whispered, 'Don't you know?'

'I was asleep. Something woke me and I saw the flashing lights, the ambulance outside the church. I was about to go down and ask if there was anything I could do.'

'You're too late. The priest is dead.'

She took her keys from the pocket of her jacket. Her hands were numb and the keys fell to the floor. Alban bent quickly to pick them up.

'The young priest?'

'Yes, Father Walter. Someone said he killed himself.'

She stared at her keys in Alban Mann's hand. He followed her gaze and after a moment's hesitation handed them back.

'Are you sure?'

'No, it was just something someone said, a tourist, and anyway . . .'

She selected the key to her front door, but Alban was still standing in her way. He asked, 'And anyway, what?'

'Nothing.'

'If you know something, you should tell the police.'

'I don't know anything. Please,' her voice was hoarse with tiredness, 'I want to go back to bed.'

'Of course.' Alban Mann stepped to one side and Jane crossed the landing, expecting to feel the weight of his hand on her at any moment. But he merely turned to watch her progress and said, 'He must have been desperate.'

The words should have sounded sympathetic, but Jane detected a warning note. She turned the key in the lock and slid inside her apartment, keeping the door ajar, ready to slam it shut if Mann made a move.

'Did you have anything to do with his death?'

'Frau Logan,' Alban Mann shook his head, but he didn't look surprised. 'You need help. I don't know how Father Walter died, I barely knew him, but I can assure you, his suicide had nothing to do with me.'

'You could have drugged him, the way you drugged me, and then slashed his wrists.'

The doctor's voice was soft and composed.

'I never touched you, and I hardly knew the priest. Why would I want him dead?'

'The same reason you might want me dead. He knew what you're doing to Anna. Did he confront you about it?'

Mann ignored her question.

'Are you sure you're okay to be alone?'

'Petra will be back tonight.'

'No she won't.' Alban Mann took a step towards her, his slippers scuffing softly against the concrete floor. 'Not unless she's changed her plans and is coming home early.' He smiled and she saw that her lie hadn't convinced him. 'There's a condition that afflicts some pregnant women. It makes them prone to paranoid delusions. It's a temporary state, but it can be disturbing for them, and for those around them.' He smiled again, his head slightly inclined so that his eyes met hers. It was easy to see how he could charm street girls used to long, cold nights and tricky punters. 'I've wondered for some time if you might be affected by it. Will you allow me

247

to help you? As a doctor? I can take you to hospital in my car, or if you prefer I could phone an ambulance. I only want to make things as easy as possible for you and for your child.' Mann took another step towards Jane. 'Getting over excited isn't good for the baby.' He was almost close enough to touch her. His voice was soft and hypnotic. 'And going out in the street late at night isn't good for either of you. Your judgement is poor. You're not thinking straight.'

Jane pushed the door almost, but not quite, shut. The police already believed Mann. He was a doctor with colleagues who would believe him too. How many phone calls would it take for him to have her shut up in a locked ward and her baby promised to the care of the authorities? Petra would fight for them both, but once the system got hold of a child, it was loath to let it go until after the harm was done.

She hissed, 'Don't even think of sending the police or anyone else to my door again. If you do, I won't be responsible for the consequences. Everything I know is written down and hidden somewhere safe.' She fixed her eyes on his, hoping the lie sounded convincing. 'You'll never find it, no matter how hard you search, but be sure that the pages will find their way into the right hands if anything happens to me.'

Alban Mann's voice was calm.

'You're a healthy young woman. You just need some help.'

'The priest was healthy, now he's dead.'

'Why not let another doctor examine you? There's a colleague I can phone.'

He held his hand out, palm upwards. Jane remembered the way he had tried to coax Anna back into their flat on the day their row had woken her in the bath, the day she might have drowned. The memory was like poison in her spine. The child moved and she said, 'You keep away from me or I swear, you'll wish you never lived.'

Jane slammed the front door and turned the locks home. She leant her back against it and sank to the floor, her heart hammering in her chest, as loud as the footsteps that pounded through her nightmares and woke her in the night.

Twenty-Nine

J ane heard the screaming on the other side of the wall early next morning. It was shrill and keening, and she knew it was because the priest was dead. The wailing was loudest in the child's room and so she drew a chair up to the wall that separated their apartment from the Manns' and sat leaning against it, wishing she could go next door and comfort Anna.

The child inside her seemed to be more active this morning. Jane hoped it wasn't aware of the cries, but it seemed imperative that she should hear them and suffer with the girl.

The conversation with Father Walter flashed back to her in fragments. She remembered the way he had switched between assurance and diffidence, from magician to small boy. Had he already intended to kill himself?

The telephone had been ringing at intervals all morning. Now it started up again. Jane stayed where she was, not even turning her head to look at the backhouse, though she could feel its presence mocking her from the other side of the courtyard. The girl's cries sounded in rhythm with the phone; they built to a peak and descended into sobs before resuming and building again. There was exhaustion in the sound.

The ringing stopped and somewhere deep in the apartment

Jane's mobile sprang into its silly jingle. It was nothing to do with her. There was no one she wanted to speak to, not even Petra. The child moved again. She wiped a tear from her cheek and sniffed, swallowing her own sobs. She didn't deserve the relief of crying. How could she have considered having a child? She stroked her stomach, hoping it could somehow feel the presence of her hands in its own small cosmos.

'I'm sorry,' she whispered. 'Really, really sorry.'

At some point she realised that the wailing had stopped. She got up from her seat, pulled the telephone connection from the wall, found her mobile and turned it off. Then she closed the bedroom curtains on the day and crawled, fully dressed, back into bed. Someone was banging on the front door and ringing the doorbell, but the chair was propped against the handle, the mortise triple-locked, and it was easy to ignore. Jane closed her eyes and let sleep claim her.

Thirty

J ane woke to the knowledge that someone was in the apartment. She hugged her stomach and whispered, 'Petra?' but there was no answer, just a sliver of light gleaming beyond the bedroom door, from the hallway she was sure she had left in darkness.

She reached out a hand towards the bedside lamp, checked herself, and pulled on her dressing gown and slippers in the dark. Out in the back court a rook cawed, but no other sounds disturbed the night. The alarm clock read 03.05. This was the time of night when beds were rolled from hospital wards, the hour most people died.

Jane tried to reassure herself it had been the child's kicking that had woken her, but she could see the light shining where she knew no light had been. She slipped her hand under the mattress, found Petra's hunting knife, slid it from its sheath and tiptoed silently from the room. The kitchen chair was still propped against the front door, the security chain still looped in place. She let out a long, shuddering sob. Her memory had been playing tricks. She had simply forgotten to switch off the hall light when she'd crawled into bed. It was hardly surprising.

Jane dropped the knife into her dressing-gown pocket and leant forward, hands on her thighs, breathing deeply. Her mobile was in the kitchen; she should switch it on and send Petra a text. She would be frantic by now. Jane straightened up, her hand on her belly, thinking again about Father Walter, imagining him crawling along the pathway from the *Kirche*, the gravel turning red as the life flowed out of him. Had Anna relied on the priest to save her from her father? How could Jane convince her that help was still available?

She shivered. There was a cold draught on the back of her neck, a hint of dampness that made her think again of the graveyard. Jane looked up, towards the source of the chill, and saw a square of blackness in and beyond the white ceiling. There was an instant of incomprehension, and then she realised that the hatch to the loft space was open. The heat of another body disturbed the air behind her, a footfall soft as a sleeping child's breath. She pulled away, but her reactions were slow and someone grasped her shoulder. Jane's shriek was cut short as Alban Mann cupped a hand over her mouth.

'Please,' he whispered, 'don't be frightened.'

Jane sank her teeth into his palm, biting until she tasted blood. He yelled and let go and she took the knife from her pocket and buried it up to the hilt in his thigh. Alban Mann screamed. His stick clattered to the floor. Jane pulled the knife out and heard him scream again.

The floor was already slithery with blood. Jane slipped and managed to break her fall with her hands. The knife had fallen with her and was shuddering point-down in the wooden floor. She pulled it free and scrabbled along the hall-way on her hands and knees. Mann was crawling close behind, too close for her to get to the front door, unbolt it and make her escape. She slid along the polished hardwood and into the kitchen, remembering too late that her mobile wasn't on the countertop next to the sink, as she had thought, but on the couch in the sitting room.

'Fuck.'

Alban Mann struggled through the kitchen door, tried to get to his feet and collapsed on to the tiled floor. He clutched his bleeding leg with both hands, breath shivering from him in long, painful gasps.

'Please,' he said, 'you've hit an artery. You have to make a tourniquet and phone for an ambulance.'

Jane held the knife in front of her, its hilt quivering against her belly.

'You broke into my home.'

'I came to see if you were okay.'

'You came to murder me, the same way you murdered your wife.'

'Why won't you believe me? I never touched Greta. I knew she was seeing another man.' He grimaced as if the memory still had the power to sear through the wound in his leg and hurt him further. 'Maybe several men. But I never harmed her. I couldn't. I'm a doctor. I save lives.'

'You're a liar. You climbed up into your attic, crept along the loft, into my flat and grabbed me. If I hadn't stabbed you, I'd be dead by now. Where were you going to put me? Under the backhouse floor beside Greta?'

Mann rubbed his hand across his face, leaving a smear of blood. His words came in gasps.

'I tried to phone you. Anna was saying you had driven the

priest to his death. I wanted to know what you'd done to make my daughter so frightened. When you didn't answer I knocked on your door. Didn't you hear me?' He grasped his leg and let out a low moan. 'Please, I'll tell the police it was an accident. No one will blame you.'

He stopped talking for a moment, his face buckling with pain. Jane wondered if she could get past him and out of the building, but he was blocking the kitchen doorway and she didn't dare.

'You have to help me or I'll die.' He grimaced, and his lips pulled back in a snarl that showed his incisors. 'Phone an ambulance, you mad bitch.'

'I don't believe you're as badly hurt as you're pretending.' Her voice was shaking, teeth beginning to chatter with shock and cold. She could still taste his blood in her mouth. 'But if you are, throw your mobile across the floor and I'll call an ambulance.'

'I don't have it with me.'

Mann looked bad, his skin sunk to the dingy grey of cheap paper, but then he grasped the door jamb and started to pull himself upright. Jane pointed the knife at him, clutching the handle with both hands. Her feet scrabbled against the cold tiles although she knew the kitchen cupboards were at her back, and behind them only wall and window, and a twenty-foot drop into the courtyard below.

'Please,' she said, 'keep away.'

Mann seemed to be gathering all of his strength in the effort to walk towards her. His eyes rolled back in his head and again he sank to the floor, his legs splayed awkwardly in front of him. He whispered, 'If you don't help me, you'll kill me.'

She couldn't go near him.

'You drugged me.'

'No.'

He shook his head, pain leaching the colour from his skin and forcing tears from his eyes.

'Why would you climb in through the loft space unless you meant to hurt me?'

The knife was trembling in her hands.

Mann grasped his thigh above the wound. His trousers were black but they must have been soaked in blood because the floor around him was red with the stuff.

'I was in bed, thinking about the priest, how sad it was that a man so young should kill himself.' He paused for a moment to catch his breath. 'I remembered two street-walkers, beautiful girls, who had attended my clinic, and who had jumped together, hand in hand to their deaths. Then my mind turned to you and I began to wonder, what if you had killed yourself too, what if you were lying here dead with your child still alive in your womb? The last time I saw you, you were so strange. I thought of phoning the police again, but what could I tell them?' He looked up at her and Jane could see him consciously trying to summon up his old charm. 'The more I thought about it, the more it preyed on me, until finally I couldn't stand it any longer. I called again and the phone rang out. I used to have keys to your flat, but I couldn't find them.' He frowned as if the loss of the keys still puzzled him. 'Then I remembered that our lofts were connected and decided to sneak in, just to make certain you were okay.' His voice was a sob. 'I only meant to check you were safe and then go away.'

'You're lying. You were going to kill me the same way you killed Greta.'

'No.' Mann rested his head against the open door, as if the effort of holding it up was too much for him. He was panting now, like a man who had run for his life and still couldn't catch his breath. 'Please,' he wheezed. 'I never touched her.'

The pool of blood was reaching across the floor towards her, staining the edge of her slippers. Jane stepped away, desperate to avoid it, and suddenly realised that her dressing gown and nightdress were already drenched. Her hands flailed against her body, trying to brush the redness from her, but they too were covered in gore. She panicked and dropped the knife. Alban Mann stretched out a hand, quicker than she thought a dying man could move, and gripped his fingers around its handle, but this time Jane was faster. She lifted a foot and kicked it from him.

'Please,' Mann said, 'think of my daughter.'

Jane looked at him and something inside her clicked.

'That's exactly what I am doing.'

She picked up the knife, put it back in her pocket, stepped over his body and out of the room.

Thirty-One

Herr Becker's graffiti was still splashed across their front door, red as the blood draining from Alban Mann's body. Jane paused in the lobby, not sure of where she was going, only certain that she couldn't stay in the apartment. The knife in her pocket hit against her thigh and the child moved in her womb. She held her stomach and mumbled, 'Wheesht now, wheesht, it's okay.' The world started to slip away, and she clutched the banister, wondering if she was about to pass out.

'What have you done?'

Anna stood in the doorway of the Manns' apartment. Her black hair hung in thick tangles around her face, as it had in the nightmare of the two of them, buried together beneath the backhouse floor. The girl's eyes were wide, her face scrubbed free of make-up. She was wearing a long white nightdress and Jane could see the silhouette of her slight body beneath it. She was only a child.

Jane stepped towards her, groping for words. 'Anna . . . we need to talk . . .'

'What have you done?'

Anna's mouth was trembling, but her body was frozen still.

Behind her, the door to her apartment swung slowly closed and shut with a bang. The girl started and her hand flew to her face.

Jane took a step forward.

'Don't be frightened . . . please . . .'

But Anna gave a gasp that was pure fear, and then she was hurtling down the stairs, her bare feet hardly making a sound on the wooden stairway. Jane followed after her.

'Anna.' Jane's voice was an urgent whisper, but the only response was the sound of the girl's ragged breaths as she fled. The girl tripped on the last step and Jane stretched out to grab her. 'Please wait.'

Anna shoved Jane hard on the shoulder, slamming her against the wall, and ran out into the blackness of the back courtyard. Jane regained her footing and followed, catching the door just before it closed, gasping as the cold air hit her lungs. The girl's pale nightdress shone through the dark and then vanished as she disappeared into the backhouse.

The backhouse was colder and darker than the world outside. Jane heard the silt of dirt and rubble crunching beneath her slippers and froze, her ears straining for any sound from above. The knife was still in the pocket of her dressing gown, a reassuring weight against her leg. Wings sounded above her. Jane moved towards them, hoping the flurry of pigeons would cover any noise she made.

The banisters were gritty beneath her hands. They trembled beneath Jane's weight as she climbed the stairs slowly, expecting them to disappear at any moment and plunge her into gravity's spin. She felt wetness between her legs and knew that the child was losing patience with the darkness of its universe and preparing to break free earlier than expected. Jane put a hand on her belly. It would be hours yet. Right now her priority had to be the girl.

The light she'd seen shining from the backhouse had always glimmered from the second floor, the place where Frau Becker insisted Greta was buried, and so that was where Jane headed. There were no candles lit on the landing, no light at all, but Jane's eyes were adjusting to the darkness and she could make out shapes in the blackness. Three doorways faced her; two of them gaped wide, the third was closed. She grasped its handle, pushed it open and slipped inside.

It was the room she had watched from the window of their apartment. Jane felt her stomach clench. She gripped the door jamb, waiting for the pain to pass, and when it was gone whispered, 'Anna, please don't be frightened, I only want to help you.' She closed the door gently behind her and ventured inside. Across the courtyard a square of light shone from her kitchen, where Alban Mann lay on the floor in a pool of blood. The thought of him tightened Jane's grip around the knife. There was a mattress on the floor tumbled with blankets. Jane nudged it with her foot and hissed, 'Anna, there's no need to be scared. He can't hurt you any more.'

She kept the knife in her hand and traced her free fingers along the window ledge until she found what she was looking for: a stub of candle and a frayed matchbook with one last match waiting for her, snug as a babe in its pram. The flame was thin and wavered in the breeze blowing through the broken pane, but it was enough to show her where she was.

It was larger than the child's room, but the same shape, a long space with the window at one end and the door at the other. The floorboards were rough and marked in places, but there were no bloodstains, no sign of Greta's tomb. The mattress sat askew in the middle of the room, an empty bottle of vodka nestling against it. In a far corner a mess of broken glass lay smashed beneath a spattered wall, as if someone had made a sport of trying to hit the same spot whenever a bottle was empty.

A delicate silk slip hung from a nail on the wall, its elegance impossible in the barren space. There was something familiar about the lace trimming its neck, the faint oyster sheen of the fabric. Jane felt an urge to touch it and crept further into the room. The slip was Petra's. Jane remembered her complaining of its loss and her own dark suspicions of where she might have left it.

The space was squalid, but there were signs that someone had tried to make it less so. Debris had been pushed into the corners, a few postcards and photographs from magazines had been pinned around the room. An amateurish mural bloomed across one wall: the outline of a girl's face, her features too poorly painted to really resemble anyone, but with long hair like Anna's. Jane noticed other, barely missed losses from their flat: a half-bottle of scent, a pair of rarely worn high heels, an evening dress that had proved too glitzy beyond the glamour of its boutique.

A bundle of carrier bags from designer shops lolled on the floor. Jane used the blade of her knife to lift one – from Das neue Schwarz – by its handles. She felt the weight of it and let the bag drop without bothering to look inside. The girl had been taking a chance, leaving her expensive treasures here where anyone might find them, but then she'd had no privacy at home, no freedom from her father.

Anna was a pale shadow crouched behind the chair, head bent, eyes closed. Jane whispered her name and the girl slowly raised her face.

She saw the terror gleaming in Anna's eyes and dropped the knife back into her dressing-gown pocket.

'I'm not going to hurt you.' Pain fired through her stomach and she couldn't speak for a moment. When it had passed Jane said, 'It was you who took the money, wasn't it? You took your father's key to our apartment and sneaked in when we were out.'

Anna started to cry. 'Please, go away. I didn't mean any harm.'

'I told you, I'm not going to hurt you.' She had never really cared about the stolen euros anyway. 'I can't leave you here. It's not safe.'

The girl drew her knees up to her chest and buried her face in them. Her sobs built, breathy and rapid, into the same desperate rhythm that had seeped through the wall between their apartments.

Jane looked down at her own blood-soaked nightclothes and took a step backwards, hoping the shadows would hide the worst of it.

'I was attacked, I had to defend myself.' She put a hand on her stomach. 'Myself and my baby.'

The girl looked up at Jane, her tear-stained face ghost-white against the dark of the room.

'Are you going to kill me?'

Anna's words were almost obscured by her sobs and it took Jane a moment to realise what she'd said.

'No, I told you, it was self-defence.'

'Ulrich never did you any harm, but you killed him.'

'Who?'

'Father Walter.'

The priest seemed a long time ago.

'I spoke to him about you, that's all.'

'Ulrich would never have killed himself. He believed suicide was a sin.'

The girl looked pale and childlike in the half-light. Jane remembered the despair of being young and said, 'I don't know why he did what he did. Sometimes people feel so bad they begin to hate themselves. Maybe he wanted to punish the unbearable part of himself.'

Anna's face was glossy with tears and snot. She shouted, 'He was a good man. He loved me.'

They were almost always good men, on the surface.

Jane's legs were beginning to tremble with cold and fatigue. She whispered, 'Then perhaps I did kill him, without meaning to. I told him you were only thirteen.'

'Why?' The word was a wail.

Jane wanted to lie down on the floor beside Anna and sleep, but she forced herself to stay on her feet. The knife was a weight in her pocket.

'Because you are.'

Another pain gripped Jane and she let out a low moan. The noise seemed to panic the girl. She edged away, pulling the chair with her, trying to keep a barrier between them.

'Please,' Jane said, 'let's get out of here.'

Anna's voice was hoarse with fear. 'If you touch me, the old man will find you and kill you.'

Jane shook her head, wondering if Alban Mann had managed to drag himself to the telephone in the sitting room. Would she be able to hear the sound of police sirens from here? It would be Jane's word against his and the girl's. Jane would be put in jail, and Alban would be free to do whatever he wanted to his daughter. What would happen to her baby?

'Your father's not going to kill me.'

'Not him. Herr Becker.'

'Herr Becker?' Surprise turned her words into an accusation. 'What is he to you?'

'Will you let me go if I tell you?'

The girl looked up, too desperate to keep the cunning from her face, and Jane saw she would say anything to set herself free.

'Yes, if you tell me the truth.'

The lie seemed to reassure the girl a little. Anna was still trembling but she brushed her hair from her face and wiped her eyes on the sleeve of her nightie. The dawn was beginning to break, the room shifting from black to grey, the pigeons stirring in their roosts, fluffing their feathers and beginning to preen themselves, like elderly ladies getting ready for an excursion into town. Anna took a long, shuddering breath.

'His wife wasn't always strange,' she paused as if remembering, 'not like she is now. When I was younger she used to babysit for me sometimes, when my father was late at the clinic. I think the old man was still working, but he was

264

always home before my father, and there was usually a present or a sweet hidden in his pocket for me.'

'You liked him?'

'Back then, yes.'

'But your feelings changed?' The girl nodded and Jane asked, 'Why?'

'He became different when the old lady got ill.'

'How?'

Anna hugged her knees closer and looked at her feet.

Jane closed her eyes as another pain seized her belly. It was as if some girls were marked with a secret brand that only abusers could see. Once they'd been used, other bastards could somehow tell, and sniffed them out to take their turn.

She took the knife from her pocket. 'I'll kill him.'

'No!' Anna clutched at her hair. 'He's just a sad old fool with a crazy wife.'

Jane turned on her, the knife still in her hand.

'Why do you keep making excuses for these men? They groomed you. Even the priest; he chose not to know how old you were. You don't look anywhere near seventeen. He knew in his heart you were too young. Can't you see that?'

Anna shrank back into the shadows, her arms wrapped protectively around her body.

'Ulrich loved me.'

'No, he didn't, he was no better than your father, no better than the skinheads you waltzed off with at the U-Bahn that day.' Jane let out a moan as another pain shot through her. 'And now this old man. He could be your great-grandfather.'

The girl hung her head, hiding her face behind her long

hair. She whispered, 'Herr Becker thinks he's my father. He had sex with my mother, half of Berlin had sex with my mother, but he seems to think he was special. I thought it was funny at first. I went along with it and asked him for money to buy clothes and make-up, but then he started to think he could order me around.'

'He didn't touch you?'

'No.' Anna's voice was barely audible. 'He began to be possessive, telling me what to do and what not to do, he was becoming even worse than my father. It was too intense, but he never touched me that way. No one ever touched me that I didn't want to.'

'Except your father.'

'My father loves me.'

'I heard him screaming at you and calling you names. I've seen the bruises on your face. When will you admit that he hurts you?'

Anna shook her head. 'Please, let me go.' She unwrapped her arms from around her body and looked up at Jane from beneath lowered eyelids, her lips slightly parted. 'We can be friends if you'd like.'

It was a look Jane remembered wearing, a self-conscious sexiness that pleaded for everything to be over soon.

She said, 'You don't have to flirt with people in the hope that they won't hurt you. Your father can't harm you any more. No one will ever harm you again.'

The girl frowned and a small crease appeared on her fore-head, just above her nose.

'What do you mean?'

'Anna . . .' It was hard to get the words out. 'Your father

realised I was on to him. He loved you and didn't want to let you go, even though he knew that what he was doing was wrong.' Jane wished she could sink on to the floor beside the girl and smooth the line from her brow, but it had gone too far for that. She said, 'He broke into my flat . . .'

The girl was shaking her head as if the news was too big for her to take in.

'I thought it was your girlfriend . . . I thought you'd stabbed her because I'd lied and told you I'd seen her with another woman . . . I thought you were after me because I'd made you murder her . . . My father would never . . .'

'He attacked me, I had no choice.'

The girl was on her feet now.

'You killed him?'

'I don't know . . . I cut him. I left him lying on the floor of the kitchen. There was a lot of blood.'

Anna jumped to her feet, pushing the chair towards Jane. She broke for freedom and ran towards the door. Jane made a grab for the girl as she dashed across the room, but a wave of pain hit her and she bent beneath the strength of it.

'No, Anna, wait.'

But the girl was sprinting away from her at full pelt. Jane recovered herself and followed on, slower than before but determined to stop her.

'Come back!' She leant over the stairwell and saw the girl descending in the grey dawn light. 'Anna, he killed your mother.'

The girl turned to look at her, their eyes met, and Jane thought she was about to climb back up the stairs and hear what she had to tell her. But then Anna's foot caught on something and she lost her balance. The girl's arms shot out, looking for a support to brace against, and she hit the rotten banister. There was no time for her to scream. The banister cracked, Anna tumbled through it and down into the well of the stair. She hit the wall once as she fell, and then landed on the floor with a quiet and final thud.

Thirty-Two

Alban Mann was lying in the hall in an ocean of blood. It took all of Jane's courage to approach him, but she did and then after a moment, she squatted beside him, held his wrist in her hand and felt for a pulse. There was nothing. She took a deep breath, hearing the hiss and flow of the air touching her lungs, and then rose and stepped over the body, all the while expecting to feel his fingers tightening around her ankle.

Her mobile was on the couch where she had left it. Jane pressed the emergency dialler. She held the phone against her chest, breathing deeply, aware of the operator repeating her spiel on the other end of the line. Then she lifted it to her ear and whispered, 'Police and ambulance. My neighbour broke into my flat and attacked me. I think I've killed him.' She paused, exhaling as another pain grabbed at her belly. She had a feeling it wouldn't be long now. 'I'm worried about his daughter. He has a history of abusing her. She's not in their apartment and I don't know where she is.' She crouched forward again and when the pain had passed said, 'I'm in labour. My baby's going to be here soon.'

Jane gave her address and then sat on the couch, grateful for the waves of pain clenching at her insides.

The phone rang, but she ignored it. She wanted to strip her bloody nightclothes from her body, but found she didn't have the strength. The door opened and she half lifted herself from the couch, expecting to see the paramedics, but it was Frau Becker, standing small and birdlike in the doorway. The old lady had wrapped a fringed shawl over her layers of dresses and an ostrich feather bobbed on top of her ragged curls.

'Is your baby coming?'

'Yes.'

'You killed him? The doctor from next door? You stabbed him?'

Jane gave herself over to another wave of pain. How could she be giving birth when she was dying? She slid to the floor and braced herself against the seat of the couch, trying not to push before the medics arrived.

Frau Becker knelt at her side. She smelt sharply of urine.

'Was he after you? Is that why you did it?'

Jane let out a moan. Frau Becker put a cool hand on her forehead.

'Don't worry. It will hurt, but soon you'll have a little baby and you won't mind.' She got to her feet and turned excitedly towards the door. 'Karl, the nice English lady is about to have her baby.'

Herr Becker's skin was the colour of tallow. He gazed at Jane in her blood-drenched nightdress and though he must have realised that she already knew, he said, 'Herr Mann is dead.' He turned his whey face towards her. 'I banged on their door, but Anna didn't answer. Do you know where she is?'

Jane rode another wave of pain and saw the old man open the collar of his dressing gown, taking deep breaths as if he too were about to give birth.

'In the backhouse, with her mother.'

The deadness was in her voice, lifeless and heavy as a corpse.

'That isn't possible.' He slumped into an armchair and his hands butterflied to his chest. 'I warned her it was a dangerous place, and she promised never to go there again.'

'Greta Muller is in the backhouse,' Frau Becker said. She got up from the couch and executed a little dance, her arms fluttering with excitement.

'Heike, be quiet,' warned Herr Becker. He was gasping for breath now. 'Is Anna okay?'

The old man had wanted to protect Anna. Jane felt a sudden urge to go to him and try to ease his breathing, but when she attempted to move, another wave of pain struck her and she was forced to steady herself against the couch.

Frau Becker kissed her on the cheek and the feather in her hair swept against Jane's damp forehead. She sang, 'Is Anna okay?' her high voice a childish echo of her husband's.

Jane said, 'She's with Greta.'

Herr Becker let out a low moan. His wife looked at him and laughed.

'Karl doesn't want us to talk about Greta.' Frau Becker stroked Jane's face with her hand. 'Greta liked to drink in the afternoon and then she would fall asleep on our couch. She looked very beautiful when she slept, like a little girl.'

'Heike, be quiet.' Herr Becker's voice was hoarse. 'Greta went to Hamburg, remember?'

'No, Karl, Greta died, you remember, she was strangled.'

'Then it was Alban Mann who did it. He killed his wife and buried her in the backhouse. Everyone knew, but no one did a thing. He found out she was unfaithful and lost his head. No one blamed him. Please,' he looked at Jane, 'tell me the girl is safe.'

Jane turned her face away from him.

'No one can hurt her any more.'

'I remember, Karl,' the old lady chirped. 'I remember that you told me.' Heavy footsteps were running up the stairs towards the apartment, loud as an oncoming invasion, but Frau Becker showed no more sign of hearing them than she did of noticing that her husband's face had flared from parchment to bright red. 'But why do I remember us laying her down beneath the backhouse floor? Sometimes I feel as if I'm there. I remember the blanket we wrapped her in, the sound of the floorboards creaking as you prised them up. Someone was crying. Sometimes I think it was me, but other times I think it was you, or maybe Greta. Perhaps she wasn't dead when you nailed her under there.'

The paramedics were in the room now and from somewhere else in the apartment came the burble of police radios. A young woman in coveralls was talking to her in soft, swift German, but Jane ignored her. She turned her gaze on Herr Becker, trying to focus on his face through the sheen of tears blinding her vision.

The old man was fighting for breath, his words hissed out in painful spasms.

'You loved poor Greta as much as I did, Heike; enough to know why Herr Mann would want to kill her, and enough

272

to invite her into your dreams.' Herr Becker closed his eyes. 'These buildings are steeped in poor Greta Mann's murder. None of us will sleep soundly in our graves until she's found.' A paramedic was trying to fit an oxygen mask to Herr Becker's face, but he pushed it away and turned his head to look at Jane. 'Tell Anna to come and see me. There are things I need to tell her.'

Jane heard Frau Becker sigh as she sat down in the free armchair, ready to watch the show unfold before her.

'I remember that he killed her, I do remember that now,' the old woman said, 'but I don't understand why I can still feel the warmth of her throat on my hands.'

Epilogue

They had painted the child's room yellow after all. Petra had found the perfect cot, hand carved by an artisan in glowing oak. Jane leant back in her chair, the child at her breast, fingers stroking the soft fuzz of his hair; swansdown and fragrant. He was eight months old now and still perfect.

She could hear Tielo and Petra in the next room. Hospital and police-station visits had given Jane a crash language course and it was her secret that now she could understand most of what they said.

The chair was turned away from the window, but she could hear the low rumble of machinery as Jurgen Tillman's builders worked on the backhouse. He'd warned her it would be months, maybe over a year of dust and noise before their new apartment would be ready, but she was content to wait, and the child seemed able to sleep through anything.

Tielo was asking Petra how Jane was; people were always asking how she was. Petra gave her usual answer: 'She's fine, madly in love with our boy.'

Our boy, hers and Petra's, nobody else's.

'Still no trauma?'

'I keep waiting for the flashbacks to start, but so far nothing. You know Jane, she keeps things close.'

There was a clatter of dishes and then the sound of chopping as Petra began preparing the salad for lunch.

Tielo said, 'Ute's convinced it was Boy that saved her.' Petra laughed and Tielo went on, his voice touched with irritation, 'I don't know why you always put Ute down, she's got a point. Women get extra strength when their children are in danger.'

'Sorry,' Petra's voice was soothing. 'I didn't mean to insult sweet Ute. Especially after the way she's picked up the reins after your redundancy.' She laughed. 'My brother the house husband – who would have predicted it? Maybe Ute's right, but Jane's always had her tough side, you know that. She wouldn't have survived without it.'

Jane whispered to the little boy, 'Your Uncle Tielo is under your Auntie Ute's thumb, and that's the best place for him.'

It was Ute who had come to see her in the hospital with clothes for the baby, while Petra battled to get a plane ticket back from Vienna and Tielo lurked in the corridor outside the ward. Ute had held the baby, examined him when Jane had asked her to, and told her that not only was he perfect, but he was beautiful. She had put her arms around Jane and told her she was safe now. Then she'd told her that Tielo was sorry for not believing that Alban Mann had tried to drug her. He also wanted to apologise for passing on what had only ever been a drunken suggestion from his sister that he should become their sperm donor, and had said that if Jane would forgive him, he would like to come in and meet his nephew.

There was a rattle of cutlery as Tielo set the table. He asked the same question he had been asking since it had happened: 'And you're really going to stay here?'

'Until the new place is ready. Why not?' Jane could almost hear Petra's shrug. 'Jane wants to.'

'I don't know how you can. I stand in here and I still see the blood. That man died right there.'

'There's no need to go on about it. Anyway, what about your place? You live above an old torture chamber.'

'That happened a long time ago.'

'Less than seventy years.'

'And I wasn't involved. Alban Mann murdered his daughter. He would have murdered Jane if she hadn't killed him first.'

The police had seemed to accept from the outset that Jane had acted in self-defence. The breached loft space and her still-on-file accusation that Alban had abused Anna told their own story, but part of her was still on the alert for the sound of heavy boots running up the stairs. Jane kissed the baby's head gently. She could hear Petra setting the knife back on the counter.

Petra said, 'Of course I'd rather move. I've told Jane, it's better to put all this behind us, but it seems important for her to face up to it by staying, and after all she's gone through . . .'

'I still think you should put your foot down. Jane's too fragile to make these decisions.'

'The counsellor says she's coping well. She's still prone to nightmares, but she's managing and taking good care of the child, so we'll stay, for now.'

Jane stroked the child's head and whispered, 'Both of your mummies love you.'

Petra went on, 'And of course, if I'm honest, I feel guilty.'

'We've talked about this already.' Tielo's voice changed and Jane wondered if he had put his arm around his sister. 'You work hard. You couldn't have known this would happen when you went away. Nobody could.'

'I neglected her. Did I tell you that Jane thought I was having an affair with Claudia from work? She found a photo someone had taken on that team-building weekend my department went on, added two and two together and came up with infidelity.' The sound of chopping started again. 'It's not just that. Jane told me that Mann was abusing his daughter but I didn't believe her. I thought it was the prospect of the baby and things in her past making her over-suspicious. Sometimes I think maybe, if I'd paid more attention and we'd tackled it together, that girl would still be alive. Instead he murdered his daughter and then came after Jane. Thank God she managed to defend herself. You know she goes to Anna's grave every day?'

'You told me.'

'She takes Boy with her. Do you think that's healthy?'

'Who knows?'

'It's one of the reasons Jane wants to stay, so she can be near Anna.' Petra sighed. 'So much death. The old man on the ground floor might have had another ten years in him if he hadn't had a heart attack. Apparently he and his wife were devoted to each other. She's had to go into a home.'

Jane kissed the child again. 'We'll go and visit Heike this week. She loves seeing you.'

Somewhere across the courtyard a man shouted and the machinery ceased its low rumble. He shouted again, a high, panicked sound that was joined by the shouts of other men. Tielo asked, 'What's going on?'

'I don't know.' Jane could hear Petra going to the window and opening it to get a better view, and then suddenly Petra was in the room beside her. She said, 'I think they've found something.'

Jane took the child from her breast and held him to her shoulder, gently rubbing his back. She and Petra went to the window together. Down below, an excited gaggle of builders were gathering. One of them pointed up at the backhouse. Jane didn't need to hear what he was saying.

She rocked the child, feeling his body grow heavy as he slid into sleep. Petra slipped an arm around her, around them, and Jane rested her head against Petra's shoulder, letting herself be held. She said, 'Maybe you should call Jurgen and tell him that work on the building's going to be delayed. I think they've found Greta Mann.'

Acknowledgements

I want to thank several organisations for their support during the writing of this book: Het Beschrijf at Passa Porta for a month-long residency at Villa Hellebosch in Flanders in 2009; the University of Iowa International Writers' Program for a residency in 2011; Glasgow School of Art and the University of Glasgow, where I was Writer in Residence between 2011 and 2012 in a post partly funded by Creative Scotland. Thanks must also go to Gisela Moohan for help with translations into German. Any clumsiness or errors in the language, which I have been told I speak with the expertise, but not the charm, of Sally Bowles, are down to me.